PRAISE FOR *KATE'S WAR*

T0014143

"... engagingly written historical drama."

—*Kirkus Reviews*

"With its well-developed characters, evocative writing, and exploration of universal themes, *Kate's War* is likely to resonate with fans of historical fiction and anyone seeking a moving story of love and resilience during tumultuous times."

—*Readers' Favorite*, 5-star review

"*Kate's War*, the story of a quiet English girl living a quiet life just outside London in the late 1930s, becomes the story of a life made larger and deeper in the run-up to the beginning of WWII. As in Henley's two previous novels, the creative life of main characters battles with the demands of daily life, and Kate's singing and teaching of music acts as a foil against the trauma of persecution and war. Henley's rich creation of pre-war England and the resilience of ordinary people called to become extraordinary make this well-written novel a wonderful read."

—Barbara Stark-Neman, author of
Even in Darkness and *Hard Cider*.

"Like a fledgling songbird, Kate Murphy makes several attempts to flee the nest before she soars. A mesmerizing and heartfelt narrative of a young woman's inner and outer battles at the cusp of WWII just south of London. Another wonderful read from award-winning author Linda Stewart Henley. Highly recommended."

—Ashley E. Sweeney, author of *Eliza Waite*.

"*Kate's War* not only illuminates a forgotten part of World War II history, it's also a beautiful story about a young woman finding her way, one that builds to a gripping and exciting ending. In this fast-paced story of strength, humanity, love, and perseverance, Henley paints a drama-filled portrait of a family's struggles at the onset of World War II. Filled with emotional wealth, *Kate's War* is a moving and revealing story."

—Laurie Buchanan, author of the Sean McPherson novels.

"While reading Kate's War, I enjoyed moving among a set of approachable characters in a world defined by the details of historical place, popular culture, language, music, and social traditions while bound by duty to family and country. Their burdens, joys, and disappointments become palpable as each passing month the exigencies of war disrupt their lives. A delightful read all the way to the exciting climax."

—Gary R. Hudak, MD, American Board of Psychiatry and Neurology

PRAISE FOR *WATERBURY WINTER*

"Henley's book is a thoroughly lovely and strangely compelling character study of a man haunted by guilt and regret who endeavors to make a new life for himself . . . This is a novel to be savored. It is warmhearted without being saccharine and abundant with grief and hope."

—*The US Review of Books*

". . . the author excels at expressing the book's larger themes through dialogue about nostalgia and youth. Overall, the book creates a suspenseful journey for characters—and readers—trying to navigate life's big questions. A reflective, witty, and fun story that elegantly crosses genres and addresses intriguing themes."

—*Kirkus Reviews*

"*Waterbury Winter* is a heartwarming story that will captivate you until the very end with its romance, mystery, and characters that readers will want to watch grow and develop. Readers will enjoy a tale that has you believing in finding the strength to better yourself and realize that your life doesn't have to be perfect to be wonderful."

—*Literary Titan*

PRAISE FOR *ESTELLE*

"For avid readers of historical fiction, this book possesses an added, almost supernatural, narrative magic. The alternating historical and personal points of view balance well, fueling the sense that many of the female characters, despite nearly a century of separation, are practically one at certain points. Engaging and swift-paced, nuanced and intricate, this book is sure to delight history and art lovers alike while serving as a strong introduction to readers new to the historical fiction genre."

—*The US Review of Books*

"A beautifully mesmerizing debut novel set in New Orleans that will haunt readers long after the very last page is read."

—*Chanticleer Reviews*

"A promising debut . . . Henley brings New Orleans to life as she braids two intriguing stories—Edgar Degas' art and dalliance with Marguerite and Anne's treasure hunt into Degas's poorly-known early history."

–*Historical Novel Society Review*

KATE'S WAR

A NOVEL

LINDA STEWART HENLEY

SHE WRITES PRESS

Published 2024
Printed in the United States of America
Print ISBN: 978-1-64742-614-9
E-ISBN: 978-1-64742-615-6
Library of Congress Control Number: 2023915780

For information, address:
She Writes Press
1569 Solano Ave #546
Berkeley, CA 94707

Interior Design by Kiran Spees

She Writes Press is a division of SparkPoint Studio, LLC.

For my father

Gordon Thallon Stewart

1919 - 2016

CHAPTER 1
Sunday, September 3, 1939

The day broke gently, misty and still, but promised nothing gentle for Kate. The plans she would announce to the family that morning would not please them, especially her mother. She lingered in bed for a few more minutes while the morning sun struggled to emerge, piercing the crack between the curtains. Then she got up and tore the window coverings open and squinted at the familiar gleam of railway tracks as they disappeared around the curve towards London. She would miss the sight, but not the sound, of trains hurtling past just a stone's throw from the house. Kate straightened her shoulders: she would go, even though leaving would unsettle her parents, deplete her paycheck, and demolish her savings. Her heart quickened at the thrill of the adventure ahead. Now she had only to let go of her doubts, fling them outside, and allow them to evaporate like steam from the passing trains.

She turned her attention to the Red Admiral butterfly perched on the windowsill. It drew its wings together, hiding their brilliant colours, then flexed and flared into the sky. Its beauty brought memories of the nickname her sister Clare had teasingly given her when they were children. *Caterpillar.* Because, despite her dearest wishes, Kate couldn't fly.

But now she could. The time had come to leave her Carshalton home, take a flat closer to London with her friend Sybil, and wing into her own life. *All it takes is courage*, she said to herself. She took a deep breath and with a quick gesture tidied her unruly hair. She would tell her parents this very day. This very minute. She pulled on a dressing gown and sped downstairs.

She found her family clustered in the living room, surprising at that time of day. Her mother still wore her grey church-going dress and shoes. Ryan, lounging in his striped football jersey, looked sleepy. How would they react when she told them her news? She opened her mouth to speak, but her father Sean held up a finger to silence her while he switched on the wireless. It crackled into life, and moments later the broadcast began. Neville Chamberlain made the announcement in his halting old-man voice.

"This country is at war with Germany."

Kate collapsed into the nearest chair. What she most feared was happening. *War.* In her lifetime.

"Oh Sean!" her mother gasped, reaching for her husband's arm. "Not again—"

"Hush, Mary Grace," he said, turning up the volume.

The Prime Minister continued, urging parents to save their children from harm in vulnerable cities by participating in an evacuation plan called Operation Pied Piper. He ended the broadcast, saying more information would be forthcoming about this and how to prepare.

Kate's thoughts whirled while the family remained huddled around the wireless listening to the news without moving a muscle. Even though it was not a surprise, it was sobering to face the certainty of war. A few seconds later, Ryan stretched his legs, and Kate caught his eye.

"Thank God you're too young to be a soldier," she said, breaking the silence. Then, looking at her father, she asked, "Will you have to serve, Dad?"

"Probably not at first, anyway," Sean said. "We'll learn more soon. The king's address comes on at six."

Dread gripped Kate's heart. *But many young men will fight and die.*

"I'll make a pot of tea and some sandwiches," Mary Grace said, her thin voice breaking, eyes brimming with tears. Kate rose to help.

Each member of the family sat quietly eating their lunch, engrossed in their own thoughts. They resorted to various activities to pass the time until the king's speech. Mary Grace cleaned the kitchen, and Sean and Ryan left to play football. Kate went for a long walk. With each footstep, she became more certain that this was not the time to announce her departure from home.

At six o'clock, the family gathered again in the living room to listen to King George. Kate moved closer to the wireless to hear.

"In this grave hour," the king began, "perhaps the most fateful in our history . . ."

Is this really happening? Fateful? Now? When I've laid such careful plans? Kate thought with horror.

". . . for the second time in the lives of most of us, we are at war."

Kate's attention wandered as she tried to absorb the full meaning of the words. The king spoke slowly, with hesitation. It was common knowledge that he suffered from a speech impediment, and Kate was well aware of the difficult task before him. She related to this, and held her breath in sympathy. As the king continued, his voice strengthened with confidence, and she relaxed. She appreciated his efforts to inspire courage in a jittery nation. She listened more intently.

". . . For the sake of all that we ourselves hold dear, and of the world order and peace, it is unthinkable that we should refuse to meet the challenge."

Kate groaned inwardly as she understood the implications for herself. *I must give up my own challenge in the interest of world order and peace.* She scrutinised the long faces of her family. Everyone sat transfixed, unblinking. There was no way she could leave home just now. Her spirits plummeted.

". . . with God's help, we shall prevail."

Sean reached over and flicked off the wireless.

"Let's hope so," he said glumly.

Kate groped for something to say. "For a stutterer, I'd say it was a good speech," she said at last. As she uttered the words, the ghost of an idea flitted through her head. Perhaps there was hope for her yet.

Mary Grace glared at her. "That's not the point. That it's a good speech isn't important. We're at war again. Don't you know what that means?" She wrung her hands, her face stricken. "We must all stay together to get through it."

Thinking that as usual her mother lacked sensitivity to a long-standing problem, Kate wanted to defend herself, to explain that she understood only too well her mother's fears about the war, but the sudden blare of air raid sirens drowned her out. She clapped her ears in fright and squeezed her eyes shut as the unearthly sounds wailed up and down the scale. When the noise ceased, Sean cautiously opened the front door. Neighbours leaned from windows, and shouts of "Blimey, are the blighters bombing us already?" and "Bloody hell!" erupted along the street. Kate attempted to push past her father, but he caught her arm.

"Don't go out. We don't know what's happening yet. We must stay inside and wait for instructions."

Kate reluctantly withdrew as the reality of the situation gripped her. Her country was at war, and her dreams and ambitions could be dashed to a million pieces. The devastation, the utter hopelessness and cruelty of war, would be here, in England. The all-clear siren sounded, one long, sustained note signaling the end of the air raid alarm. She clapped her hands to her ears again, knowing that it signaled the beginning of a new and inescapable kind of alarm. However would she adjust, as adjust she must?

CHAPTER 2
September 1939

They drew the blackout curtains tight each evening, but life continued eerily as usual. Kate was happy to retreat to her part-time job teaching singing at St. Bridget's School for Girls. From work, she phoned her best friend Sybil to commiserate about the end of their plans for a flat together. Each day Kate arrived home to the sound of her mother's heavy sobbing in the kitchen as she grieved at the onset of another war. Kate sympathised, but couldn't bear witnessing the red eyes, sunken cheeks, and shuddering shoulders. Most days Kate slipped into the house quietly and stole up the stairs to her room.

At the end of the week on Friday, she wanted to sit at her piano. She needed to practice and craved the calming effect music always had on her. But she didn't dare. She knew her mother hated the constant repetition of passages that didn't always sound musical, and Kate didn't want to add to the tension in the household. She sighed and threw her satchel on the bed, kicked her shoes off, and lay down. An hour remained before tea time at four, and she would stay out of the kitchen until then. She stared at the ceiling, her mind restless, until a knock disturbed her thoughts.

"Can I come in?"

She pulled herself up, opened the door to Ryan, and fell back on the bed. He shut the door and sat down beside her. She mussed his hair. At thirteen, he was too old to cuddle with any more. He'd grown tall and lanky, and his voice sometimes cracked, switching from a boy's high pitch to a new deeper tone. His dark hair flopped around his ears, and his brown eyes snapped with anger.

"She's at it again. I wish she'd stop. She's so dramatic."

"I know. I hate it, too, but I try to understand. She's our mum guarding her chicks, just like your old pet hen, remember? She clucked and chased her babies around the garden, and scolded them when they ran too far."

"I understand all that. But Hickory was a chicken and didn't know any better."

"Look, everyone's on edge these days. They're saying the threat of an invasion by Germany is real. And we live on the outskirts of London, so that puts us at risk for bombing. The government wants to protect the children. That's you!"

"I'm not a child," he snorted, "and I don't mind getting out of the house. It's so depressing these days, with Mum afraid, and the bomb shelters, blackouts, and talk of air raids. You know about the Operation Pied Piper thing. I'd like to go to the countryside where there's more space. My school mates feel the same."

"Are any of them leaving?"

"Not yet. Billy might soon."

"Where will he go?"

"They haven't told him. Everything's a secret. At school they gave us all a sign-up letter to bring home today. That's what got Mum going again. The envelope said 'From His Majesty's Government. Urgent.' She broke down and cried buckets."

"You didn't tell her you want to leave home, did you?"

He shook his head. "Not yet."

Kate nodded and gave him a feeble smile.

"That's best. We need to let things settle down for a bit. I'd think Dad's not against the idea of evacuation, and Mum may come around in time."

"You have all the luck. You can make your own decisions. Don't you want to get out of here?"

Kate grimaced. "Come on, Ryan, how can I justify both of us taking off?" *Especially now Clare's married,* she thought. "Mum wants to keep the family together," she continued. "If you go, I stay."

"But you're twenty! You don't have to live at home anymore. If I were you, I wouldn't hang around for a minute. I'm going to leave school next year anyway."

"Fine, if that's your decision. No one's going to stop you from growing up." She mussed his hair again. "And I'll miss you, too, little brother, when you do."

He grinned. "Aw. Let's arm wrestle."

They made right angles of their arms on the bed and clasped hands. Kate presented her stronger left arm. For a few minutes they swayed one way, then the other, until Ryan tightened his grip and slammed his sister's forearm onto the mattress.

"You're strong, for a girl," he said.

"You forget I'm a swimmer, or used to be."

"Hmm. Like Mum. Hard to imagine now."

It *was* hard to imagine. At his age, the former Mary Grace O'Donnell had been a competitive swimmer. She learned to swim in the sea near her parents' home in Sussex, in Selsey, on the South coast, fearlessly plunging into the water at all times of the year. She had taught Kate early during summer visits there, but by the time Ryan was old enough the family no longer spent holidays in Selsey, or anywhere. Things changed for the family, and Mary Grace, no longer challenging herself to confront white-crested waves, lost her powerful arm muscles. How sad, Kate thought, that her mother's now softer body did nothing to soothe her constantly skittish mind.

"I wish I could swim as well as you," Ryan said. "Maybe you can coach me."

Kate inhaled sharply. *He doesn't remember. Thank God for that.*

But she would never forget. Because of her, he had almost lost his life. She was only ten years old: how could she have taken her three-year-old brother on the rowing boat, without permission? A sudden storm came up, rocking the vessel out of control. She heard herself scream as she lost an oar, then clutched Ryan in the terrifying moments as the boat capsized, turning everything upside down. Mustering her strength, she scrambled to employ the lifeguard's manoeuvre for rescuing non-swimmers that her mother had taught her, and she held her little brother's head to her chest as she swam on her back, frog-kicking her legs, whisking him to safety. Mary Grace, watching helplessly from the bluff, had never forgiven Kate for her reckless behaviour and, to avoid traumatising Ryan, told Kate never to talk to him about it. Kate would live with her guilt forever. She had often been tempted to talk to Ryan about the incident to find out if fear prevented him from learning to swim well when he was younger. But she respected her mother's wishes. It was one of many instances where Mary Grace had banned discussion of unpleasant things, further constraining their already tenuous relationship.

She shook her head to clear the memory and heard the end of Ryan's comment, ". . . anyway, I wish we lived closer to the sea."

She sighed. "Mum does, too. Sometimes I think that's all she wants—to live by the coast again, away from all the noise and grime of the city. And now from the bombing."

"Maybe so. Maybe that's what we all need."

Ryan pushed himself up from the bed and left the room.

Kate hadn't told him her other secret. She'd received a letter that day from their older sister Clare, sent to St. Bridget's, probably because she knew their mother would want to know the contents of the letter if she posted it to the house. The letter ended: *Please come and stay with us. You can escape that terrible war, and start your singing career. There are tons of opportunities in New York. Besides, you need to get away from home. Your loving sister, Clare.*

An awful dilemma. Kate would love to leave the about-to-be war-ravaged country behind and start an exciting new life. But, as she told Ryan, how could she abandon the family, especially if he left as well? Clare understood that, most of all, more important than anything, Kate still entertained hopes to sing professionally. Kate wanted to shine on stage, have a rousing effect on the audience, and pour her soul into her singing. Perhaps she should do that in America. On Broadway. Why not dream big? If only she didn't have that accursed problem, she might do anything. Kate folded her arms around her chest, protecting her secret. She'd have to overcome her big problem first.

Her mother's tense voice called from the stairwell.

"Kate, are you home? It's tea time."

"Coming." She tugged a comb through her hair, now matured to a subtle auburn, and smoothed the loose curls. As a child, she'd endured endless teasing because of its bright colour, and she winced as she untangled a knot, remembering the time her English teacher had scolded her for describing herself as "fair-haired" in an essay. "You're a redhead," the nun scoffed. Her schoolmates had laughed. But Kate liked her hair now. She slipped into her shoes and went downstairs.

The kitchen table, set for four, stood in a corner of the small room. There was hardly space to open the pantry door if four people sat down, and when Sean took his place next to it, he could not easily get out despite his still muscular, lean frame. He liked the seat because it afforded a view of the window and robins and bluetits eating crumbs on the windowsill. He acknowledged Kate with his usual ready smile, one that inched to the corners of his eyes. Ryan had inherited the feature, and a grin tugged at the edges of his mouth too as he joined the family at the table.

"Smells good, Mary Grace," Sean said. "What's the occasion?"

Kate had to admit, it did smell good, with cheesy and bacon aromas and a hint of garlic. Her mother was a superb cook.

"Quiche," Mary Grace said. "I found the recipe in my French cookery book. It's not what we usually eat, but with all the talk of rationing, I thought we should enjoy it while we can. It uses lots of eggs and cheese. Very nutritious." She glanced at Ryan. "Good for a growing boy."

"I don't care what they ration as long as it's not marmalade," he said. "What else would I have on my toast?"

Mary Grace wore an apron over her tan skirt and white blouse. Her greying hair, once thick and glossy, had lost its sheen, and she kept it short, allowing only a few tight waves to hug the back of her ears. Kate noted the flushed, tear-stained cheeks that made her mother appear hot and uncomfortable as she poured cups of tea. She set the pie dish down on the table along with a plate of bread slices and butter.

"*Bon appétit.* Help yourselves," she said, cutting the quiche into equal portions.

"How was school today, Ryan?" Sean asked.

The boy groaned. "Same as yesterday. More air raid drills and maps of Germany showing how close it is to our shores. They're building a shelter in the school grounds."

"Is that so? Already?" Sean said. "I heard on the news they were going to install those around the neighbourhood. Some people are getting them for their back gardens, too. They're called Anderson shelters. We may get one. We'd have enough room, I believe, if we gave up part of the vegetable bed."

"Enough of that talk," Mary Grace said quickly. "I won't give up my vegetables. We might need them."

"And what about the hen house? We must keep that. We could keep chickens again, for eggs," Ryan said, "though I might not be here to take care of them."

Whoops, Kate thought, as their parents stopped eating and stared at him.

"What did you say?" Mary Grace asked.

He blushed. "Sorry. I just meant that, um, chickens can live a long time."

Kate sat rigid in her chair, hands clasped tightly under the table. Their mother, her small face crumpled, scraped her chair back.

"We'll talk later, young man," Sean said. "Meanwhile, finish your tea."

Kate watched her mother's tortured expression. Before she could offer any words of comfort, a torrent of hiccups surged to Kate's throat. Mary Grace stood up immediately and patted her firmly on the back. Kate struggled to hold her breath to stop the uncomfortable contractions, but the hiccups didn't abate. The whistle of a train passing mere yards from the back of the house drowned all the sounds in the kitchen. *Clickety clack, clickety clack*, the train stuttered as it thundered by. The entire house shook, rattling crockery and glasses in the cupboards for several minutes before the noise faded out of earshot.

"The five o'clock to London, right on time," Sean said, glancing at the clock on the wall.

Kate's spasms subsided, and she cursed to herself as she rose to remove her plate from the table. *Those blasted hiccups again.* She coughed.

"Delicious. Thanks, Mum."

"I'll leave the dishes for you," her mother said as she left the room.

"Ryan, make yourself useful and help dry," Kate muttered as she handed him a tea towel.

Sean eased himself out of his chair. "Time for the news." He went into the living room to turn on the wireless.

Once they were alone, Kate said, "Big mistake, Ry. You'll get further if you let Dad talk to her first."

"Yeah. It sort of slipped out. I couldn't help thinking how I'd miss the chickens if we got some. I won't say another word, although if she's read the evacuation application forms I gave her from school, she'll see what's up."

"She will, but there's still time to make decisions, isn't there?"

"I don't know. We don't know anything. There might not even *be* an invasion."

"I'll talk to Dad. He might have more information."

"All right."

As soon as they'd finished doing the dishes, he bolted from the kitchen, leaving her to her melancholy thoughts. Despite her efforts, she still hadn't overcome the awful hiccupping problem, the one that stopped her from achieving her goal of attending music school. She would never sing before an adoring audience. But she heard the king's speech. Somehow, he had overcome his stammer, enough to speak well in public. *Maybe there's hope for me yet.* She piled the dishes neatly in the cupboard, then joined her father in the living room to hear Vera Lynn singing "When You Wish Upon a Star" on the wireless.

However, much as she loved Vera's voice and as many times as she had wished upon a star, she couldn't rid her mind of the dreadful moment the hiccups ruined her chances for a singing career.

Just turned eighteen and full of hope, she'd won an audition at the Royal Academy of Music. She anticipated fulfillment of her biggest dream, studying music. Her father encouraged her, but she refused his offer to accompany her to the tryout, saying she would prefer to go alone. She entered the recital hall with its high ceilings, rising rows of velvet-covered seats, and lights flooding the stage. Standing tall to heighten her five-foot-four frame, Kate faced a panel of six men and women sitting in the front row below her. She could hardly see their faces. Despite telling herself to relax, she felt her throat tighten and her pulse quicken as she waited. Silence hung in the air like fog.

"You may begin when you're ready," one of the adjudicators called.

She folded her hands in front of her and nodded to the pianist. The opening chords of her song rang out. She took a deep breath and opened her mouth to sing.

"Early one morning, just as the sun was shining . . ." Kate began, and paused. She knew she was singing off-key. The piano accompaniment continued for a few seconds, then came to a halt. Kate cleared her throat.

"Excuse me. Let me try again," she said.

The pianist replayed the introduction, and Kate sang.

"Early one morning, just as the sun was shining, I heard a maid singing in the valley down below. Oh, don't deceive me . . ." *hic, hic, hic . . .* She stopped. The hiccups intensified until they sounded like dishes rattling in the kitchen when the train passed by. She felt her face flush and panic rise through her veins. Her legs shook as she glanced at the piano player.

"Miss Murphy, perhaps you should have a glass of water and try again later," one of the judges boomed.

Hic, "Yes," she replied. *Hic.* "So sorr-*hic*-y."

She stumbled to the wings and down the steps leading off the stage.

Still hiccupping, she shuffled up a side aisle to the back of the performance hall to locate a lavatory and some water. *Why did this happen now, of all times?* Kate asked herself angrily. She had lost her opportunity for both a scholarship and the chance to study at the Royal Academy of Music. Her long-held dream crashed in a few short minutes. Even though she might control the tears, she couldn't control her hiccups. She'd no idea those could happen to her on stage. Before, she'd only experienced occasional episodes, mostly when she ate too fast at mealtimes. But she started off-key as well. That was probably unforgivable, and she had only herself to blame by neglecting to hear the piano's first note in her head as she began to sing.

Kate told herself she simply wasn't cut out for a performance career. She couldn't face the ordeal of another audition and had done nothing to further her dream of a singing career since then. She had settled for leaving home instead.

But with that plan thwarted, she would take steps to achieve her other goal. She must start by finding a cure for her hiccups. Rephrasing the king's words, it was unthinkable that she should refuse to meet the challenge of winning her own private war.

CHAPTER 3
September 1939

K ate woke in fright after a muffled whistle invaded her sleep. *Am I dreaming*? she asked herself. But the noise continued, then stopped abruptly, ending with the front door slamming shut. She let out a sigh.

"The blooming kettle again, blast it all." Her father's voice downstairs confirmed her suspicion. She'd wait for things to settle down before going down.

"And a fine good morning to you, Katie," he greeted her later, looking up from the newspaper. The scant remains of an Irish accent enlivened his words with a musical tone that bore no trace of his earlier anger. She always liked him for that: he had a quick temper, something she shared, but he didn't harbour grudges. He'd come home grumpy from work recently, and she wondered why. She knew he didn't love his accounting job at the Royal Mail service, but he had uncomplainingly held his position for years. Perhaps he secretly wished he had more singing in his life, and had curtailed the desire because of his strong sense of duty. Or maybe he missed his onetime more adventurous life as a lifeboat sailor. She started to speak, but saw he was engrossed in his reading. Someday, she'd ask him.

A blackened kettle sat on the stove. She looked at it with suspicion and filled a pot of water to boil for tea. "Where's Mum?"

"Out buying a new kettle. It's the third one she's burned out in as many weeks. She was in the garden and didn't hear the whistle. Waste of money, buying kettles, but she can't be without a kettle now, can she?"

Kate suppressed a giggle.

"What's going on? Anything new in the paper?"

"Not much. So far, nothing has happened. The air raid alarms after the war announcement did nothing except scare people. But there's a town meeting this week where they might give us more information, and I plan to go to that."

"Will Mum go?"

"No. She already fears the worst."

"True. How will she get through this? She's practically having a nervous breakdown already, burning out kettles and so on. She'll be in the loony bin if the bombs fall."

"Kate, she has good reason for fearing another war. Remember her brother died at sea during the last one, a terrible loss for her."

Kate heaved a sigh, chastened. *How would I feel if I lost Ryan?*

"Don't underestimate your mother. She finds strength in working to keep the family going, preparing meals, tending her garden."

"Yes. That's exactly the point. That might change. You know the government is advising families to save their children's lives by sending them away. I think Ryan wants to go."

Sean set down the newspaper.

"Now, that's a different matter. I heard what he said at tea time, but he can't be serious."

"I don't want to put words in his mouth, but I believe he sees evacuation as an exciting opportunity."

Her father ran his hand through his thinning hair. "Oh dear. That will give your mother all kinds of grief."

"I understand lots of children react the same way. The schools encourage them."

"Strange thinking, I must say, although I do understand the

excitement of going to a new place. After all, I left Ireland at fifteen, though my sister Siobhan stayed, and was a comfort to our mother."

Kate cringed. There it was again—the notion that she, the daughter, should remain at home, while the son would be allowed to go away. Despite what Ryan said about her good fortune because of her age, he was the one who had all the luck. He could follow his dreams with fewer obstacles, she surmised, imagining her father's adverse reaction to her leaving. She didn't have an acceptable excuse, like marriage. Clare was lucky, too. Only she, Kate, had missed out on the proverbial luck of the Irish. But then she scolded herself. *Feeling sorry for myself won't help. I'm a grown-up.*

"I expect we'll hear more about evacuation in the coming weeks, then," she said.

"Thank you for the tip about Ryan," Sean said. "I'll have a conversation with him, but for now, best keep this to yourself, my dear."

Kate had planned to make bacon and eggs for breakfast, but lost her appetite. Despite her refusal to dwell on inequity within the family, she couldn't help feeling slighted. In her mother's absence, at least she might practice the piano. The old upright stood against the wall in the dining room, taking up most of the space. Her maternal grandmother Ellen had left it to her five years ago. She had given Kate elemental lessons as a child, saying she had a natural gift for music, and Kate had continued to study classical music with Sister Joseph Mary at St. Bridget's. After lifting the lid, she slid onto the piano bench and ran her hands over the worn ivory keys. Playing the piano was one of the rare instances where she could relish her left-handedness, believing the dexterity made playing easier. In any case, music cured even the worst heartache.

For the next hour, her spirits revived as she made progress with the John Field *Nocturne in B flat* she'd been working on. It always gave her great satisfaction to master a new piece, and she worked on it with determination. The Nocturne allowed for expression, especially where the chords ran up the scales chromatically. She loved hearing the notes unfold as a piece progressed and then, as her playing improved, adding dynamics and phrasing to bring it to life. The Nocturne challenged her, especially the more difficult passage in measure eight. She repeated it twenty times. That was why her mother didn't like listening to practice sessions, Kate reflected ruefully. But, regardless of her limited skills, Kate always valued music's power to transport her to a better place, something her mother didn't understand.

Her practice session over, Kate went upstairs to take a bath. Relaxing in the steamy water, she anticipated the day ahead. She wanted to talk to Sybil. Perhaps they could go dancing, a pleasant distraction. She immersed herself in the suds, inhaling the fragrance of the lavender bubbles. Thank goodness they still had water and an intact house. There couldn't be a war without bombs and so far, none had fallen. It all seemed unreal. Her father was right that she lacked her mother's all-too-vivid knowledge about wartime. Kate forced herself to empathise. How afraid Mary Grace must have been, pregnant in 1918, and wondering if she and her first baby Clare would survive. But Clare had thrived, and as she grew up, met all her mother's expectations. She had gone to nursing school, and planned to live and work nearby. Until she met Stan, now her husband. An American lawyer from New York. That had not been part of her mother's plan for Clare's future, a disappointment she might never overcome.

After the bath, Kate towel-dried and brushed her shoulder-length hair, keeping it loose, unlike on weekdays at the school, when she wore it pinned back. It framed her face with soft, shiny curls. After applying lipstick and mascara and checking her image in the mirror, she deemed herself presentable. She felt some pride in maintaining her reputation as a pretty girl and didn't mind making the effort necessary to do so. Making arrangements with Sybil meant finding a phone box, but now she was hungry for lunch. Downstairs, she found shepherd's pie from the previous day in the pantry. Perhaps her father would want some as well.

"Dad, I'm heating leftovers from yesterday," she called upstairs. "Will you have some?"

"No, thanks, I'll wait for your mother. She'll have something in mind for us. By the way, I liked whatever you were playing, but you forgot the Irish songs," he said, as he came down to the kitchen.

"That was a nocturne by John Field, a composer from your homeland, Dad, who influenced Chopin. I can play songs for you next time, though."

Her father loved popular music, especially tunes that reminded him of his childhood home, songs like "My Love Nell" and "Molly Malone." Kate wished she could interest him in classical music as well, though she loved catchy tunes as much as he did.

Lunch was the main meal of the day, and usually the family ate it together on weekends, but today Kate wanted to get out of the house. She couldn't stand all the waiting: for her mother, for her life to start— even for the war, for God's sake. Everything seemed to move in slow motion. She turned on the oven and placed the potato and meat dish inside. She speculated about why it was taking her mother so long to buy a kettle. Perhaps she wanted one with a louder whistle, one she would hear even if she was pruning roses in the garden. The clock read one o'clock, the usual time for their meal. Kate finished her lunch, rinsed the plate, and called to her father in the living room.

"Just going out to make a phone call and run some errands, Dad," she said. "Back soon."

She took a raincoat from the hall coat rack and stepped outside. The sky threatened rain, but at least she could enjoy the fresh air, away from the house and its stifling atmosphere. The nearest red telephone box stood on Water Road, two streets away. She scurried along the pavement on Holly Road past blocks of houses like her family's. All nineteenth-century stone semi-detached dwellings, the ones on her side of the street were blackened by soot from the railway that ran behind them. Most had tiny gardens in front. A few, like the Murphy home, thanks to her green-thumbed mother, glowed with flowers. But most were dull and lifeless, paved or landscaped with small pebbles. A modest but friendly neighbourhood, she knew the people on both sides. She had lived there all her life, and as she trundled along the familiar street, she hardened her heart and told herself she would not spend the next twenty years there.

Upon entering the phone box, she deposited the coins and dialed her friend's number.

"Sybil, we need to talk. Want to go dancing tonight?"

"I'd love to go. At the Strand? At eight? See you there."

Kate assented and hung up, and the coins clanged deep into the instrument. The rain hadn't started yet, and she took a different path home. A row of shops stood around the corner. She'd buy a postcard to send to Clare. That way, she could acknowledge her sister's invitation without long explanations for her refusal. She groaned as she remembered Clare's last words before she left for America. "I'll be waiting for you. You will always have a home with me, Caterpillar."

Clare, more mature, though only one year older, had given her sister the nickname when Kate was six. She had brought a caterpillar home on a cabbage leaf, saying she wanted to watch it turn into a butterfly. It did eventually, but she hadn't been there to witness the metamorphosis. After emerging from its cocoon, the butterfly had flown from the windowsill through her open bedroom window one spring day while Kate was at school. She was devastated. But even now, at twenty years old, she wasn't a butterfly. Not free, like Clare.

As their mother's favourite child, Clare wielded considerable influence in the household and had a calming effect on Mary Grace's fragile nerves. Clare always knew exactly what to say, and in the three months since her departure, home life had become unstable, with occasional ferocious arguments between Kate and her mother that seemed to come out of nowhere, like summer thunderstorms. These disagreements, often about such trivial matters as how much milk to pour in cups of tea, dissipated as quickly as they began, but they electrified the air for hours. Recently, Kate had made strong efforts to control her temper and avoid confrontations, resigning herself to the notion that she and her mother didn't understand each other, and probably never would. But she missed Clare and her reassuring presence.

At the tobacconist's shop, she inspected the rack of postcards. The suburb of Carshalton had some historic buildings, including her school, part of which had been a Georgian private mansion. A few cards pictured those on front and others showed scenes from the surrounding Surrey countryside. They weren't interesting. Why would Clare want to be reminded of her home town when she lived an exciting life in New York City? She chose a postcard of a London bus, red and cheerful.

"Will that be all, love?" asked the storekeeper. "How about a newspaper? There's news about the war in the *Evening Standard*."

"I'll take one. Thanks."

Her father read the newspaper regularly, but not the *Evening Standard*. Everyone was starved for information about the war. She paid for the items and left the shop. Pedestrians passed her on the street—mothers pushing prams, dirty-kneed boys in football jerseys, and people of all ages pulling dogs on leads. Everyone seemed to be in a hurry, trying to get home before the rain. *Or the bombs that might fall from the sky any minute,* she thought. Or did she only imagine the urgency? As she passed the florist's shop, she thought guiltily of her mother. Perhaps flowers would cheer her up. She purchased a bouquet of pink carnations. *That's enough splurging for now,* she told herself, clutching the stems as she inhaled the spicy fragrance. She needed to keep some change for the dance hall.

At home, the house smelt of bangers and mashed potatoes.

"I hear you've had your lunch, Kate," her mother greeted her. "Sorry I was late. Long queues in the shops, and everyone's talking about the war."

Kate handed her the flowers.

"Lovely, but Kate, dear, you shouldn't be spending your money on me," Mary Grace said, sniffing the flowers as she filled a vase with water and set it on the kitchen table. "I see you're all dressed up. Will you be home for supper?"

"No. I'm meeting Sybil Thorndyke at the Strand."

"Are you sure that's wise? It's dark out there. People get hurt because they can't see. And should you be out having fun when the rest of us are in hiding, preparing for war?"

Kate bit back her tongue at the provocative comment. Perhaps her mother's state of mind was incurable, and the flowers hadn't helped at all.

Sean stepped into the room. "Hello there, Katie. My, you look fetching in that green dress. Matches your smiling Irish eyes. You're going out, I'm guessing."

She smiled. She basked in his admiration. "Yes, Dad. By the way, I picked up a newspaper."

She passed him the folded paper. He took it eagerly, smoothed it out, and gasped. "Lord help us! The Germans torpedoed a liner, the *SS Athenia*."

"When? Where?" Kate asked.

"On September third, the day we went to war, off the coast of Ireland. One hundred twelve passengers lost."

Mary Grace crossed herself. "God save their souls," she said, placing her hand on her chest.

"So it seems the war has begun," Kate said, frowning. "Here we are, three weeks later, and only now learning about this. So much for people calling it the Bore War because nothing has happened. And U-Boats are sinking *passenger* ships, for goodness sake."

"I expect air warfare will come our way soon," Sean said glumly. "The Germans have Messerschmitts, I hear. Many of them. Frightening."

"We're vulnerable, being close to the railway," Kate said. Her mother's hands were already shaking as she arranged and rearranged the flowers and muttered to herself. "I'm going dancing tonight, anyway," Kate continued. "No point sitting around waiting for bombs."

"Take the big torch, and keep it pointed down," her father said. "You'll need it after dark in the blackout."

Kate took the torch. If the war had started, perhaps she shouldn't go out, as her mother warned. But she wanted to see her friend and have fun, war notwithstanding, and after a moment's hesitation, she stepped outside.

CHAPTER 4
September 1939

K ate usually took the number 407 bus to the Saturday night dances at the Strand, a fifty-minute ride from the stop at the corner of Holly Road, but she could barely make out the dimly lit signs on the buses. It was dusk, and she waited in the familiar neighbourhood, which had taken on a strange, unearthly quality. No streetlights, no chinks of yellow warmth escaping from windows. An occasional car with masked headlights passed by, wheels swishing on the damp road. Alone at the bus stop, she shivered and looked around warily. *Mum was right. The place is creepy in the dark.* The bus finally appeared, brakes squealing as it drew to a halt. She paid her fare and took a seat at the front, away from the few other passengers. Raindrops dribbled on windows misty from the damp interior. Her nose wrinkled at the fusty smell. *Wet wool or soggy dog?* she wondered.

Kate went to the dances at the Strand as often as possible. She, Sybil, and several girls from their schooldays enjoyed seeing one another there. Sybil's gold curls and quick smile enhanced her vibrant personality, and thanks to her father's position as a highly placed diplomat, her parents could afford to buy her fashionable clothes. During their years abroad, they had left Sybil in the care of the good sisters at St. Bridget's. Now they lived in one of the more respectable areas of Carshalton. Sybil had attended Oxford to read mathematics, but moved back to her parents' home afterwards.

Kate and Sybil met when they were eleven. Assigned to the same table for lunch at school each day, they discovered Sybil detested fish, which Kate loved, and Sybil enjoyed pork chops, which Kate abhorred. The school provided no choices for lunch and did not permit pupils to bring food from home. Furthermore, the rules required girls to eat everything on their plate. No waste, the nuns said. This regulation inspired Sybil and Kate to eat the food that the other disliked. They became adept at completing the quick manoeuvre of tipping a serving of fish or meat from one plate onto another without attracting the watchful eye of the nun in charge, and they learned to keep straight faces while doing so, though sorely tempted to giggle.

Sitting at lunch together each school day, Kate and Sybil developed a close friendship. Some of the older girls disapproved of their lunchtime antics, but they could usually be convinced that the swaps were for the best because the entire table would be punished if they employed a popular alternative for disposing of disliked food. They would pile plates on top of leftovers, crushing them, so they wouldn't be noticed when the nuns removed stacks of plates from the table. At various times everyone had been guilty of that behaviour. School food was not always tasty— inedible grub, some said—and Kate invited Sybil home often for a better meal on weekends. Mary Grace always welcomed her, sharing her own memories of unsatisfying school meals, and telling Kate how much she enjoyed Sybil's lively personality and good manners. *Everyone likes Sybil*, Kate recalled, with a slight twinge of envy.

In the smoky dance hall, Kate bought her entrance ticket and headed for the washroom to change her boots for pumps suitable for dancing. She shook off her raincoat, checked her appearance in the mirror, and re-applied her lipstick. Then she joined the throng dancing to the sound of the live band. Sybil waved and came over to her. In her red dress, she shone like a lone poppy among a field of khaki uniforms.

"Glad you got here in all this rain," Sybil said. "I should have thought to collect you in the car. I can take you home, anyway."

"Thank you. You look smashing. Is that a new frock?"

Sybil nodded. "Mummy got it, don't know where. Let me buy you a drink. What'll it be?"

"Gin and tonic, please."

Kate rummaged in her handbag for some money, but Sybil stopped her.

"Drink's on me. I've got news, something to celebrate. Find a table and I'll be back in a sec."

Sybil vanished into the throng and Kate located an empty table. The band's songs filled the room and a huge rotating ball in the ceiling cast shards of light on the dancers. She tapped her foot to the beat and began to enjoy herself. People swirled around, women with skirts flying, men mostly in uniform. She didn't see anyone she recognised but hoped to find a decent dancing partner, join the fray, and lose herself in the music. Sybil reappeared bearing two glasses. She handed one to Kate.

"Cheers," she said.

"So what's the news?"

"I know this may come as a shock, but I hope you can be happy for me." Sybil set her glass down. "I'm going to America next month. Boston."

"Are you?" *So no flat together.* Even though Kate realised the flat was no longer possible, she hated to see the last shred of the bold idea die. She took a deep swallow of her drink to hide her dismay and resentment, then forced a smile. "It sounds exciting. Tell me more."

"Mummy has a distant cousin who lives there. They think it's safer overseas, and Doris has invited me to stay for the duration of the war. Mummy's coming, too."

Kate watched as a slight frown crossed her friend's forehead. *Does she want her mother there? Wouldn't she rather share the flat with me, as planned?*

Sybil swept the bright curls from her clear grey eyes.

"I don't know how long Mummy'll be there," she continued. "Daddy will stay here to work. As he's a diplomat, they can't spare him. We have tickets on RMS *Aquitania*, and we'll leave from Southampton next month."

Kate sat stupefied. She hadn't expected that her best friend would leave her, and so soon.

"That's news, all right. But aren't you afraid?" she blurted. "Haven't you heard about the *Athenia*?"

"No. What's the *Athenia*?"

"A liner that a U-boat torpedoed just a few weeks ago. She went down in the Atlantic. Over a hundred passengers drowned."

Sybil scowled and shrugged. "I suppose that might be our fate, but if we're here, we could die anyway, or who knows what might happen when there's an invasion. Daddy's sure there will be one. After all, the Germans marched into Poland."

"Well, I do envy you. I'd love to go to America. Actually, Clare invited me to New York."

"Splendid! Are you going?"

"No. I can't leave Mum now."

"That's a shame," Sybil said. "So, you're going to wait out the war, here in Carshalton?"

"What else can I do? I'll miss you. Who will I go dancing with?"

"Sorry if I've let you down. This damn war is disrupting everything, I'm afraid."

Kate made no reply, but looked down at the table and reached for her glass.

Sybil touched her friend's hand. "Drink up, and let's get out on the floor. It'll cheer you up."

Kate downed her drink and got up to dance. Two men approached them. The taller one, blond and handsome, in uniform, said, "Nice to see such attractive young ladies here tonight. I'm Colin." He bowed slightly to Sybil. "Would you like to dance?"

"With pleasure. I'm Sybil, and this is Kate."

The dark-haired man wearing an ill-fitting suit held his hand out to Kate.

"I'm Barry," he said. "Want to dance?"

On the dance floor, Sybil and Colin blended into the crowd. Barry didn't steer Kate far from the edge. He danced awkwardly, and she kept herself as far apart from him as she reasonably could.

He tried to pull her closer. "Hey, is something the matter?"

"It's just so hot in here," she said, wishing the song would end. His hands were sweaty, and he looked hardly older than a boy.

Eventually the music stopped, and he released her. *Thank goodness.* He was not the kind of dancing partner she enjoyed, someone who would swing her around with confidence. But when she returned to the table, he followed.

"How about another drink?"

"No thanks," she said, taking a seat.

"Well, I need one. Back in a minute."

She watched him amble towards the bar. His skinny build and large feet reminded her of a stork. *Where's Sybil?* She didn't want Barry as her sole companion for the evening. He reappeared with a glass of ale and sat down beside her.

"Cigarette?" he asked, offering her one.

"No, thanks."

He lit one for himself and took a deep drag. She noticed dirt under his fingernails.

"Tell me about yourself," he said. "Do you live nearby?"

"Yes. You?"

"I live in Sutton. Work in a garage there."

"Oh. So you're not joining up?"

"Not if I can avoid it. I don't approve of war."

"Of course not. No one does," she said. Sutton was two miles away, so he was a local. He had soft brown eyes. She couldn't imagine him as a soldier. He took a swig of his drink and leaned back. He looked a lot more comfortable sitting down, and she found herself feeling more kindly towards him. The music became louder, making conversation difficult, and she gave him a weak smile and shrugged her shoulders. After a while, Colin and Sybil, pink-cheeked and out of breath, returned to the table. Sybil smoothed her dress and leaned back in her chair.

"Colin, where are you stationed?" Sybil asked.

"In Pirbright. I'll be leaving for Belgium soon."

"Has the fighting actually begun?" Kate asked.

"In Poland it has. The Germans are going to attack the French, the Belgians, us. Everyone."

"It's ghastly," Sybil said. "I'm not waiting around for the Nazis to come. I'm off to America soon."

"You're running away?" Colin asked. "Not sure that's best. Churchill doesn't approve of evacuees, you know. He says people should stay and defend the homeland."

Sybil glowered. "Well, he can stay. He's the First Lord of the Admiralty, so it's his job to protect the country. I've no wish to die or live under German rule."

"Uh, no. Would you like to dance again?" he asked her.

"Not really. I could use a cigarette, though."

Colin pulled a packet from his pocket and offered her one. She held it between her fingers and waited for him to light it. She inhaled, then blew out the smoke.

"Thanks," she said.

Kate regarded her friend and envied her attitude of bored nonchalance, but knew she herself could never get away with such an affectation. They sat for a while without talking, and Kate tapped her foot in time to the music. Barry leaned closer to her, his eyes eager.

"I can tell you like music. Want to dance again?"

"No, thanks. Do you like music too?"

"Yeah. Play the violin a bit."

This surprised her. He didn't look like most musicians she knew, with his dirty fingernails.

"Really? How did you learn?"

"At school. They had a wonderful music teacher. He took me on, gave me free lessons."

"You must have impressed him then," she said.

A shy smile reached his eyes.

"I teach singing at St. Bridget's," she said.

"Do you, now? So you're a teacher." His face lit up. "I've always had a soft spot for teachers. Tell me more about yourself."

Kate shifted back in her chair, away from him. "I only teach part-time."

She turned to Sybil and raised her eyebrows.

It was the secret getaway signal they used when they met men they didn't care to get to know better. Sybil yawned. "I've had a long day. Hate to leave you chaps, but I have to go home now."

She eyed Kate. "Ready?"

Kate nodded.

"Too bad. The evening's barely begun," Barry said.

"Good luck with the war," Sybil said to Colin.

The women grabbed their raincoats and cut through the crowd.

"Glad we left," Sybil said. "I couldn't wait to get out of there, either. The last thing I need is a lecture about why I shouldn't go overseas."

"I didn't care much for Barry. He was coming on too strong," Kate said. "And he was a terrible dancer." She didn't add that she wasn't in the mood for dancing now. Sybil's news had upset her more than she wanted to admit.

"Better luck next time," Sybil said cheerfully. "Let's come again on Saturday."

"All right. Perhaps you shouldn't dress up so nicely. That red dress is like a beacon. You'll attract all the wrong types."

"Maybe so, but I like red. It's my favourite colour. And I like admirers. One day I'll find the right one."

They switched on their torches, shining them on the ground as they had been told to do. All the buildings around were dark shapes, with drawn curtains or brown paper taped over the windows to block the lights. The damp air smelled peculiar, like mouldering mushrooms, Kate thought, as they splashed through the puddles. A faint rumbling sounded in the distance. Kate caught Sybil's arm.

"Is that the sound of planes, or bombs?" she asked shakily. She could feel a hiccup on its way. She stopped and bent to touch her toes in an effort to curb it, then stood up. After a few moments, the hiccups stopped.

"Sorry," she said.

"So, you still haven't kicked the old habit? Don't worry. It's only thunder," Sybil said. "Here comes the lightning."

A white flash illuminated the sky and the buildings around them.

It's not just a habit. If only it was, I could control it. "Nerves trigger them," Kate said, "and these days, there's plenty. At this rate, I'll be hiccupping for years."

She didn't elaborate. She hadn't told Sybil that she never experienced long episodes of hiccups until her relationship with Tony ended. *Tony.* Her first and only love.

"You'll outgrow them," Sybil said.

But will I outgrow them both? Kate questioned silently. Her friend had an amazing ability to think things through quickly, an attribute Kate admired but didn't share. Sybil's mind ran like clockwork, never missing a beat about what she wanted or thought she deserved. Perhaps she was right, and the dreadful hiccups would disappear. But if not . . . she recalled the king's speech. *How had he conquered his speech impediment?* Time to find out. Sybil, with her connections to high society, might know someone who could help.

The rain poured, and they sprinted to the parked car. "I hate these blackouts," Sybil said, driving slowly. "Dash it all. I can't see a thing. Another reason for getting out of here. They're going to ration petrol. Soon we won't be able to see anything or drive anywhere."

"That's the least of my problems, since I haven't got a car," Kate said. "What will you do with this one when you go away?"

"Leave it in the garage. Daddy'll still be here. His job will provide him with transport, but he can use it if he wants. He has diplomatic privileges and goes to Whitehall all the time. Very hush-hush."

"What did Colin say about Churchill not approving of evacuations? Is that true?"

"'Fraid so. Daddy says so, anyway. Churchill says wars aren't won by evacuation."

"Most people think it's a good idea to save the children."

"Right, and there's nothing to stop parents who want to send them away from doing so."

"Not true. Money. Most people can't afford it."

Sybil looked at her, but made no response. Soon they reached 59 Holly Road. Kate turned to face her friend. "I wanted to ask you. Do you know anyone who has connections to the royal family?"

"I know a few people who move in those circles. Why do you ask?"

"I'd like to find out who treated the king for his speech disability. He must have had a good doctor or some kind of specialist. There may be someone like that who can cure my hiccups."

"I can ask around."

"Would you, please? And thanks for the lift," Kate said as she opened the car door. "See you next week?"

"Right. I'll collect you at half past seven."

Kate waved briefly as she unlocked the front door. As she looked over her shoulder at the car's blood-red tail lights receding into the distance, the unexpected sadness of losing a friend overcame her. She adored Sybil, even though they lived in different worlds. But Sibyl had said she would help if she could, and her status in society might prove useful.

After all, the war hasn't really started yet, she reasoned, and with some assistance she might yet succeed at meeting a cherished goal.

CHAPTER 5

September 1939

The next morning, Kate found her mother sitting at the kitchen table wearing her blue dressing gown and fluffy slippers and nursing a cup of tea.

"Morning, Mum," Kate said, giving her a quick kiss.

"I've been thinking about the garlic," her mother said.

"What about it?"

"It's almost time to plant it. October. That's next month."

Kate met her mother's sea-green eyes but held her tongue. She didn't want to remind Mary Grace that there might not be a garlic bed this year, that they might need it for an air raid shelter instead.

"Is there any more tea?" she asked.

Her mother glanced at the clock.

"I made it two hours ago. I suppose we should make a fresh pot."

"You got up at five? Couldn't you sleep?"

"Well, it's so dark with the windows covered that you can't tell when it's morning. It's like living in a cave. That's why gardening's good. It calms me down. The smell of the sweet earth."

"But it's morning now," Kate said. She opened the curtains. Sunlight streamed through the window. Her mother blinked as the soft rays caressed her face.

Kate shook her head slowly as she filled the new kettle with water. Her poor mother. How would she withstand the bombs? She was the one who needed to be evacuated.

That evening, Sean announced he would attend the meeting at the town hall on Wednesday at five.

"Can I come?" Kate asked.

"I don't see why not. How about you, Ryan?"

"Can't. Football practice doesn't end until half past five."

"All right. Kate, we can walk over together."

"Have you got any idea what they'll tell us?"

"Not really, except that we'll hear the usual reasons for evacuation. I hope they'll tell us more about the air raid shelters."

"We don't need our own, do we? They've made a big one at school," Ryan said.

"Of course we do," Sean said. "Remember, we're right beside the railway line. We might not have time to get to the community ones and anyway, they might be full. We can all fit in the Anderson shelters they're offering to families, and we can equip it with things we'll need."

Kate watched Ryan's mouth droop. He probably considered the shelter at his school a good opportunity to be with his friends. They had installed one at St. Bridget's too, but she agreed with her father that it would be better to have one closer at hand.

On Wednesday, Kate looked around the large room overflowing with men and women all chattering loudly. A group of men in hard hats clustered around a podium on the stage talking and gesturing.

"Standing room only," Sean said. "We should have come earlier." Taller than most, he could see over the heads in front of them.

"You're too old, or I'd lift you onto my shoulders," he teased.

She liked him for those shared memories and was always proud to accompany her handsome father on the rare occasions when they went to events together.

At exactly five o'clock, a man took up a microphone. "I'm Paul Jenkins from the County Council." The room quieted. "You've all seen the Air Raid Precautions wardens in your neighbourhood. If not, you should meet yours. You might already have an ARP booklet. If you don't, we've got some here. Read it thoroughly. We will distribute gas masks this coming week. There are instructions on how to use those. Finally, we're taking orders for Anderson shelters. We recommend them. They're only about six feet by four and will fit in a small back garden. You should inform yourselves about the location of public shelters in schools, libraries, and other public buildings. We'll pass out lists of these as well. Any questions?"

"The war's not here yet. Why all the fuss?"

"Yeah, why all the fuss?" others echoed. The crowd became noisy as people talked amongst one another.

The councilor roared into the microphone. "We're here to inform you, not to frighten you. The government has taken the position that we must prepare for the worst. That's why we're having air raid drills in the schools and night blackouts. Also, and I don't mean to alarm you further, here in Carshalton we're only nine miles south of the centre of London. I don't need to tell you what that means."

The crowd mumbled. A woman sobbed.

"Blimey O'Reilly," rasped a gruff voice behind Kate.

"What an arse," someone else muttered.

Kate blocked her ears and the councilor held up his hand. "Quiet, please!"

The noise abated.

"There's one more precaution that most of you are already aware of. Evacuation."

At this, several people began shouting.

"One at a time, please!" the councilor yelled.

"Yeah, what about it? Only the wealthy can go. What about the working classes?"

"He's right. It's all about privilege. Why doesn't the government do something?"

"Hey, speak for yourself, mate. Not everyone wants to leave. I don't. Give up my home and go to some place in the countryside to frolic with the cows? Not me."

"All right everyone. We may have different opinions about this," the councilor boomed as the microphone screeched. "All I can say is stay calm. We're British. That's all for now. Please talk to us about any questions. But only to us. Keep your mouths shut otherwise. You know the government's slogan: 'Careless talk costs lives.'"

Someone played a trumpet rendition of "There'll Always Be An England," prompting people to sing. Others jeered. Kate joined the singers, her voice loud and clear. She never panicked when singing with a crowd. After the song ended, most applauded, some cheered, and the meeting concluded.

Sean said, "Let's go and see a warden about the shelter. We can pick up some information, too."

They made their way to the front of the room. Kate examined the leaflets while her father talked to a warden. She found it hard to accept that they would need to wear gas masks and spend time squatting in shelters smaller than a greenhouse. Perhaps Sybil had the right idea. Life would go on better in a place not threatened by war.

"Our local warden is George Bolton. Goes by Mr. B," Sean told her. "He says they'll deliver a shelter by the weekend. Best prepare your mother. I'll take her out for a nice meal. That's an extravagance, and she won't like any of this, but it'll soften the blow."

But maybe not, Kate thought. *The flowers didn't.* She responded, "While you're at it, you might want to tell her that Ryan wants to be evacuated."

Her father groaned. "He can't. Not yet, anyway. Where would he go?"

"The school has plans. They're outlined in the information he brought home the other day."

"What information?"

"Oh for God's sake. Didn't Mum show it to you?"

"No, she didn't. I'll ask her about it."

"This isn't going to be easy, is it?"

"No. But don't worry too much, my dear. It'll be all right," he answered, patting her shoulder.

Kate wasn't reassured. Her mother may have survived the last war, but now she was older, and more fragile. And their home close to the main train line to London might be an easy target.

CHAPTER 6
September 1939

K ate readied herself for school as usual on Monday. She pinned her hair back and dressed in a dark skirt and white blouse, then added a necklace in an attempt to look more mature. School rules didn't allow the girls to wear jewelry when in uniform. Even so, Kate looked young, barely older than some of her pupils. In fact, she was only a couple of years ahead of those in the sixth form, and several of them planned to go on to university, as Sybil had done. Like many of the lay teachers at the school, Kate was Catholic, with a good education, but no university degree. She considered herself fortunate to have a teaching job at such a young age without more credentials, and sometimes she envied the other teachers' experience and education. Attending the Royal Academy of Music would have given her those credentials along with a higher salary, but she had lost that opportunity and tried not to dwell on it.

Kate checked her pigeon hole in the school office and picked up an envelope addressed to her. She tore it open and read the note dated the previous week.

Dear Miss Murphy,

I came to see you but you weren't here. I would like to talk to you about my daughter Hannah who is in your music class. I will come to see you after school on Tuesday, if that is convenient.

Sincerely,
Mrs. Sarah Bell.

Hannah. *Who is she?* Kate wondered. Probably the small dark-haired girl, about twelve, who wanted to join the school choir. This early in the school year and with no individual instruction, a music teacher couldn't easily get to get to know her pupils well. This would be a good opportunity, and she liked talking to parents about their children.

Kate's first class, singing for the third form, started at ten o'clock. The girls, aged twelve and thirteen, were giggly. She had to choose the music carefully because if the songs had even the slightest reference to love or romance, the girls would whisper among themselves as they laughed, and lose attention. After the bell rang, the pupils filed into the assembly hall, where rows of chairs surrounded the piano. They took their assigned seats.

"Good morning, girls," Kate said.

"Good morning, Miss Murphy," they chorused.

"We'll warm up with the C major scale."

She played the scale on the piano and the girls' sweet voices rang out, "Do re me fa so la ti do."

"Very good. Now sing softly at first and gradually get louder. Does anyone remember the musical term?"

"Crescendo!" someone called.

"Correct. Raise your hand so I can see who you are."

A small girl in the front row did so.

"Your name, please?"

"Hannah."

"Thank you, Hannah. Hannah Bell, is that right?"

"Yes," she smiled.

So this was the girl whose mother wanted to talk to Kate. Now she would pay Hannah some attention before that conversation took place.

Kate had a two-hour break before her next class. Though she worked every day, she had a lighter load than most teachers, with correspondingly lower pay. But she enjoyed teaching and the opportunities it provided for her to stretch herself musically. The previous spring, she'd proposed a performance of Handel's *Pastoral Cantata* to the headmistress Sister Mary Joseph. Kate would direct it and coordinate all aspects, including sets and costumes, and now she planned to use ticket sales to support the war. She only hoped enough pupils would remain at the school to sustain a chorus.

Kate crossed the quadrangle and entered the lay teachers' staff room. Furnished with comfortable leather couches, armchairs, and tables, the space glowed with light from lamps near bookshelves lining the walls. Kate enjoyed sitting there with the camaraderie of fellow teachers. Some took an interest in her and offered advice. The school's teaching staff consisted mostly of nuns, who had their own staff room somewhere deep in the recesses of the convent for relaxing between classes. *Or more likely praying*, Kate thought.

Today she would spend some time in the staff room going over the Handel score.

"Hello there," the grey-haired French teacher greeted her. "Have a cup of tea. I've just made a fresh pot."

"Thank you, Mrs. Fitzgerald," Kate replied as she sat down on the couch next to the older woman. "That's quite a stack of papers," she noted. "Are you marking exams already? It's so early in the term."

"Not exams. My contribution to the M.O."

"And what is that?" Kate asked.

"Mass-Observation diaries. Don't you know about that programme?"

Kate nodded. "I've read about it in the newspaper. Doesn't it seem like spying, writing about other people and sending in your observations to be published?"

"I don't spy. I write a diary entry each day about what I've been doing. It's an important social research project. You should try it."

"I don't know," Kate said. "Not much to write about these days, even though we're supposed to be at war. The Bore War. No bombs, no invasion."

"What do you mean? There's always plenty to write about. Have you heard the latest about evacuations?"

Kate shook her head.

"Sister Mary Joseph told me they might arrange for the entire school to go to Devon—all the girls at St. Bridget's between ages eleven and fifteen."

"Lord help us. Then only the fifth and sixth formers would be in school. We would lose our jobs."

"I think so. There's a staff meeting today after school."

"But I have to practice with the choir. I won't be able to attend."

"You'll have to cancel choir. There should be a note in your pigeon hole about this. I understand Sister announced the meeting at this morning's assembly. The children have all been given information to take home and permission forms for their parents to complete."

"What are things coming to? We can't plan anything anymore," Kate said, thinking about the cantata. And about Ryan. Would his school be evacuated as well?

"War is coming, Kate. You can be sure of that," Mrs. Fitzgerald said, as she got up to leave.

Kate flinched. What awful news. She couldn't imagine how these children would feel leaving their parents and going somewhere new. Where would they live? It was an extraordinary plan. Maybe something worth writing about.

The meeting took place exactly as Mrs. Fitzgerald had imagined. The headmistress explained that information about evacuation to a safer place in a rural area would be sent home with pupils the next day. The exact destination for the children was unknown at the present time, but if enough parents signed the forms, arrangements would be made for the entire school to evacuate. Parents would not be allowed to accompany their children. Teachers were given copies of the forms and information along with notices that their jobs might be terminated if large numbers of pupils left.

As she listened, Kate's throat tightened. Her world was crumbling around her, not from enemy attacks, but from the assault on her dreams and goals. No escape for her—but her friend, her brother, perhaps also her pupils, would leave her behind, sitting at home with Mary Grace for company. Kate drifted home dispirited. She relied on the teaching job for her small income, and that might disappear. She worried all over again about Ryan and her mother. And worst of all, how would she live her life without music? She heard no answers, just a faint whisper of trees in the wind through the open window. *Sotto voce,* subdued, *like my stalled musical career,* she thought.

When she arrived home, the unusual sound of women's voices rang in the kitchen. She peered around the door to see Mary Grace at the table across from Mrs. Warren, their next-door neighbour. *At least Mum's not crying.*

"You're home, Kate dear," Mary Grace said. "Have a cup of tea with us. Pamela's telling me more about the ev—you know, what everyone's talking about . . . the Pied Piper plan."

Kate understood. Her mother couldn't bring herself to say the word.

Pamela Warren had wispy hair held back with clips on each side of her head. The hairstyle made her small head seem smaller, like a rabbit.

"Pamela tells me she won't send little Michael away. He's only five, old enough that she wouldn't be allowed to accompany him. Rachel is seven and wants to go, but only if she can take her canary. She says it's an exciting adventure. They're all going together from school."

"So you'll let Rachel go, but not Michael?" Kate asked, looking at Mrs. Warren.

"My husband says that's best. Better to keep one at home, at least. I couldn't bear to part with both of them. Your mum understands that."

"I do," Mary Grace answered, touching the woman's arm. "I won't let Ryan go, either. Fortunately, Kate's over the age limit, and anyway, she doesn't want to leave. She's far too attached to her job and the girls at school."

"Actually, Mum, I may not be able to teach much longer," Kate said. "We had a meeting today, and they're considering letting all the children go together to somewhere in the countryside. I can't teach if there are no pupils."

Her mother held a hand to her throat. "Jesus, Mary, and Joseph. Whatever's next? You mean, the nuns *want* the children to leave?"

"They didn't say, only that they trust the Lord will protect them, wherever they are."

Her mother crossed herself.

"We've been given information," Mrs. Warren said. "There's a list of things the children must take in suitcases. They'll have to wear name tags and carry gas masks. It will cost a lot to equip them all, and some can't afford it. That's another reason my Bill says we should only send one."

"When will you know if she's leaving?" Kate asked.

"Maybe not until the last minute. I've been told sometimes children have to leave directly from school without time even to say goodbye to their parents."

"That's inhuman. You poor dear," Mary Grace said.

"I'm keeping a diary about all this. It helps to write it all down."

Kate looked at the woman with new respect. "Are you participating in the Mass Observation Project?" she asked.

"May as well. They need volunteers. Gives me something to do instead of fretting about things I can't change. Sometimes they publish my entries in the papers, and it's exciting to see my words in print."

"Good luck, Mrs. Warren," Kate said, then turned to her mother. "Mum, I could use a bath. I'll be back to help with the tea things."

Upstairs, she turned on the hot water to draw her bath, wondering again what small luxuries like this would disappear once the war really began. She crossed to the window and gazed at the back garden. Her mother's tomatoes shone brightly along the sunniest wall and a row of string beans grew on a tall support nearer the house. The garlic bed lay bare, the earth freshly turned, ready for planting. Interesting that her mother grew garlic, the only person she'd heard of who did that. It wasn't an herb used in England, where people preferred more bland seasonings, but Mary Grace had acquired some cloves from the local greengrocer, a Frenchman, along with a French cookery book, and she liked trying out new recipes. Kate sighed. The freshly prepared garlic bed made the perfect place for an air raid shelter. A train surged by like a slick black monster, rattling her thoughts and shaking the house. She wished the railway line were anywhere but here.

Later, she gave some thought to contributing to the Mass Observation Project. It might be a useful exercise and she had the writing skills to do so. But after giving the matter further consideration, she quickly dismissed it. How could she write about such private matters, like her concern for her mother and Mrs. Warren's state of mind as they considered sending their children away in a desperate attempt to escape the war?

CHAPTER 7

September 1939

K ate met Mrs. Bell after school in the front office on Tuesday. A short woman with untidy hair, her face seemed frayed like the brown cardigan hanging over her loose dress and scuffed shoes. Her eyes darted around when Kate came near, as though she feared someone followed her.

"Thank you for seeing me, Miss Murphy," she said.

"Let's sit outside, since it's so warm today," Kate said.

She led the way through the halls. From Mrs. Bell's wide-eyed expression as the extensive grounds and manicured lawns stretched before them, Kate guessed that the woman had used the school's side entrance when she came in.

As they sat on a bench absorbing the view, Kate's mind slipped back to the only time she had entered the school through the main entrance. Sybil's father had driven the girls along the curving driveway lined with rows of mature chestnut trees that ran from the wrought-iron gates to the Georgian mansion at the bottom of the hill. The impressive approach presented views of the house, spreading lawns, and lake. Sybil once told Kate that the only reason her parents had sent her to St. Bridget's was because of its beautiful setting. "Is beauty enough to compensate for the nuns and their strict, silly rules?" she'd asked.

Kate watched Mrs. Bell swivel her head from side to side. *Who or what is she afraid of?* she wondered.

"How can I help you, Mrs. Bell?" she said at last.

"Please call me Sarah. As I told you, it's about my daughter Hannah, you see. She is good at the singing, I think. She likes it very much. I hope you can perhaps help her with it."

"In what way?"

"I thought you could maybe give her some private lessons. She would like to improve her voice. I can pay, a little."

"I don't know, Mrs. Bell . . . Sarah." Kate paused. "I have no formal training myself, and I only teach singing to groups." Noting Sarah's crestfallen expression, Kate continued, "I'll be happy to hear her sing, and she may wish to audition for a cantata that we hope to perform later this year. But as you know, the school might send the younger girls away."

"I have heard this. But if they stay . . . "

"Well, if they stay, she can try out for one of the soloist parts."

"*Ach, ja.* Very good. That will be something for starting, anyway. Thank you."

Kate hesitated. Would it be appropriate to ask the question buzzing in her head? She had to know. "You're from Germany, aren't you?"

Sarah hesitated in turn before answering. "Yes. But Hannah, she speaks English well. She has been here since many years now. She was seven when we came."

"Ah, I see. The cantata we hope to perform is by a composer called Handel."

"*Händel!* A German composer! *Wunderbar!* We will come and hear it."

"Ah yes. The German pronunciation. Do you live nearby, in Carshalton?"

"We do. But my husband, he can't work. He had a good job in Berlin but not here. Temporary Refugee Aliens, they call us. Only one person in a family is allowed to work."

"I wasn't aware of that. So you work?"

Sarah nodded and dropped her head. "Thank you for your time," she said. "Hannah said you are kind. I am certain you can help her."

"I'll do what I can."

Kate watched Sarah go back into the school, retracing her steps. Sarah was about thirty-five, she guessed, though she had tired eyes and appeared older. Her cracked fingertips reminded Kate of scorched tree trunks. *There must be more to her story than she told me . . . but maybe I don't want to know.*

Kate shivered and shook her hands as though scattering water on dying embers.

Constant discussion of evacuation broke up the school routine. Teachers were instructed to collect permission slips from the girls. Parents clamoured for further information and Sister Mary Joseph scheduled meetings during and after school. Kate attended one, wondering how much longer she'd be able to teach. St. Bridget's held fond memories. Sister Mary Joseph, who taught singing before she became headmistress, had encouraged Kate when she was in school and given her many solo parts in performances.

"Welcome, everyone," Sister Mary Joseph said to the group gathered in the assembly hall. "I expect you have questions, and I'll do my best to answer. But first, let me explain that we don't yet have all the details of the proposed evacuation. What we do know is that children who participate will be taken to a safe place in Devon where there are foster families willing to take evacuees in. We won't find out ahead of time what families your children will stay with. Each child will take a postcard stamped and addressed that the host family will send back with contact information."

The crowd jostled and murmured. From the back, someone shouted, "Are you saying that we're to send our children away without knowing where they're going?"

"That's what we've been told," the nun replied.

"Can't we go with our children to meet the families?"

"No. Escorts will accompany them and make sure each child is settled."

"What happens if my child doesn't like the family she's with?"

"I understand there will be a way of checking on the children and reporting on the success of each placement."

"Can we visit our children?"

"We don't know about that. Possibly."

"Will the children go to school there?"

"Yes. It's my understanding that they will attend local schools and every effort will be made to send our girls to Catholic schools."

The audience again talked among themselves and the noise level grew louder. Kate looked around at the parents. She caught sight of Sarah Bell, but otherwise didn't recognise many. *How awful this must be for them.* Sister Mary Joseph lifted her hand, and the crowd slowly quieted down.

"You understand it's by no means certain that the entire school will evacuate. Only children under the age of sixteen can go. And only if most parents want them to. If not, we'll keep the school open as best we can. But you must understand that the proximity of the premises to central London makes us all vulnerable to bomb attacks."

The crowd protested, their cries resounding in Kate's ears. "Not fair . . . damned Nazis . . . warmongers . . ."

"Hush," Sister Mary Joseph said, holding up a hand. The buzz died down again, and she continued, "For that reason city officials are encouraging people to save their children by sending them to a safer place. We don't want to lose a whole generation of young people. That happened in the last war."

"Right. Let's save the children," a man shouted.

The headmistress held up her arms in a supplicant gesture. "I trust the Lord will show us the way. This is a most difficult decision for us all. I must ask you to return your permission forms by the end of next week. Please note that they must be signed by both parents."

Kate closed her eyes and let dismay overwhelm her. She hadn't realised how much pressure the city officials were placing on parents. With a deep pit in her stomach, she felt sad for everyone. She filed out of the hall with the others and dawdled home. It was no surprise that her mother was becoming unstable as she contemplated whether it would be safer for Ryan to go away than stay at home. Until now, Kate had taken the view that her mother had a tendency to over-react and expect the worst. Now it seemed the government implied that parents who refused to evacuate their children were foolish as well as unpatriotic. The country didn't want to lose its young again. That made sense. She began to think there was no real choice.

Ryan would have to go.

CHAPTER 8
September 1939

The next morning Sean knocked on Kate's bedroom door.

"Kate, are you up?"

She rolled over in bed and swung her feet to the floor.

"Just barely," she said as she opened the door.

"I wanted to tell you I'm taking your mum out for supper tonight. I'm going to talk to her about Ryan leaving."

"Very well. Good luck," Kate said.

"Another thing. They're delivering the air raid shelter tomorrow. You might want to take her out for a walk or something."

"Are you going to let her know about that, too? She'll go mad when they take over her garden. Please don't make me be the one to tell her."

"Fair enough," he said and rushed downstairs, off to work. Her father was considerate, one of the reasons she adored him. He'd always been a good husband and father.

Half an hour later, she encountered Ryan in the kitchen eating toast and marmalade.

"Good morning, Miss Murphy," he said.

She shot him a withering smile.

"Going to school today?" she asked.

"Yes. Not for long, though. Dad's agreed. I'm being evacuated."

"For sure?"

"It's all decided. Dad's going to talk to Mum and get her to sign the form."

God help us. It's really happening. She struggled to keep her voice steady. "What do you know about this? Where you will go?"

"No idea. The school has arranged it. All the children are meeting at the train station in Sutton. Next week, sometime. There's a list of things to take. Mum will have to get those for me."

"Oh Ryan. I'm not sure this is the best plan, but I know it's what you want."

"It's better than staying here getting bombed to smithereens," he said, gesticulating wildly. "Come on. You know it's no fun around here."

She made an effort to smile. "With you gone, that's true, little brother."

She understood his excitement and wanted him to be safe, but as she viewed his lean, lengthening limbs she feared he would go away a boy and perhaps not return until he had grown into a man. Her mother would miss out on the little that remained of his childhood, and so would she.

Kate rose early on Saturday. The Anderson shelter would arrive later that day and she needed to decide where to take her mother. In the kitchen, Mary Grace was already up, drinking tea. Kate sat down beside her.

After a while Mary Grace said, "Hardly slept at all. Ryan's leaving."

"I know. I'm sorry."

Her mother sniffed and held a handkerchief to her eyes. "Your father says he wants to go and we shouldn't keep him here. He's so young," she said in a small voice, burying her face in her hands.

Kate put her arm around her mother's shoulder.

"I'm still here," she said.

"You're not like Clare, though. I miss her, and I'll miss Ryan."

Kate withdrew her arm. *But you wouldn't miss me,* she thought, feeling a stab of pain. *My careless mother, trampling on my feelings again.* "For God's sake," she snapped. "Will you never stop comparing me with Clare? I'm sick and tired of you moaning and groaning about how much you miss her. I miss her too, Goddammit."

Mary Grace's face turned pink and her hands flew to her throat. "Stop swearing and show some respect, Kathleen."

Kate left the room, buttoning her mouth. *I will, when you do*, she thought. She did not want to be drawn into another explosive argument, today of all days, and she chastised herself for losing her temper. But her mother wasn't fair. She had never appreciated Kate in the same way as Clare and wasted no opportunity to tell her so. *Trapped. Goddamned trapped.*

Mary Grace called after her. "Kate, wait a minute."

Kate halted at the foot of the stairs.

"I'm sorry," Mary Grace said. "That was thoughtless of me. I'm grateful to have you here. Really. But everything is so difficult now. This war is tearing families apart and making us all behave like crazy people."

Especially you, Kate thought. But there was no point in dwelling on longstanding hurt feelings. She was a grown-up. She took a firm grip of her feelings and returned to the kitchen.

"All right," she said, with a tight smile. *A truce for now, but someday . . .* "Let's go shopping. Ryan will need some things to take with him. Perhaps he'll want to come. We can take the bus to Sutton, go to Shinners, and then to Lyons for tea. Why don't you have a bath before we leave? It'll make you feel better."

"Yes, that sounds nice." Mary Grace looked towards the window, blinking back tears. In a strained voice she said, "How will we know that he'll have enough food where he's going?"

"We won't, but they're saying the real shortage is in the cities. Most people haven't got gardens or land for growing their own vegetables, as we do. Or did."

Kate regretted her words the minute she said them. How could she have made as thoughtless a comment as her mother's? Mary Grace's garden helped keep her sane, and she would lose it soon to make room for the air raid shelter. Her mother wheezed and dabbed again at her eyes.

"Sorry, Mum," she said, sighing as she got up to refill their cups. More tea would ease all worries. What was it the government had said? *Tea—a metaphor for carrying on.*

Mary Grace left, and a few minutes later Kate heard the sound of running water. She never ceased trying to make her mother see that she, Kate, was a worthy daughter, but lately, Mary Grace was the one who needed mothering. The day promised to bring new challenges, ones she would rather avoid. But now the truth about Ryan was out in the open, and they all needed to adjust.

Kate and Mary Grace took the fifteen-minute bus ride to Sutton without Ryan. Kate wasn't surprised when he declared he had no interest in shopping for clothes.

"What do they want him to bring?" Kate asked.

Mary Grace consulted the list. "A complete change of clothing, sleepwear, an overcoat, and sturdy shoes."

"That's all? It sounds like only enough for a weekend stay."

"Everything has to fit in a suitcase or rucksack. Ryan said he prefers a rucksack, and he asked for an extra pair of shorts for football. He'll need those, because he always gets so muddy."

"How can we buy him shoes if he's not with us to try them on?" Kate asked.

"He told me he doesn't need any new ones and would rather have a pullover. A blue one."

Kate smiled. Blue was Ryan's favourite colour.

They bought clothes and a rucksack at Shinners on High Street. Kate loved the old place. The ground floor displayed clothes on racks, and the carved railing of the first-floor balcony and domed ceiling above added old-fashioned grandeur to the setting. It bustled with shoppers like themselves, many buying for child evacuees. Carrying their packages, Kate and her mother strolled down the street to Lyons for tea and crumpets. They had always enjoyed shopping together and, despite their recent conflict, they assiduously kept the truce and avoided any talk about the war.

When they arrived home a few hours later, Sean met them at the front door. "The men are finishing the installation of the bomb shelter. You might want to have a look at it."

They detoured around the side of the house to the back garden. There, barely two feet high, sat a four- by six-foot shed. Two city workers were digging a ramp at one end to allow access.

"It's much smaller than I imagined," Mary Grace said.

One of the men stopped shovelling.

"Yes, love. It's buried, see. Most of it's below the ground. It's six feet high inside. Are you the lady who lives here? Will you be wanting a garden on top? We can shovel some soil there so you can grow things."

Mary Grace smiled.

"I'd love that," she said. "I didn't know that was possible."

"They want people to grow food, don't they now. Victory gardens, they're called. Digging for Victory."

"I'll be happy to dig a victory garden. Can we see inside the shelter?"

"Course you can, soon as we've finished the pathway."

He resumed digging.

"Better than I feared," Mary Grace said.

"I agree," Kate said. "Much better."

They watched while the men finished making a sloping entrance to the door. Then the foreman opened it and beckoned for Kate and Mary Grace to go in. Despite the dark interior, they could see two benches lining the walls with shelves above. Galvanized corrugated steel panels formed the walls and curved roof. It smelled like an odd mixture of sweet earth and a whiff of garlic.

"There's room for six people. You can even sleep in there," the man said. "Cosy, ain't it?"

"Safe, anyway," Kate replied.

"We'll read the instructions in the Air Raid Precautions book and learn what supplies we need," Mary Grace said. "I can see it makes sense to have this shelter near us. I just hope we never have to use it."

The workers piled soil on top of the structure and soon a foot of freshly dug earth neatly covered the roof.

"We're all finished here now, and we'll be on our way," the man said.

"Thank you for helping us," Mary Grace smiled.

Kate followed her mother into the house. From the window, she scanned the garden. Still plenty of room for vegetables and flowers. *That went better than I feared. Maybe Mum will come through this after all, digging for victory.*

CHAPTER 9
September 1939

In all the excitement, Kate had almost forgotten her date with Sybil to go dancing. Maybe, she dared hope—just maybe she had good news and was acquainted with someone who knew how to cure hiccups.

Sybil arrived promptly at half past seven.

"Ready?" she asked.

"Ready to go, but not sure I'm ready to see some of those chaps we met last week again."

"I agree. I want to talk to you about that."

Kate gazed at her. "Is something the matter?"

"Not really, but I would prefer not to go dancing tonight. Thought we might go to the cinema instead. *Goodbye Mr. Chips* is playing at the Palace Theatre. Starts at nine. Interested?"

"Fine, but why don't you want to go to the Strand?"

"I'll tell you more in the car."

"Okay. Let me tell Mum I'm leaving. Come inside for a minute," Kate said.

"Righty ho. I'll say hello to her," Sybil said.

Mary Grace was stirring a steaming pot on the stove.

"Good evening, Mrs. Murphy," Sybil said. "Whatever you're making smells divine."

"French onion soup," Mary Grace said. "Nice to see you, Sybil. It's been a while. Would you like some?"

"Thank you, but I've already had my supper."

"Have you finished your studies at Oxford?"

"Yes. I sat my final exams last term."

"So you have a university degree? Quite an accomplishment, I must say."

"Thank you," Sybil smiled. "I'll admit it took a lot of swotting."

"I imagine so. What are you going to do with your education?"

"Nothing. I went to university because I happen to love mathematics and wanted to learn more. They're shortening the course requirements now because of the war."

"Interesting. Anyway, I understand you're going to America soon."

"That was the plan. We'll see."

Kate looked at her questioningly, then at the clock. "We have to get to the cinema before the film starts. I'll be back before midnight, Mum. Don't worry about me. Sybil's giving me a lift."

"That's good," Mary Grace said, with a nod. "Better to drive than lurk in the dark streets these days."

In the car, Kate faced her friend. "All right. Talk. Why don't you want to go dancing?"

"Partly for the reason you mentioned, and not wanting to see Colin again, but also because I'd like some entertainment that doesn't involve meeting new people, since I'll be leaving soon."

Sybil fumbled to fit the keys in the ignition.

"This isn't like you," Kate said. "You're always so comfortable in social situations. What's going on?"

"There's been a change of plans. I'm not going to America."

"What? Why ever not?"

"Something came up. I can't talk about it."

"What on earth . . . are you eloping, or something?"

Sybil chortled. "No. Nothing like that. I'm going away, but not overseas."

"Why all the mystery?"

"Look, I'm not trying to deceive you. There's something called the Official Secrets Act. I'm sworn to secrecy, and I don't know a lot about what I'll be doing. It's to do with the war effort. That's all I can say."

"Oh. When?"

"This week. I've probably told you too much already. Let's go to the cinema and enjoy ourselves."

Kate settled back in the passenger seat trying to take in the new information. Sybil started the engine. Then she turned it off again.

"You know, I feel badly about letting you down," she said. "I suppose you rely on me for a social life. I have a friend who only needs a little persuading and she'll go dancing instead of me, I'm sure."

"That's kind, but I have other people I can invite." *But who*? Kate wondered. She didn't want to sound pathetic. She continued, "I enjoy *your* company, and I'll miss you."

"I think it would be good for you to meet Lydia Rand-Smith anyway. She has connections."

"With a name like that, I suppose she would. What sort of connections?"

"She's mad about music and knows people who play for charity events. Maybe she could arrange a singing gig for you."

"My goodness, that would be splendid," Kate said quickly, then thought, *now I really must find a way to stop hiccupping.*

"All right. I'll get in touch with her before I leave. Too bad you're not on the phone. I'll send you a note with her number."

"Thank you. Now how about that film."

The cinema walls were lined with posters. One showed a picture of a soldier talking to a young boy holding a toy sword. The caption read "Leave Hitler to me, sonny—<u>You</u> ought to be out of London."

"Ryan's going," Kate said, "Mum is distraught but has accepted it."

"Why is she distraught? All the mothers I know are used to their sons leaving. They send them off to boarding school at seven."

"That's upper-class boys, not us. Most children in our neighbour-hood go to local schools as day pupils, not boarders."

"Well anyway, he'll be safer out of London, just as the poster says."

Kate didn't reply. She wasn't sure she agreed, and Sybil's words reminded her again that they lived in two different worlds. Where was she going? Perhaps to a holiday place for the well-to-do. That wouldn't surprise her in the least, she thought, then caught herself. *What am I doing, becoming cynical and disgruntled with my best friend when she's just shown she's looking out for my best interests. Everything's upside down.*

As much as she enjoyed *Goodbye Mr. Chips*, she couldn't dispel the dread that overcame her as the names of former schoolboys who died in the last war were read aloud at the end. She thought of all the young men who were being sent to fight now, including those she and Sybil had met at the dance. After the film ended, the organist played some chords and invited the audience to sing. He struck the opening bars of the national anthem, and Kate stood up: "God Save our Gracious King . . ."

"You have a gorgeous voice, my friend," Sybil said. "You really must pursue that singing career you've talked about for so long."

"Thank you. Maybe after the war."

"Why wait? You could be the next Vera Lynn."

"I wish."

She refrained from mentioning the serious obstacle that would thwart her chances for singing professionally. Sybil was well aware of it, and Kate accepted her friend's comment as a kind gesture after their disappointment about the flat.

"Good luck to you, and drop me a line when you can," Kate said, as the car drew to a halt beside her house. Her throat felt dry as she swallowed to prevent a hiccup. Sybil reached to give her a hug, and Kate's eyes filled with tears. Sybil turned to face her. "Don't be sad. Remember when we ate each other's lunch at school? We got good at being sneaky. We never told, and they never guessed. It was good training."

Kate smiled despite herself. "Good training for what?"

Sybil put her finger to her lips. "Bye," she said.

Kate climbed out of the car and watched it disappear into the night. *Why all the secrecy? What is Sybil up to?* But now she would lose two important people in her life, at least temporarily . . . well, she hoped temporarily. She couldn't help wondering if she would see either of them again.

She turned and walked slowly to the house. As she crossed the threshold, a quiet hiccup erupted from within her, forcing her to inhale deeply. "Damn it all," she rasped.

The next morning, Mary Grace appeared downstairs in her church-going dress and hat.

"Aren't you two coming with me to Mass?" she asked Kate and Ryan.

"Not today," Kate said, and Ryan shook his head. Sean, who rarely went, didn't raise his head from the newspaper.

Five minutes after she had gone, an explosion followed by the crash of breaking glass sounded outside.

Kate jumped. "What's happening?" she shrieked.

Angry voices from the house next door penetrated the room. Kate and Ryan opened the window and poked their heads outside. Tendrils of smoke rose from the front garden. Mr. Bolton—Mr. B, their local patrolling Air Raid Precautions warden—had dismounted from his bicycle. Wearing a hard hat, he stood beside the fence of their neighbour, Mickey Brickhouse.

"What do you mean, I can't 'ave my own grenade?" Mickey shouted.

"Mr. Brickhouse, they're dangerous. The *government* is supposed to provide ammunition for the war, not private citizens."

At that moment a train arrived, hooting and roaring its way along the line behind the houses. Kate and Ryan pulled their heads inside and slammed the window shut.

"Two trains this time, one from each direction," Ryan shouted over the din. "I hope they're short ones. I want to hear more about Mickey's bomb."

After the rattling subsided, they opened the window again. The warden stood still, hands covering his ears. He opened his mouth to speak, but Mickey's dog jumped at him, baring his teeth and barking.

"Get down, Pinocchio!"

Mickey opened the gate and grabbed the dog by the collar.

"Stop that noise! No barking!"

The dog sat, quivering and staring at the warden.

"Sorry, 'e's a good dog, well be'aved, mostly."

Mr. B stepped back and took out a notebook. "Got any more of those things, have you?" he said.

"Not at the moment. I can make more, though."

"Hey, this is exciting," Ryan hissed to Kate.

"Shush," she said, leaning out to hear better.

"Whoa, hold on a minute," Mr. B said. "*You must stop.* Understand?"

"Cor blimey. I'm only trying to 'elp the war effort. Do my bit." Mickey held his hands, palms up.

"Have you got a shelter yet?" Mr. B asked. "That might be the best way to protect yourself and your family."

"Ain't got no family. Missus died a few years back. Anyways, can't afford one."

"It's free for people like you. I'll talk to the authorities."

"Not sure I want one. Takes up space the dog needs out there."

"The shelter doesn't take up much room. The Murphys got theirs yesterday. You can see for yourself."

Mickey shrugged and wiped his face with a grubby hand. He had several days' growth of beard and his trousers hung loosely around his waist.

Ryan shut the window and laughed. "Man's a character, a real cockney. They should let him have his bombs if it makes him feel safer. He knows something about explosives. Told me he used to work in a factory where they made them."

"They do have to regulate things like that," Kate said. "I'm not keen about people making their own bombs around here."

"It's not really a bomb, just a grenade. I like Mickey. He's funny. Sometimes shows up to play football with me and my pals."

"He plays football?"

"Not well, but he runs fast. He played a lot when younger. We had to ask him to stop bringing his dog because he kept chasing the ball."

"Odd that I never knew all those things about him," Kate said.

"Well, you wouldn't. Your world is all filled up with music and looking out for Mum."

She couldn't disagree. She did live a narrow life. *What else had she missed out on?* Mickey had lived next door for how many years now? She couldn't remember. His wife had died—she did remember that—but she hadn't gone to the funeral, as Ryan had. She had missed important things staring her right in the face. For too long.

CHAPTER 10
October 1939

K ate arrived home from work to find a letter from Sybil with the promised phone number for Lydia Rand-Smith. Before she had a chance run out to make a call, Sean summoned the family to the kitchen.

"Gas masks," he said, handing one to each of them. He read the instructions aloud. "We're supposed to have them with us at all times. You'll take one when you leave, Ryan. It has a loop so you can hang it over your head and keep your arms free."

Kate gagged as she pulled the helmet over her head. It reeked of rubber, and the mouthpiece moved in and out as she breathed.

"They're horrible," she said. "Smell like rotting fish."

Ryan took his mask off and wrinkled his nose. "These things make you look weird, like some sort of prehistoric animal. But I've got everything I need to take with me now. We may leave on Saturday."

"As soon as that?" Mary Grace asked.

"I think so. I'll know tomorrow."

Mary Grace set the kettle on the stove. Kate watched her fight back tears and felt a pang of empathy.

"We still have to equip the shelter with supplies," Sean said. "First aid kits, water, food, candles, books, playing cards, more torches, lanterns. Anything to help us survive and pass the time."

"Sounds like barrels of fun," Kate said with a frown. "I'd rather stay in the house and play the piano to drown out the sound of the bombs."

"You're such a dreamer," Ryan said, laughing. "That's my sister, playing the piano amidst the rubble."

On Saturday, Ryan knocked early on Kate's bedroom door.

"Ain't you shamed, you sleepyhead?" he said, quoting the Robert Louis Stevenson nursery rhyme.

Time to rise. He'd always quoted those rhymes, Kate remembered, stretching as she got out of bed. As a small child, he'd repeat lines he'd memorised. But she sang the words. To her, that's what gave the poems soul. A dull ache settled deep inside. He'd leave his childhood behind him when he left, and he would take part of her own with him as well.

"Are you coming to the train station to see me off?" Ryan asked.

"Of course. What time are we supposed to be there?"

"At eight. Mum's already downstairs, wearing black."

"Well, she would. This is a sad day for her."

"But she shouldn't grieve as though I'm dead. I'm going away so I can live!"

She got out of bed, then reached inside a drawer on her bedside table.

"Look Ry, I've got something for you."

She held out her hand, offering a small blue jewel. He took it and examined it carefully. "The moonstone! I'd forgotten all about it."

"You used to believe it had magical powers. You would hide it, remember? I had to search for it after you gave me clues. I always found it."

"Yes, even when I put it up the chimney with tape," he said with a crooked grin. "You got all sooty, looking for it."

She smiled at the memory. "I want you to have it. It'll bring you travellers' luck."

"Thanks," he said, blew her a kiss, and stuck it in his pocket.

"Don't lose it. I want you to bring it back to me someday. And I don't want to go searching the countryside for it."

"All right. I'll guard it with my life."

"Just guard your own life, please. And don't go messing with explosives like Mickey."

"I'm not stupid," he growled. "Don't worry. I'll write. They told us at school we should send a letter home every week."

"You do that. Mum would appreciate it."

Kate's mind swung back to the day she had received the sky-blue stone. Smooth and cold, round on top and flat on the bottom like a half-full moon, it felt good in her small hands. She was nine years old, staying with her grandmother Ellen in Selsey for a few weeks that summer. They often enjoyed watching swallows careen and swoop at the water's edge. One blue-sky day Ellen said, "You have musical wings, Katie. You should always soar like those birds. Aim for the moon." From her pocket she drew a shimmering stone whose colour seemed to float skywards. Placing it in Kate's hand she said, "This is a moonstone. It's a rare thing and came all the way from Burma. Keep it safe to remind you of your dreams."

Kate smiled at the memory. She still missed her grandmother since her death five years earlier. But she had more practical matters to deal with now and didn't want to dwell on diminishing dreams of fame and freedom. She dressed quickly and joined Ryan and their mother in the kitchen. Mary Grace had prepared a substantial breakfast of eggs, bacon, fried bread, tomatoes, toast, and marmalade, which Ryan downed quickly. After eating, he eased his arms into the rucksack straps and hung the box containing the gas mask around his neck. Mary Grace pinned the label with his name, age, address, and school to his overcoat and gave him a cheese sandwich and an apple. He crammed a cap on his head. Kate made a mental note to remember him as he was, a bright-eyed boy eager to leave home with a white label on his lapel like a sales item at a shop. He looked like all the other boys she'd seen who were being evacuated, but he was her brother, and special, and her life would be different, a bit emptier, without him. She blinked back tears.

She followed her family to the bus stop, hanging back two steps so her parents could have these last minutes with Ryan. The Harris twins, Tom and Francis, were already there, waiting beside their mother. They would take the bus to the train station to see the children off.

"It's a sad day, this one is," Mrs. Harris said.

"Sad for you, Mum, but exciting for us," said Tom.

"Ryan's excited, too," Mary Grace said.

Mrs. Harris looked at her. "I just 'ope they don't separate my boys."

Mary Grace regarded her sympathetically, but said nothing.

"Come here, son," Sean said. "You're going to need some money for the journey. Use it wisely." He thrust some pound notes and a few shillings and other coins into Ryan's hand.

Ryan pocketed them immediately. "Thanks."

The three boys raced around throwing conkers fallen from a large chestnut tree. The late September sun shone through yellow leaves, spreading warmth like a kind hand on a shoulder. *Just when we need it most*, Kate thought. Finally, the red double-decker bus appeared, brakes screeching as it slowed and stopped.

"Fares, please," the conductor said as they climbed inside.

Mrs. Harris inhaled loudly. "Do we 'ave to pay? The boys are going to be evacuated. Thought it was free."

"I'm afraid not."

"So that settles it. You're not going," she said to the twins.

"But we want to! We've been looking forward to it," Tom shouted.

"Here, take this," Ryan said, handing some change to Mrs. Harris.

"Thank you kindly," she said, reddening.

"Tommy and Francis are my friends. I want them to come along, that's all."

Sean nodded with approval and silently handed Ryan another half crown. Kate noted Mrs. Harris's flushed cheeks and hoped she didn't feel humiliated by Ryan's offer. The war was making things especially hard for the working classes, and she hated to think of the woman's hurt pride adding to sadness of the boys' leaving.

They took seats in the back of the bus and jolted their way to the train station where a throng of a hundred or more boys stood at the entrance surrounding a teacher who wielded a sign saying ST. PETER'S SCHOOL.

"That's us. There's Mr. Simmons, the maths teacher. I hope he's going with us," Ryan said, speaking loudly so that he could be heard above the noise. "They told us some teachers would escort us. I'll go and find out."

He disappeared into the crowd. Boys and parents jostled together in the chaos, many carrying suitcases, small children bearing rucksacks almost as big as themselves, others screaming in their mothers' arms. Mary Grace and Kate, unable to press forward, stood on their toes, searching for Ryan. Sean shoved his way into the crowd.

"Move back, please. Only evacuees should proceed to the platform," came an announcement from a loudspeaker.

Mary Grace shouted into Kate's ear. "He's gone, and I didn't even have a chance to say goodbye."

"It's easier this way, Mum." *Maybe he wanted it this way.* "Perhaps he'll wave to us from the train."

Mary Grace held her handkerchief to her eyes. They could see the mass of boys following the school's sign as it moved towards the platform. They could make out heads of the teachers, some of whom Kate recognised, as they herded the boys onto the train. Mothers sobbed and some of the smaller children clung to their skirts, refusing to be parted. Sean materialized from the throng and stood beside them.

"Couldn't reach him," he said.

"Please don't send me away," a small boy pleaded. He looked no older than five.

His mother picked him up. "You're right, Harry, this is nonsense," she said as she turned and strode out of the station with her child.

People pushed and shoved, and women wearing Women's Voluntary Service uniforms struggled to pass out sweets. Kate watched the scene in horror. The trains hissed, the steamy plumes spreading soot and fumes over everyone within reach.

After what seemed like hours, the carriage doors ceased banging shut and the only onlookers in the station were family members of evacuees. The whistle blew, and the train slowly puffed away from the platform. Boys hung out of windows waving, most smiling widely.

The family didn't see Ryan. They waited until the train disappeared, a small dot in the distance. Mary Grace clung to Sean. Kate felt tears trickling down her cheeks. With an effort, she straightened herself.

"Let's go home and have a cup of tea," she sniffed. It wasn't a panacea, but what else could they do but carry on?

CHAPTER 11
October 1939

Kate followed the course of events at school anxiously. Few St. Bridget's parents, it turned out, were of a mind to send their children away. The school remained open, evacuation plans abandoned. Boarders stayed on, while a handful of families made their own arrangements to send their girls elsewhere.

On a drizzly autumn afternoon, she sat in the assembly hall with her notebook and a piano accompanist holding auditions for lead roles in the Handel cantata.

Hannah Bell stood by the piano, her small hands pressed to her sides. Her silvery soprano voice offered a pure tone with a wide range. After hearing several older girls vying for the part, Kate chose Hannah for the lead role of Flora, the head shepherdess. Kate posted the list of soloists on the assembly room door.

"Thank you, Miss Murphy," Hannah said the next day, her eyes shining.

"You'll have to work hard," Kate warned her. "I'll give you extra coaching, but you must practice on your own."

"I'll be happy to do that. Thank you again, Miss Murphy."

Kate hadn't seen the girl's mother since their talk a few weeks earlier and felt pleased she could help Hannah. She herself had sung many solo roles in musical productions at school before the dreaded hiccups upended her singing, and even if she couldn't perform these days, she liked supporting the aspiring young singer. She understood the exhilaration of performance: when she'd stood with lights focused on her, releasing her entire being into her singing, she felt alive, and important. It was as though taking up space on stage gave her full ownership of her life.

A week passed with no postcard from Ryan. Mary Grace twisted her hands and roamed the house at night like a pale ghost. She barely slept. Kate noticed the dark circles around her eyes and wondered why she hadn't contacted the school authorities to learn more. They had been told to be patient, that no news was good news, but the wait became agonising. Mary Grace planted her garlic on top of the shelter and went to church every day. Sean worked long days and relied on Kate to keep her mother company until he arrived home. At least, unlike some, he still had a job.

One day, choosing her words carefully, Kate suggested her mother might take on volunteer work to occupy her time.

"What would I do? All I know about is cooking and gardening. And swimming, but that's not helpful."

"Mrs. Harris volunteers with the Women's Voluntary Service now that the twins have left. You might find out if there's something you could do there."

"I'll consider that," Mary Grace said, brightening. "It would be better if I spent my free time more usefully than sitting around grieving."

"I agree. Let's see where you can sign up."

Kate missed Ryan more than she expected. She had always enjoyed her role as older sister, and he amused her with his high-spirited bantering. She hoped he had been assigned a good foster family, or billet, as they called it. Sometimes Kate and her parents listened to Winston Churchill on the wireless. His speeches encouraged everyone to persevere. So far, not one bomb had fallen on London. The Americans dubbed it the "phony war," but Kate imagined it was just a matter of time before things became all too real.

After work one day, Kate remembered Sybil's letter with Lydia Rand-Smith's phone number. She had forgotten it amidst all the recent happenings. Time to contact Lydia. Kate stopped at a phone box on her way home and made the call.

She introduced herself. "This is Kate Murphy, a friend of Sybil Thorndyke's."

"Kate . . . now I remember. You're her old school friend, aren't you?"

"I am. I'm phoning to ask if you would like to meet me on Saturday. Sybil said you might be persuaded to go dancing."

"Dancing? Where?"

"We usually go to the Strand in Kingston. They have good bands there."

"I've never been, but it would be a new adventure. It's not my usual sort of venue, you understand, but why not? Shall I meet you there? What time?"

"At seven. How will I know you?"

"Let's see. I'll be in a pink twin set and pearls."

"I'll find you."

Kate understood the Strand was not the type of place that Lydia Rand-Smith would frequent. She spoke with a distinctly upper-class accent. Surprisingly, Lydia had agreed to come. Perhaps she would consider the outing a kind of social experiment, daily life for the masses. *Like the Mass Observation Project*, Kate thought wryly.

On Saturday, she prepared for her evening out. She wore her green dress and tied a ribbon in her hair. As she sat in the bus on the way to the dancehall, she wished she had a car. She'd taken public transportation all her life, but a car would more convenient, especially at night.

When she arrived, couples were already moving in time to the lively music. She waited by the entrance searching for Lydia, and soon saw her holding a coat over her arm, looking distinctive but out of place, wearing a pink twin set and pearls.

"Lydia? Pleased to meet you," Kate said, extending her hand.

"How do you do? My goodness, this place is popular. Positively crawling with people. Where do we go from here?"

"We pay for our tickets, then hang our coats in the cloakroom. We can get a table inside."

"Righty ho."

Kate watched as Lydia paid for her ticket. Tall and slim, she held herself well. *Probably had lessons in deportment*, Kate thought. The confidence of the upper classes always impressed her. They found a table.

"What will you have to drink?" Kate asked.

"How about a Singapore Sling?" Lydia suggested.

"I've never heard of that. I don't know if they serve it."

"Oh dear. Well, what are you having?"

"Gin and tonic."

"All right. Make that two."

As she pushed her way towards the bar, Kate almost collided with a man standing in line.

"Sorry," she said.

"Kate! I hoped to see you. I'm Barry. Do you remember me?"

"Yes, of course. Hello."

"Are you here alone? May I buy you a drink?"

"I'm with a friend."

"A girl friend, I hope?"

Kate nodded.

"Well then. I'll buy one for both of you."

Kate cursed herself inwardly at the offer. Now she would have to talk to him, and wouldn't have a chance to get to know Lydia. She should have thought things through better. Perhaps the evening would be a disaster.

"Thank you," she said. "Two gin and tonics, please."

He paid for the drinks and handed them to her. He bought ale for himself.

"Where are you sitting? May I join you?" he asked.

She led the way. He looked slightly better than the last time she had seen him, almost handsome. His white shirt appeared crisp and his brown coat fitted well and matched his eyes. They reached the table where Lydia sat, but before Kate could speak Lydia exclaimed, "It's Barry, isn't it? What brings you here? Are you playing?"

"No. I don't play here," he said.

"I meant to ring you. We're having another event next week. Can you come?"

"I think so."

"Good. Usual time, usual place. Now, do sit." She smiled, a perfect white-toothed smile, and pushed a chair out with her toe. "Barry often plays at our charity events in Esher," she said to Kate. "He's an excellent violinist."

"Really?" Kate said.

She contemplated Barry with new respect and remembered he told her he played. He had under-stated his skills. They sipped their drinks and Kate tapped her foot as the band's rhythm picked up.

"Would you like to dance?" Barry asked her.

"I would. Please excuse us," she said to Lydia.

"Of course," Lydia replied, relaxing in her chair and lighting a cigarette.

Barry steered Kate into a space on the crowded floor and held her firmly. He seemed more comfortable than before and swung her around with more assurance. His hair smelled of shampoo and his face appeared freshly shaven. He kept perfect time to the beat of the music and she began to enjoy herself.

"How do you know Lydia?" he asked

"I don't really. We've just met. She's a friend of Sybil's, who came with me last time."

"I remember her. Has she left for America?"

"No. She went somewhere else. To the country, I think."

"Out of harm's way. Can't say I blame her. But I'm surprised to see Lydia here. It's not her kind of place."

"So I understand. Maybe she'll meet someone to dance with and have a good time. The band is good tonight."

"Yes. The drummer is a friend of mine."

They danced for two songs and when they returned to their table, Lydia wasn't there.

"I hope she hasn't left already," Kate said.

"She wouldn't leave without telling you. Probably dancing. Tell me more about your interest in music. Do you play an instrument?"

"Piano, a little."

"I can give you the name of a good piano teacher, if you'd like lessons."

"I can't afford them. Anyway, I'd rather have a singing tutor."

He beamed. "Ah, you sing. I'll have to talk to Lydia about that. Can you manage songs like Vera Lynn's or Gracie Field's—you know, popular ones?"

"Yes. I often listen to them on the wireless."

"Let's see what I can do."

Kate glanced at him with new appreciation. She had underestimated him in more ways than one. "Thank you," she smiled.

At that moment Lydia arrived, pink-cheeked and breathless, accompanied by a tall man in an army officer's uniform.

"Haven't had this much fun in donkey's years," she said, sitting down. "This is Nigel. Pull up a pew."

He joined them at the table.

"It's a fine evening. Does a fellow good to see all you lovely ladies," he said. "Let me treat everyone to a round of drinks."

He stood up and cut through the crowd to the bar.

Lydia re-applied her lipstick. "I might come here again. The band's good. Everyone's full of high spirits. It's contagious. The events I'm used to attending are more, shall we say, formal."

"I'm glad to hear this," Kate said. "You're always welcome."

Barry moved closer to Lydia as though sharing a secret. "Kate can sing," he said.

"Is that so? We'll have to talk more about this. I need soloists for charity events. May I have your phone number?"

"I'm not on the phone, I'm afraid. But I can give you a ring or meet you somewhere, if you have time."

"How can people get by without a telephone?" Lydia muttered. "All right. I'd like to hear you audition. Can you come to my house? Perhaps Barry can accompany you on the piano. How does that sound? Next Friday evening at seven? Montrose House in Esher."

"I'll be there," Kate said.

"Let me collect you. I have a car, and I know the way," Barry said.

"You've got a car?" Kate asked, raising her eyebrows. "That's kind of you. We'll need to decide the repertoire."

"Yes. Where do you live?"

"Near St. Bridget's. 59 Holly Road."

So Barry has a car. I must have underestimated him, Kate thought for the second time.

Nigel placed a tray of glasses on the table. "Singapore Slings, all round. Hope that's all right," he said.

Barry winked at Kate. "Lydia's favourite."

Kate scrutinised the glass. An orange slice floated in the brownish liquid. "Quite fancy. What's in it?"

"Many things: gin, Cointreau, fruit juice, cherry liqueur . . ."

She took a sip. "Not bad."

They each raised a glass. "To England, and a quick victory," Nigel smiled.

"Hear, hear," they chorused.

Turning to Barry, Kate said, "Where's your friend Colin? Have they sent him to Belgium yet?"

He scowled. "Yes. It's only a matter of time before I'm conscripted, too. I believe they're taking us in order of age. Colin is twenty, and I'm twenty-one."

"If you really don't want to go, why don't you claim exemption as a conscientious objector?"

"I could, but I wouldn't. I'd never live it down. My brother's signed up. He's in the air force."

"Is he flying Spitfires?"

"Not yet, but he will. He's training."

"That's impressive." Her father had told her the planes were difficult to fly, but a good match for the German Messerschmitts in combat. But still, a shiver ran up her spine. "What do your parents say about your joining up?"

"They'll never know. They died a few years ago, in a car accident."

"Oh. I'm sorry."

Kate observed his downcast eyes and a wave of sympathy swept over her. He would have been a teenager when they died, perhaps not much older than Ryan. She wanted to ask if he lived alone but didn't want to pry. She suddenly became aware that Lydia and Nigel were talking and laughing, oblivious to her conversation with Barry. Lydia was clearly enjoying herself.

"Let's dance," Barry said, taking her hand.

The spinning crystal ball over the dance floor cast shards of light onto the dancers, lending them an unreal quality, their arms and legs moving in slow motion. Kate felt light-headed and dizzy. *Probably the alcohol but not an unpleasant sensation.* She let herself melt against Barry and allow the music and light to lull her into unaccustomed tranquility. She was a little sorry when the music ended and they returned to their seats. Lydia and Nigel were still engaged in conversation, their heads close together.

"Let's go outside for a breath of air," Barry suggested. He took her arm and ushered her through the door. She took a deep breath. "Smoky in there," she said. "I'm glad I don't like cigarettes."

"I don't either. Unhealthy habit. I've given it up."

Maybe we have more in common than I imagined, Kate thought. After a while, chilled by the night air, they went back inside. The evening was coming to a close. As the band stopped playing, the crowd thinned.

"I need to go, or I'll miss the last bus," Kate said. "Lydia, thank you so much for coming."

"You took the bus? What time is it? Heavens, it's past eleven. Hang on a minute. My driver will be waiting outside. We'll give you a lift home."

Kate and Lydia said goodbye to the two men and stepped out into the night. Kate's head swam. Was it the cold or had she felt Barry's eyes on her as she left?

Lydia motioned for Kate to sit beside her in the back seat of the Daimler.

"What a fine evening. Thank you for inviting me," Lydia said.

"My pleasure. You seemed to get along well with Nigel."

"Yes. We're acquainted with a lot of the same people. Perhaps you and I can come again sometime. Now you'll need to give my driver some directions."

The car crawled through the gloom to Holly Road. Kate thanked Lydia for the lift, adding, "I'll see you on Friday."

She had enjoyed the evening and its pleasant surprises: liking Barry, and finding Lydia to be a decent person who might even offer her an opportunity to sing. But could she get through the audition without the blasted hiccups interfering? Kate desperately hoped so, and wanted to succeed, but hoping was not enough. She must take steps to ensure a flawless performance. But how?

CHAPTER 12

October 1939

It had been three weeks since Ryan left.

"This is outrageous," Mary Grace fumed one morning. "No word from him or his host family. We don't know where he is. Somewhere in Devon, that's all. What if he's lost? Killed? What if we never hear from him again?"

She lowered her head and ran her hands through her hair.

"Let's hope for the best, Mum," Kate said. "No news is good news, remember? I'm sure we'll hear from him soon."

Her mother raised her head.

"You don't know that. You're just repeating the nonsense the government keeps saying. They're not telling us the truth. We've got no sense of what's really going on."

Kate said nothing. Privately she agreed. She poured her mother a cup of tea. "Has Mrs. Harris heard from the twins?" she asked.

"That's one of the reasons I worry. She *has* heard. They separated them."

"*What*? I thought the school said they'd keep siblings together."

"Looks like they lied."

"That's terrible. What's Mrs. Harris going to do about it?"

"Nothing. What *can* she do? She doesn't have money for the fare to go and see them. She heard from Francis, but not Tom. Francis's family sent a friendly letter, she said."

Kate touched her mother's arm. What could she say? She went

upstairs to get dressed. This was all very difficult. Kate wished there were something she could do to ease her mother's anxiety, but hearing that the Harris boys had been sent to different homes only reinforced her notion that anything could happen. They would have to wait and see, painful though the wait might be.

Since it was a school holiday, it would be a good time to look for some volunteer opportunities for her mother. She'd seen the Women's Voluntary Service Centre on High Street. She flew downstairs and grabbed her coat. "Mum, let's go out. Are there any food items we need? Bread? Vegetables?"

"We do need some bread, and I'd appreciate your company."

At the bakery, they paused at the window to admire the plates of buns, cakes, and custard tarts. "At least they haven't started rationing food yet, though I expect they will," Mary Grace said. "I remember that from the last war. No pastries. Butter, margarine, sugar, and meat were all rationed."

"They've increased the prices, though. Look at the cost of those cakes."

"We don't need to buy a cake. Let's treat ourselves to some iced buns," Kate said.

The shop smelled comfortingly of yeast and butter.

"Morning to you, Mrs. Murphy," the baker said. "What'll it be today?"

"Six iced buns and a loaf of brown bread, please."

"Certainly. How's your young man? Left with the school, didn't he?"

"He did. I don't know. I haven't heard."

Mary Grace's hand shook as she took the paper bags the baker handed to her.

"My boy William likes his billet. Says they've got a big house and a tennis court. Might learn to play. Sounds nice, if you ask me."

"He must be one of the lucky ones, then," Mary Grace said tersely.

They left the shop, the bell on the door tinkling behind them. Kate, eager to comfort her mother, said, "That was so unfeeling of him, Mum. He knows we haven't heard from Ryan. I had to bite my tongue."

"I did, too. Maybe I'll bake my own bread from now on."

They continued strolling past the row of shops. They slowed in front of the Women's Voluntary Service Centre and a large sign reading REGISTER HERE TO HELP US.

"Let's go in," Kate said.

Her mother stared at the sign for a while.

"Come on," Kate said. "You don't know what they need. You might be able to do something to help Ryan and the other evacuees."

"Good point."

Mary Grace pushed the door open. Inside, a woman wearing glasses sitting at a table greeted them. "Hello there. How may I help you ladies?"

"My mother is interested in volunteering," Kate said.

"Splendid! We can always use another pair of hands. Do you like cats?"

A small orange cat curled up in a chair watched them with green eyes. Mary Grace bent to stroke it and it purred gently. Across the room a black cat sat on the floor, ignoring them.

"I like cats," she said, looking puzzled. "But why are they here, and is this what you do, care for cats?"

"No," laughed the woman. "It's not all we do. We take them in sometimes when men leave to join the forces and there's no one to take care of their pets. The black one is called Coal and this one's Marmalade. We sort and distribute clothes and provide treats for evacuees at the train station."

Kate flashed on the image of Ryan at the breakfast table with his beloved toast and marmalade. She hoped her mother wouldn't get distracted and lose her fragile interest in volunteering.

"Do you have a child who has gone away?" the attendant asked.

"Yes. My son Ryan left in September," Mary Grace said in a small voice. "He loves marmalade." She bent to stroke the cat again. Kate held her breath. Maybe her mother's emotions would prevent her from volunteering in this place.

"We could certainly use your assistance," the woman said. "And you'd be helping children like your son. We ask people to commit to working several hours a week. There's a large room in the back where we accept and sort the clothes. There are a lot of needy families and, as you must be aware, evacuees are required to take extra clothes when they leave."

Kate heaved a sigh of relief. The woman had said exactly the right things.

"It's a good cause, and I'd like to volunteer," Mary Grace said firmly.

"Very good. Please fill out a form with your information, and we'll decide on a rotation. Can you start tomorrow?"

Mary Grace nodded and completed the form.

"I'm Alison Whitney," the woman said, offering her hand. "I look forward to working with you."

"That was easy," Kate said as they left the Centre. "Perhaps you'll make some friends there. It's better than sitting around all day by yourself at home."

"You're probably right, dear. I need something to do to take my mind off Ryan."

"I miss him, too," Kate said.

As she expected, the house had become dreary in his absence. Perhaps they should get a cat, one from the volunteer centre. She could already envision Marmalade sitting in her mother's lap by the fire.

Back at home, Kate sat down at the piano to practice songs she might perform at the audition. She'd made her way through a few favourites when a knock at the door interrupted her.

Mickey Brickhouse stood on the doorstep. "Sorry to interrupt, miss, but I was wondering if you could 'elp me out."

"Help you how, Mickey?"

"With the apple trees. I've got three of the bloody things in my garden out back and the fruit's ripe. Can't stand to see it go to waste."

"So you want to know if we'd like some? Is that what you're asking?"

"Yeah, that, but there's something else besides." He gave a toothy smile. "Trees need picking."

"I see. You mean you want some help picking the apples."

"That's the ticket. Seeing as your brother ain't around no more, I don't 'ave anyone to go up the trees and bring them down, see."

"Ryan helped pick your apples? I had no idea."

"Yep. Used to come over with a couple of 'is friends and pick the lot. Ate some, too."

"Aha. Now that I think about it, he did leave apples in the kitchen sometimes. I didn't know they were yours." *Why do I know so little about what's going on right before my very eyes?* "I'm not sure I'm much good at picking, not as good as he would be, but I'm willing to have a go," she said. "Mum would love some apples for pies."

"That's not all they're good for. Cider's better."

"You mean apple juice?"

"No. The real stuff, the 'ard kind."

She raised her eyebrows. "With alcohol? Don't tell me the boys drank it."

He winked and smiled, and she noticed the gap between his two front teeth. "Oh, I understand. They did drink it. Payment for their services."

His smile widened.

"Do you intend to make cider again this year?" she asked.

"Course I do. Just need to get them apples down. You're welcome to 'ave some yourself, and your family. I'd pick them myself, only I got a bad knee. Got 'urt playing football. Shouldn't 'ave competed with those young lads."

"All right. I'll do what I can. How about tomorrow at two?"

"Thanks, miss. I'll be expecting you."

After he left, Kate couldn't help smiling to herself. No wonder Ryan had never told her he picked apples. How much had he and his friends drunk? Not enough that she'd noticed, anyway. She wished all over again that he hadn't left home.

After work the next day, Kate changed into dungarees and an old blouse and started for Mickey's house. From the front window, he motioned for her to go round to the back garden. An Anderson shelter almost blocked the way.

"Put it up myself, I did," Mickey said. "Comes in sections that fit together. Glad to 'ave it, but I don't expect to use it against the bombs. Far better as a place to ferment my cider. It's dark, and the temperature's just right."

"But if you fill it with barrels of cider you won't be able to use it yourself, for protection, will you?"

He cackled. "That's all right, love, it'll be better in there with something to drink. Might as well go out 'appy, don't you think?"

"I suppose so. Please show me what to do about the apples."

"You'll need a ladder, I expect. Your brother didn't—'e was good at climbing the trees, but you'll find it 'elps you to reach the higher branches. I've put one 'ere for you."

The three trees were loaded with apples. Some were green, but most had already begun to turn bright red. She knew they were almost over-ripe, and a few had already fallen to the ground.

A ladder leaned against one of the trees and Kate stepped onto the first rung. She hesitated.

"Just go on up. Take this bucket. When it's full you can pass it down to me and I'll give you another."

"How many apples do you need for the cider?"

He scratched his chin. "Well, let's 'ave a think. There's plenty of them this year, but they're small. I'd say about two 'undred and fifty."

"That many?"

"Yep. That's about right for five gallons."

"I suppose I had better pick them all, then," Kate said.

"If you can, that's best. Any leftovers are good for eating raw or cooking. You can take some 'ome, if you like."

"Thank you."

She mounted the ladder with the bucket and started pulling fruit off the tree. Most of the apples almost fell off on their own without any need to twist them. Soon she had filled the first bucket. She descended the ladder, passed it to Mickey, and ascended again with a new one. As she worked, she inhaled the sweet smells of sap and apples and began to enjoy herself in the leafy bower. A blue sky showed like patchwork through the branches, and a gentle breeze ruffled her hair. Glad she had tied it back, it would have become caught in the twigs if loose, but she should have worn a hat. She could get used to this work. She hummed to herself, climbing higher, and reaching for the farthest hanging fruit. Soon she had finished picking all the apples from the first tree.

The second tree, smaller, with green apples, proved easier. Mickey deposited all the pickings into a large barrel. He moved the ladder to the third and largest tree.

"That one's oldest, and the best. Look at them apples," he said.

Kate stood back to see. Festooned with reddish-orange orbs, it reminded her of a leafless Christmas tree.

"What variety are they?" she asked.

"Cox's Orange Pippins," he said. "Don't get no better than them for cider. Need to be sweet for the fermentation. But to get the pollination you need different kinds of apples. The others are Bramley and Granny Smith's."

"How do you make the cider?"

"It takes a while. 'Ave to wash them, cut them up, puree them, strain the pulp, make starter from the yeast, cook it, put everything in a jar and wait until it bubbles. Then you add sugar and let it sit. That's when I'll put it in the shelter."

"How long until it's ready to drink?"

"Two to three weeks. Would you like to try some?"

"I would. When it's ready."

She resumed her work. Finally, she had only one more high standing branch to pick. To reach it, she had to step partly off the ladder. She kept one foot on it and moved her weight onto the other as she felt for the branch. She knew in a flash she'd made a mistake. The branch began to bend and she lost her footing, falling to the grass with a thud, screaming from shock and pain.

Mickey knelt beside her.

"Oh dear, love, are you 'urt? I'm so sorry. Can you get up? Let me 'elp you."

She lay on her side, conjecturing if anything had broken. Her foot lay twisted underneath her. The pain was excruciating.

"I can't get up. I've hurt my ankle," she said.

"Stay there, love. Shall I find a phone and call an ambulance?"

"Perhaps so," she mumbled, groaning. "And get my mother, please."

"I'll do that. So sorry. Should've pruned the bloody tree last spring."

She lay helplessly on the damp grass, hoping help would arrive before dark. Her thoughts turned to soldiers at the front, lying wounded, perhaps with no ambulance to rescue them, a situation too painful to contemplate for long. She closed her eyes, acutely aware how quickly things could change for the worse. In the blink of an eye.

A few hours later Kate sat at home in the living room, her broken ankle in a cast, propped on a stool. They had given her some medicine for the pain. Her father learned at work about the accident and came home early. He handed her a glass of whiskey.

"This'll help, just a small shot." he said. "How about listening to the wireless for a bit? Take your mind off things."

"It's all right, Dad. Let's not learn more bad news about the war. I've been worrying about school. I won't be able to teach if I can't get there. It would probably take me an hour on crutches."

"True. What did the doctor say?"

"He said I should stay off my foot for a couple of weeks. For the first few days I'm supposed to keep my foot elevated."

"That's good. You've been working too hard. You spend a lot of time at that school of yours, working for a pittance."

"I don't mind. I like the girls and rehearsing for the performance. This accident is a real nuisance, though. I'll lose time for preparing."

"It's your left foot, at least. That means you can still use the right one for pedaling on the piano."

"I've considered that. I'll practice. Now that Mum's working at the WVS she's out of the house a lot, so I won't annoy her."

Sean patted her on the shoulder. "I do wish she liked music more and shared your interest, Katie. Why don't we spend some time together, you and I? It's a good opportunity. We can sing on weekends when she's working. Haven't done that in a while. Good Irish songs."

"Good suggestion . . . but dash it all, I forgot. I'm supposed to audition on Friday. Now I won't be able to. I can't imagine giving full attention to singing when I'm standing on one leg."

"You have an audition? Where?"

"At Lydia Rand-Smith's. She's a friend of Sybil's who organises musical events."

"That's mighty nice. She'll wait until you've recovered, don't you think, and give you another opportunity?"

"I hope so. So disappointing, though."

"Don't worry, Katie. Irish eyes are always smiling, aren't they now?"

"Even when I'm falling out of apple trees?"

"Even then. As I said, you have time to do other things." He smiled, encouragingly. "I want to thank you for taking your mother to the volunteer place. It's good for her."

"I know. She likes it there. Tell me, Dad, how she got to be so fearful. She wasn't always like that. I remember when she taught me to swim. I loved that. Never nervous in the water, she swam even in winter, when the icy waves crashed over us, sweeping us under."

"You're right." His face took on a faraway expression. "When we first met, she was different. We both loved the sea. She had thick dark hair and bright eyes. She enjoyed the out-of-doors and learned the names of all the wildflowers. Always walked in the woods, especially in spring, at bluebell time."

Kate warmed to the image of her mother, young and beautiful, tripping carefree through the bluebells.

"She was enchanting, and we shared a love of the countryside as well. I grew up in a rural place in Ireland, you'll be remembering."

"And you worked at a lifeboat station in Ireland before you came here as well as in Selsey. I've never understood why you both moved to Carshalton."

"She wanted me to give up the dangerous work on the lifeboat. After she lost her brother at sea, she became afraid that she would lose me as well."

"All right, but do you imagine all the years of city living have somehow broken her spirit?"

Her father shrugged. "I suppose so. That, and the death of her brother. She never talks about it, but they were close, and she took it very hard. It's one of the reasons she's so worried about the war and the bombing. We all remember it. Then, as you know, her parents died, Clare has moved to America, and now Ryan's gone."

"So she feels abandoned." Suddenly it seemed so clear. "Yes, Dad," she said gently. "Let's plan to sing together soon. By the way, I've been meaning to ask. Do you wish you had more time for singing?"

"I sang often when I was younger, with a men's choir. But work keeps me so busy these days. It's all right. I enjoy hearing you. That's what parents do sometimes. They live though their children."

He planted a kiss on her forehead and left the room. So that explained her father's generous support of her singing. But not her mother's dislike of it. *Abandonment.* Kate's mind shifted back to the time she felt abandoned. Not abandoned, exactly, but dismissed after her grandmother Ellen died. Kate had developed a special attachment to her, much more than Clare. Yet their mother had chosen to have Clare help sort out the house in Selsey. It had been a bitter disappointment. Why hadn't she spoken up, told her mother how much Grandma Ellen's house meant to her? But she knew why: her mother hadn't thought Kate practical enough, and would have told her so without hesitation.

Then Kate remembered Barry and his offer to take her to audition at Lydia's, and how she wouldn't go and needed to tell him. She didn't know where he lived or worked. Perhaps her mother could phone Lydia and ask her to relay a message to Barry about the injury. The familiar tightening of her throat signalled the start of a hiccup. She swallowed hard, stalling it, as she contemplated the possibility that her hiccups were an early sign of nerves. *Her mother's nerves.* Kate recoiled at the new and unwelcome theory. She did not want to end up like her mother.

CHAPTER 13

October 1939

K ate spent the next two days sitting in the living room with her leg propped up. The doctor had given her crutches, and she practiced getting around. She used one to climb upstairs while holding onto the banister. Mickey brought a pail of apples over and her mother made a pie. Kate mulled over the idea of talking to her parents about Ryan drinking cider but decided against it. They likely didn't know, and she didn't want to risk compromising the relationship with their neighbour. She wondered again at her ignorance about her brother's life. Not surprising that he'd teased her, labeling her a dreamer with a head full of music.

She listened each day to the news on the wireless. Broadcasts told everyone to take precautions, get shelters, keep the blackout, and practice wearing gas masks. All familiar warnings, but they seemed futile. They had scarce information about the war's progress in Europe, or about when to expect bombs in Britain.

"Mum, I need your help," Kate said. "I'm supposed to go to my new friend Lydia's on Friday, and I need to tell her about the accident. Would you please give her a ring and tell her I can't come? Here's the number. And please ask if she would be good enough to let Barry know he doesn't need to take me there in his car."

Her mother regarded her with a half-smile as she took the paper with the phone number. "Barry? Who is he?"

"Just someone who knows Lydia and who was going to accompany me."

"He was going to accompany you, you say? Do you mean while you sing?"

Kate nodded but offered no further information.

Mary Grace shrugged. "Fine. I'll phone soon."

The next day, Mrs. Bell paid a visit.

"They gave me your address at the school. I hope you will excuse my boldness, but I wish for you a good recovery and to ask a favour." She handed Kate a bunch of daisies. "I want to tell you how excited Hannah is with her part in the *Händel* cantata. But she worries she is not good enough, and you are not in school to help her. If it is not too much trouble, can she come here to practice with you? I can pay for the lessons."

"She's been doing well, but I'd be happy to see her here, and you don't need to pay me," Kate said. "Please have her come over after school sometime soon."

"Many thanks, Miss Murphy," Mrs. Bell said.

She nodded deferentially, and shuffled out of the house.

Kate still hadn't learned anything about the circumstances of Hannah's family. Perhaps the girl would explain in the privacy of Kate's home. For the remainder of the week, she tried to quell her impatience as she rested her leg. She wanted to be out and about. The lost opportunity to audition at Lydia's irritated her, and she had done nothing to address the hiccup problem. To distract herself from what she was missing, she filled her time by practicing the accompaniment for her school production. Then she turned to the Chopin piece she wanted to learn. She had mastered the Field Nocturne and needed a new challenge. She set the score for the Chopin prelude in front of her, then played the first few measures with her right hand.

Her mother interrupted her. "I rang Lydia this morning to tell her you can't keep the Friday appointment. Not friendly, is she? Very hoity-toity. Where does she live?"

"In Esher. I hardly know her, but she was pleasant enough when I met her. She's a friend of Sybil's."

"I always liked Sybil. Have you heard from her since she went away?"

"Not a word. She told me she can't talk about it."

"I don't know what to make of it all. Everything's a secret. We can't even discover where our own children have gone . . ." her voice faltered.

"Mum, it's all right. Ryan can take care of himself. Try not to worry so much. It won't help him, wherever he is."

Mary Grace sank onto a chair, and Kate gazed at her mother with resignation. *Why do I keep telling her to stop worrying? It's hopeless, like throwing water into the ocean.*

"Everything's changing before our eyes, but we can't see it," Mary Grace said. "I think I'll go crazy before it's all over. I can't even cook a decent meal for you and your dad now that I'm spending so much time at my volunteer job."

Now she's talking about going crazy. Whatever's next? Kate thought, and said, "Mum, we're glad you're so busy. And speaking of food, if there are some apples left, how about making another pie?"

Mary Grace perked up. "We might just have enough. How about helping me? You've never shown much interest in cooking, but since you're home these days, it might be a good opportunity for you to learn to make pastry."

"All right." Kate sighed. *As usual, there's no point in practicing when she's around, anyway.*

She rose from the piano bench and hobbled into the kitchen with her crutches, then positioned herself at the table, propping her injured ankle on a chair.

Her mother fetched flour, salt, butter, lard, and a rolling pin from the pantry. "We'll make the pastry first and let it rest while we prepare the apples." She measured the ingredients into a bowl. "The important thing is to keep everything cool and not overwork the dough."

She worked quickly, rubbing the fat into the flour with her hands. Then she poured a few teaspoons of water into the mixture and stirred it with a knife.

"See how it binds together? You only want to mix it to that point. If you overdo it, the pastry'll become tough instead of flaky."

"Sounds difficult, Mum, even though you make it look easy," Kate said.

"You have to get the feel of it. It takes some practice. I'll let you do it next time. For now, best if you watch to see how it's done."

"You're right. Funny, how I never learned this."

"As I said, you were never interested. Not like Clare. She has the makings of a true baker."

"True," Kate said. But the familiar stab of pain shot through her. Clare and her mother were bakers. Practical. Not dreamers.

Mary Grace glanced impatiently at Kate. "Well, you can learn. It'll be fun to do this together. You can help with the apples." She pushed them towards Kate and handed her a sharp knife. "Just peel and core them, then cut them into even slices."

Kate got to work. Soon she had filled a bowl with the pale green fruit, now turning brown. She hardly noticed Mary Grace rolling out the pie dough and lining a pan with it. Her thoughts turned to the happiness she'd felt at the tree top before she'd fallen. Like music, for a while it had transported her to a different, more beautiful world. Not like the work-a-day kitchen. Soon the pie baked in the oven, its apple fragrance emanating more strongly as the minutes ticked by.

A knock sounded at the front door and Mary Grace left to answer it. Kate overheard voices, her mother's and a man's deeper tone.

"I'm sure she'll be happy to see you," Mary Grace said, "but she's had an accident."

Moments later, Barry appeared, holding a bouquet of red roses.

Kate took a deep breath. "Hello. What a surprise," she said, taking the flowers. "Thank you."

"I wanted to see how you are. Sorry about your ankle. How are you feeling?"

"Better every day. It's nothing. I'll be back on my feet soon."

"I hope so. Too bad you had to miss the audition, but I'm sure there'll be another opportunity," he said, staring at her cast.

"Do you think so? Perhaps Lydia will contact someone else in the meantime."

"Possibly, but she's always in need of musicians. Many of the younger ones have gone to war."

"I suppose so."

Mary Grace swept flour off the table and handed Kate a damp cloth to wipe her sticky hands. She placed the roses in a vase and set it on the table.

"Please excuse the mess, Barry. Kate dear, why don't you sit with your friend in the living room and I'll bring you some biscuits and tea." She glanced at Barry. "Or would you prefer coffee?"

"Tea would be lovely," he said. "That pie smells good. Home cooking—haven't had any for ages."

"So you don't have family here?" Mary Grace asked.

"No. I live by myself now. Not strong in the domestic department. Mostly I just make beans on toast."

"Well then, you must stay for supper. Nothing special, I'm afraid. Toad-in-the-hole."

"Sausages in batter. I'd love that. Thank you, Mrs. Murphy."

Kate limped out of the kitchen using the crutches. Sitting across from him in the living room, Kate appraised his appearance. He wasn't wearing a tie, and his pullover hung loosely on his thin body. He folded his arms, hiding his hands, but she could still see dirt under his fingernails. She wished the clock didn't tick so loudly, making her painfully aware of the minutes passing while she didn't know what to say.

Mary Grace arrived, clattering the tray down with the tea and biscuits.

"Supper will be ready in an hour," she said.

Barry smiled his thanks and passed a cup to Kate.

"Did you work today?" she asked at last.

"Yes. It's not been as busy since they started rationing petrol. People aren't driving much, so cars don't need repairing."

"How did you learn your trade?"

"My dad had the shop. When he died, my brother and I inherited the business. I've always liked messing around with engines. I'd be an engineer if I could get the training."

"Wouldn't you rather be a musician?"

"Not really. There's no money in it. Don't get me wrong, I love music, but I need to earn a living."

"I understand that," she said. "Teaching doesn't pay well either. That's why I'm still at home."

"Where else would you live?"

She lowered her voice, looking towards the kitchen. "In America. My sister's there."

"So why don't you go?"

She appreciated his interest but couldn't confide in him. Not yet, anyway, "It's not easy," she said. "Maybe someday."

"I'll be leaving any day now to join the army," he said. "I'm surprised they haven't called me up already."

"What will you do with the garage if you go?"

"Don't know. Nothing. Just want it to still be there when I get back. I hope my car survives. I'd hate to lose that."

"What make of car have you got?"

He looked at his shoes, then met her glance. "It's a nice one, actually. A Bentley."

"That *is* nice."

He regarded her with the glimmer of a smile. "My one asset."

She let the remark pass. *He probably has more than one*, she thought. Musical talent, at least. "Perhaps we could practice our songs," she said. "The piano's in the dining room."

"Why not?" he agreed.

Kate stood up, reached for her crutches, and crossed the hallway. He followed and sat down at the instrument.

"What do you want to sing?"

"How about 'We'll Meet Again.'"

Barry played the introduction. "How's that for the key?"

"A little lower, please. I'm an alto."

He started again.

"That's good." Kate threw a brief glance at him, impressed that he could transpose keys at will. She'd do her best to impress him. Standing as straight as she could, she leaned against the piano for support and held her injured foot off the floor. Then she took a deep breath and began singing. Barry followed her tempo, playing softly, allowing the sound of her voice to shine through. When the song ended, they exchanged glances and burst out laughing.

"We're quite good, I'd say," he said. "You've got a lovely tone, smooth and rich like butter. Every bit as good as Vera."

"Don't be silly, but it's nice of you to say so."

"I mean it. I take it you're not professionally trained, but you have a natural ability. Your phrasing and dynamics are good. Have you considered studying at a music school?"

"I have. I'd love to, but now with the war, it's not possible. And . . ." she hesitated. "I have a problem with hiccups when I'm nervous. I'll stick to teaching the school choir for now."

She glanced sideways at him. Perhaps he wouldn't accompany her now that he knew about her affliction.

"Don't give up your dreams," he said firmly. "Never do that."

A relief. He doesn't seem concerned. "Thanks for reminding me. Anyway, I smell food. Let's go and see if Mum needs any help."

They ate in the kitchen, Barry sitting in Ryan's usual seat. Sean wasn't home, having announced earlier that he would have a pint with friends at the pub after work.

"So good to have home cooking, Mrs. Murphy," Barry said. "Thank you for inviting me."

"You must come again. It's a pleasure to have company."

They chatted until the meal's end, Mary Grace doing most of the talking.

"Would you like a hand with the dishes?" Barry asked.

"No, but thank you for asking," Mary Grace said.

Barry stood up to leave. "Don't move. I can let myself out," he said to Kate. "Give me a ring at the garage when you're able to get about a bit more. Here's the number." He handed her a business card.

Mary Grace escorted him to the door and returned to the kitchen.

"Kate, you sly creature. You never said anything about a boyfriend. How did you meet him?"

Kate felt herself blush and crossed her arms.

"He's not my boyfriend. I hardly know him," she said, staring past her mother at the window.

"Maybe he thinks differently. After all, he brought you roses. *Red roses.*"

Kate guffawed. "He did, but that's because he's kind. He's a friend of Lydia's. I met him at a dance."

"He seems nice. Very polite. He plays the piano and has rather an impressive car. I saw it by the curb. How did he get a car like that, I wonder. Aren't you interested in him?"

"Not really. He's just a friend."

"I don't know what's the matter with you, Kate dear. If I were in your shoes, I'd pay him some attention. Most of the nice men your age are off to war."

"And he will be, too, soon enough," Kate retorted. "Anyway, with this darn foot I'm not going anywhere anytime soon. Definitely not to the dance hall. I'm not much fun these days."

She hated Mary Grace's intrusion into her private life. She certainly didn't want an unsolicited opinion about a man whom her mother had only met once. After helping with the dishes, Kate made her way upstairs to bed. Although grateful to Barry for visiting, she didn't consider him a boyfriend. He was a talented musician, and she had no objection to friendship. But he didn't make her flutter inside, as Tony had.

She would have preferred to keep her relationship with Barry to herself, of course. But her mother would have found out anyway. Kate groaned. Ryan had been able to get away easily with activities he didn't want their mother to discover. *How did he manage it?* Because he was a boy? She tried to remember if Clare had kept any secrets. But no—because of their close relationship, she had always confided in Mary Grace—until she decided to go to America. That had surprised them all. Kate, on the other hand, had told Clare about Tony, with strict instructions not to say a word to anyone. Only Clare had known about Kate's broken heart, and had been a great comfort, lending her a shoulder for crying and telling her the end of the first love affair was the deepest, cruelest cut.

Kate laboriously climbed the stairs to bed. She settled under the covers taking care to avoid putting any pressure on her foot. She didn't need any more pain in her life. Barry was a chance she couldn't afford to take. Anyway, she wouldn't fall for a man just because her mother approved of him.

CHAPTER 14
November 1939

K ate's impatience didn't make her foot heal any faster. She tried to use the time constructively. With Mary Grace now spending more hours at the WVS Centre, Kate was free to devote herself to her piano, practicing the songs she hoped to perform. Her strong voice rang hiccup-free through the empty house. If only she could find her way to singing on stage.

The family talked every day about Ryan. Mary Grace said she'd heard at the Centre that most parents had received postcards from host families, and some children had sent letters as well. It became harder and harder for Kate to find comforting words to say. Mary Grace grew quieter as the days wore on with still no word from Ryan.

Then one day the stamped postcard he had taken with him arrived. Kate spied it on the doormat among the other mail, folded and torn around the edges, as though it had been thrown away. She sat on the stairs to read it.

Dear Mum, Dad and Kate. I'm here in Kingsbridge. I'm fine. Love, Ryan.

Not much information. Not even a date, she thought. The post-mark was illegible. He'd been away for six weeks. But then she saw something else. On the side of the card, barely discernible, appeared a drawing of a half-round sphere like a crescent moon. An X crossed the image. She gasped. The moonstone! Crossed out! It must be a message. Something was wrong.

She sat for a few minutes catching her breath. It would be some hours before her mother got home, and Kate considered going out to give her the news. As she stood up, she rejected the foolish idea. The news could wait. What would they do about the situation, anyway? They didn't even know where Ryan stayed, only that he lived in Kingsbridge, a place she had never heard of. This war was all about waiting: waiting for bombs, waiting for air raids, waiting for the invasion, now just waiting for her parents to get home. She limped into the kitchen to make a pot of tea.

At five, Mary Grace arrived home. "Such a busy day at the Centre," she said, taking off her coat. "They're giving away poppies for Remembrance Day tomorrow." Then she saw Kate's white face.

"What's wrong? Are you ill?"

Kate handed her the postcard.

"From Ryan? At last!" She read the scrawled words. "That's his handwriting!" she said, her eyes brightening. "He's in Kingsbridge, in Devon. That's good. A lovely place on the coast, an old market town. He'll be all right there. The card is damaged. Maybe it got lost, and that's why it took so long to get here. I knew Ryan wouldn't keep us worrying for so long. What a relief!"

Kate nodded. "It's good to know where he is."

She didn't want to spoil her mother's moment of happiness by telling her fears about Ryan's billet and the hidden message he might have sent. Her mother hadn't noticed the small moon. It would be better to wait and tell her father about her suspicion that something had gone amiss.

Kate retired to her room after supper. She read until she heard the front door click shortly after ten. She crept to the stairwell and called down softly. "Dad, is that you? We need to talk."

"A'right, daughter. Be there in two shakes of a lamb's tail," he said, his voice slurring.

Blast, she thought. *He's drunk.* No point trying to have a conversation now. Her father rarely went to the pub. But she had heard him mention he planned to celebrate a friend's birthday that evening. They must have enjoyed themselves, staying until closing time.

Sean mounted the stairs, holding onto the banister.

"So what is it you have to tell me, Katie," he said. "Can it wait till tomorrow?"

"Yes. That would be best. Good night, Dad."

He tipped his cap, and Kate went back to bed. Sleep didn't come easily, and she read her novel *Rebecca* until after midnight. Her dreams wavered between ghostly images of Manderley and the moonstone. In the morning she rose early, hoping to catch her father before he left for work. He came into the kitchen as she sat eating breakfast. He had dark circles under his eyes and slumped into a chair.

"How are you this morning, Dad?" she asked. "How about a cup of coffee?"

"Sounds grand, thank you. Do I remember you wanted to talk to me about something? About Ryan? Your mum told me. We got a postcard, and he's all right."

"Maybe. Did you examine it carefully?"

He gazed at her uncomprehendingly.

"I suppose not, then," she said. "If you look at it closely you can see the coded message. Mum didn't notice yesterday, and I didn't want to mention it, but I think he's having trouble with his billet."

"What are you talking about? He said he's fine."

"He and I have an understanding. I gave him a gift, a moonstone, before he left and told him it would keep him safe. He drew a picture on the card of a crossed-out moon. I'm sure he's trying to tell us that something's wrong."

"Hmm. Interesting. Upsetting, if you're right."

"I didn't want to tell Mum and make her worry."

"Good daughter, always looking out for her. I know she'll want to go after him if you're right and he's in trouble. Let's think about this awhile. I might stop by the school to find out if they know anything."

"Thank you, Dad. I'd do more myself, only I'm house-bound just now."

He patted her hand. "Don't you worry. I'll come up with something. Now, how about that coffee?"

She stood up to fill the kettle with water.

"Today's Remembrance Day," he said, pinning a red poppy on his jacket as he left. "Don't forget the two minutes of silence. For your uncle. And for all the others."

"Of course," she said, lighting the stove and putting the kettle on to boil.

Kate spent the morning in a state of frustration. She wished she could do something useful and for the hundredth time cursed herself for her carelessness in falling out of the tree. Her mother's buoyant mood didn't help because it was misplaced. All the same, Kate wouldn't tell her the truth until she and her father had a plan. At eleven o'clock, the church bells rang, and they stood in silence for two minutes out of respect for the men who had died in the first World War. Catching Mary Grace's sober expression, Kate contemplated whether her mother still missed her brother. Of course she did. He would never come back. After the two minutes had passed, Mary Grace left for the Centre, saying she'd be home at the end of the day. Kate promised to start supper.

The weather turned cold that afternoon. Alone in the house, Kate stared at the grey sky and bare trees rattling in the wind. The shelter, covered with brown earth, now held twenty garlic cloves. The plants wouldn't emerge until spring, and wouldn't be ready for harvesting till summer. Such a long time away, and who knew what would happen in the meantime.

At four o'clock Kate answered a knock at the door. Hannah Bell stood outside waving a sheet of music. "Good afternoon, Miss Murphy," she said. "My mother said you could help with my singing. Would this be a good time?"

"Yes, it would. Come in."

Kate appreciated the timely distraction. The girl took off her coat and hat and Kate noticed the school uniform she wore looked a size too small. She wondered why the school hadn't given her a larger one but remembered that parents had to pay for part of the cost. She led Hannah into the dining room, then set the music score on the rack and sat down at the piano.

"Have you been practicing at home?" she asked.

"I have, but I'm not sure I'm getting the rhythm right. We don't have a piano to accompany me, you see."

"You need to count," Kate said. "Can you read music?"

"Not really."

"All right. We'll go over this and I'll help you, but you'll need to understand time signatures and learn to count if you want to be a real musician. How's this for the tempo? One, two, three . . ." Kate played the opening bars and Hannah sang, softly at first, then with fuller volume. As they ended the piece, Kate clapped. "Very good. You need to be sure to keep your voice strong in this song. Be sure to enunciate the consonants—*bright, tight,* and so on. Sound the Ts at the end. Take a breath before each phrase. Does that make sense?"

"Yes. Can we go through it again?"

"Here's something else important to remember. Listen to the piano, and hear the first note in your head before you begin singing. That way you won't start out flat." The terrible image of her audition for the music school passed through her mind. She had forgotten that simple device, and it had cost her dearly.

Hannah took a deep breath before singing.

"Better." Kate said afterwards, smiling. "Let's go over the first lines again. It's essential to make a strong start."

After practicing for a while longer, Kate announced, "You'll do fine at the performance."

Hannah gave her a shy smile. "When are you coming back to school?"

"As soon as the cast comes off. In another week, I hope."

"Does it hurt?"

"Not any more. But difficult getting around."

"I broke my arm once. They called it a green stick fracture. What a funny name."

A green stick fracture. Like a moist, green branch, too flexible to fully break, just like a child's resiliency. Or so she hoped. For Hannah, especially. "Did it hurt?" she asked.

"Not too much. It got better quickly. The worst thing about it was no one was home when it happened, and I had to wait until my parents came to go to the hospital."

"Yes. Waiting is difficult, especially if you're in pain."

"My father had gone out to buy bread. My mother works, every day except weekends. She cleans houses. She's always tired when she gets back."

Kate gently touched the girl's forearm. "Your mother must work hard to support you."

Hannah pursed her lips. "Too hard. And Papa wants to work, badly. He used to have a good job."

"In Germany, you mean."

"Yes. I hardly remember it. We can't go back unless they deport us. It's not safe. *Mutti* believes some people will punish us there."

"Deport and punish you? How?"

"She won't tell me."

"No? Well, you're here now. And you're going to be a star in the cantata. Wait and see."

"I hope so. I want to make my parents proud."

"Would you like something to eat before you go? My mother makes tasty cakes."

"Yes, please."

In the kitchen, Kate set out plates and cut the Madeira cake her mother had made the day before. Hannah delicately broke off a piece to taste.

"Scrumptious!" she said, and finished her slice.

"Would you like another piece?"

"Rather. It's jolly good. We don't have cakes like this at home. My mother doesn't bake anymore. She says the ingredients are expensive and we should eat simple, nutritious things like potatoes and eggs."

"No bacon?"

"No bacon. We don't eat pork. This cake is yummy."

"Madeira cake. Would you like to take some home with you?" Kate asked.

"I'd love to. It'd be a treat for *Mutti* and Papa. Thank you, Miss Murphy."

Kate wrapped several slices of cake in brown paper. "Come again if you need more help," she said, giving Hannah a brief hug. After Hannah left, Kate sat for a while, thinking over the conversation. She liked the girl. Her modesty, honesty, and complete lack of guile were appealing qualities. Now that she knew Sarah worked as a char lady, she understood how the family might struggle financially. So why didn't they eat bacon, one of the cheaper and more available meats? Kate had been aware of Sarah's nervousness when they met at school, but why did Sarah fear that the family would be deported? Kate resolved to learn more about the family's circumstances and to do whatever she could to help. She guessed that her own family's difficulties were far fewer than the Bells'.

Kate opened the pantry to see what she could come up with for supper. Perhaps macaroni and cheese. She took out a package of noodles and grated the cheese. Her parents would be home any minute. As she set the table, Sean arrived, followed by Barry.

"Look who's here, a friend of yours," her father said. "This young man tells me he came to see how you're getting along."

Kate smiled. "Hello, Barry. So you've met my father. As you see, I'm still wearing the cast."

"Well, offer him a seat, lassie, and give him a pint. You like ale, don't you?" Sean asked.

"I do, sir. Thank you. How's the foot, Kate?"

"Getting better at last." She passed out bottles of ale to the men, and they sat down at the table.

Sean leaned forward. "Katie, I've learned a few things about Ryan. We'll have to tell your mother. Barry, you may know that our son's an evacuee. It turns out he and the other boys had no assigned host families when they arrived in Devon, in Kingsbridge. They all got off the train, lined up on the platform, and then the families who met them there chose the one they liked. That's why the Harris twins were separated. Their hosts only wanted one boy, and the escorts had no authority. The school has no information about where anyone ended up. The boys and hosts had strict instructions to send the postcards home as soon as possible. That's all we know."

"That sounds ghastly," Kate said. "Maybe Ryan ended up with a horrible family."

"That's possible, and may explain his message to you."

"The only way to find out would be to go and see for ourselves, then. But Mum won't want to go alone, you have to work, and I have a broken foot."

Barry had listened quietly to the conversation, but now he spoke up. "Perhaps I can help. I've got a car. I could drive Kate and Mrs. Murphy."

In the Bentley? Kate thought. *Splendid.*

"That's a right kindly offer," Sean said. "Are you sure you can do this?"

"Absolutely. I can close the garage for a day or two. There's not much work anyway, and I have plenty of petrol."

"Plenty of petrol, you say? But it's rationed. You may not have enough to get you to Devon and back. That's a long way."

"With respect, sir, I have special access, being in the car business."

"Ah, that's all right then. I'm sure my wife will appreciate the offer."

Kate could hardly believe her ears. "How soon can we leave?"

"As soon as you like. Tomorrow, even."

"Kate, how about a pint to celebrate?"

"I'd prefer some of Mickey's cider, actually . . . oops. I wasn't supposed to say anything."

Sean laughed. "So the old fellow makes apple cider with his fruit, does he? It doesn't surprise me. Good for him."

"It's not ready yet, and he gave me a sample," Kate said. "But I'll join you with some ale, please."

Barry left as soon as he finished his drink, saying he needed to buy fuel and prepare the car for the trip. He'd collect them at ten o'clock the next day.

When Mary Grace arrived home, Kate quickly finished preparing the meal and told her about the plans, carefully avoiding expressing any fear about Ryan's billet.

"Thank the Lord," she said. "Your friend Barry is an angel. I knew I liked him the first time I saw him."

Hmm, I'm not sure he's an angel, Kate thought, *but he knows how to be useful.* Or maybe he was a kind of an angel. Despite years at St. Bridget's, she didn't really know much about angels.

CHAPTER 15
November 1939

K ate and Mary Grace had just stepped out of the house with their suitcases when, good as his word, Barry pulled the car up to the curb at the stroke of ten. "Ready to go?"

"More than ready," Mary Grace said.

He lifted their suitcases into the car's boot.

"What a shiny car," Mary Grace said.

"I keep it waxed. Good for the finish," Barry said proudly. "Climb in."

"Would you like to sit in the front, Mum?" Kate asked.

"No, thanks. You two sit together."

Mary Grace settled into the back. "Leather seats. What luxury," she sighed contentedly.

Barry helped Kate into the front seat before settling himself at the wheel. He started the engine and drove to Carshalton Road, the main artery that would take them south.

"Do you know the way?" Kate asked.

"Not exactly, but I have maps. Here, take a look. I may need you as navigator."

"How long will the trip take?"

"Depends on how often we stop and how good the roads are. I expect as we get closer to Devon they may become narrow country lanes. I'd say five hours, so we should be there by mid-afternoon."

"Mum says the town is small, with only a few thousand people, so it should be easy to locate Ryan."

"We can ask. I imagine most people there know about the boys' arrival. If he's going to school, we'll find him there."

"He's supposed to be attending a Catholic school. If we arrive by four, we should catch him when he comes out."

"That's what I was thinking. I'll drive as fast as it's safe to do."

Kate turned to watch him at the wheel. He drove with confidence, and the Bentley rode smoothly. She relaxed gratefully into her seat.

"Tell me more about your car," she said.

"I've had it for two years now. A customer used to bring it in, and I always did the work. I appreciated its quality and good looks—"

"It's a lovely car," Kate interrupted him.

Barry continued. "The owner, a doctor called Robin Hartley, became a friend. He treated my brother when he had a bad case of the flu and took us out for meals sometimes. Robin acted like a father. He always kept the car in immaculate condition and when he died, he left it to me."

"Nice heirloom. You said you'd have no trouble getting fuel for this long trip. How's that?"

"We apply for coupons, which are rationed. Customers who don't use theirs often give them to me when they can't afford to pay for work I've done."

"But don't the people at the petrol stations check for names?"

Barry laughed. "They're supposed to, but they don't. You'll see. Anyway, if we use someone else's for the trip, it's for a good cause, isn't it?"

"I'll say. You can hear how happy Mum is."

Mary Grace was humming softly in the back seat. Kate twisted her head to smile at her.

"I could fly to the moon today," Mary Grace beamed. "I only hope we learn that our boy's all right. In any case, we're going to see him. I know we'll find him. I can't wait."

The trip progressed without difficulty. The November fog lifted to reveal the gentle Surrey landscape of fields, woods, and streams interspersed with cosy villages. Autumn leaves clung frailly to boughs. Barry drove carefully, observing the speed limits, and as the hours sped by Kate and Mary Grace became drowsy. They passed through Surrey and Hampshire and entered Somerset. The countryside along the way became increasingly rural, with fields of cows and sheep and acres of ploughed farmland.

"Are you hungry?" Barry asked after a while. "Ready for a break?"

Kate stirred. "Uh, yes, I think so," she said, yawning. "Mum, how about you?"

Mary Grace was fast asleep.

"Mum, wake up. Barry asks if we need a break."

She jerked and rubbed her eyes. "A break? Where are we?"

"Just outside Yeovil, "Barry said.

"Still a ways to go, then. I would like a break, actually."

Barry pulled the car into the parking lot of the Cheek and Jowl pub. Mary Grace produced a bag of sandwiches while Barry went into the pub to buy drinks.

After eating their meal and making use of the washroom, they resumed the journey, and the afternoon wore on. When they reached the Devonshire border the landscape changed again. Copses and rolling hills gave way to wild, open moorland and remote villages. The road narrowed. Tall hedgerows on both sides obscured their view.

Mary Grace leaned forward. "I remember this area so well. It reminds me of my childhood. We used to go to Devon every year on holiday. We could hardly wait to get to the water and sailing. Perhaps that's what Ryan's been doing."

They passed Exeter.

"Kate, could you check the map?" Barry asked. "There's a turning we need to take somewhere soon towards Kingsbridge."

Kate unfolded and examined the map.

"I think we have to go a few more miles. We'll pass through part of Dartmoor first. That's exciting—I've always wanted to see it. It's full of mystery and stories of smugglers. Very romantic."

"Not all of it is romantic. There's a jail there, too," Barry said, "and I take it you won't want to stop and visit."

Kate agreed, smiling.

The light suddenly faded, and raindrops splashed on the windscreen. Barry turned on the wipers. They waved back and forth, squeaking softly. Everything turned grey.

"It feels like night already," Kate said. "How will we see Ryan in the dark?"

Mary Grace pressed her face against the window pane. "We will find him. I'm not leaving until we do. The Harris boys are there. They're sure to know where he is."

Soon theirs was the lone car on a road that wound though the bleak moorland flanked by eerie skeletal trees and grotesque shapes of boulders. The horizon disappeared into the dank mist.

"Really creepy," Kate said.

"I love it," Mary Grace said unexpectedly. "My father used to make up ghost stories about the moor and scare us half to death."

I never knew that, Kate thought, and shivered. Suddenly a white shape leaped from the roadside in front of the car. The headlights caught it, and Barry slammed on the brakes. The car skidded, swerved, and came to a stop. Mary Grace shrieked. Kate froze.

"It's all right," Barry said. "Just a sheep. Damn near killed it."

"Place gives me the willies," Kate said. "It reminds me of *The Hound of the Baskervilles*."

"I remember that story," Barry said. "Let's get going. We'll be out of the moor soon. Kate, please keep an eye out for the sign to Kingsbridge."

Fifteen minutes later, they saw the sign and turned towards their destination. Barry parked the car under a clock tower in the town's central square. He stepped out, wound a scarf around his neck, and opened Mary Grace's door. Kate and Mary Grace buttoned their coats, and Barry held an umbrella over them. The wet cobblestones shone as the travellers surveyed the scene.

"Exactly as I remember it," Mary Grace said.

"Lots of charm," said Kate.

Mary Grace threw back her head and inhaled. "Smell the sea air. How I've missed it!"

A jumble of buildings and shops surrounded the square. The Kings Arms, a white-walled pub with paned glass windows, stood nearby.

"Let's see if they have accommodations." Barry said.

They traipsed in, Kate managing her crutches with speed. Dark but warm, the pub had low beamed ceilings and upholstered benches around wooden tables deeply etched with initials.

The innkeeper leaned across the counter. "How may I help you?"

Barry made reservations for two rooms and asked the whereabouts of the Catholic school.

"No Catholic school here," the man said. "The local school is about a mile away on Duke Street." He pointed to the right.

"No Catholic school? That's bad news," Mary Grace said. "I thought they told us . . ."

They filed out of the building and turned towards Duke Street.

Kate looked up at the clock tower. "Almost half past three. School will be out soon. We're in luck."

They drove down the street to the school entrance. A few boys came out dressed in green uniforms.

"We'll have to ask every boy we see if he knows Ryan," Kate said. "The older boys, around his age."

"How old is he?" Barry asked.

"Thirteen. He's tall for his years, and thin. Has thick dark hair."

"I have a better idea," Mary Grace said. "Let's ask at the school's office. They should be able to tell us if he's registered and possibly where he lives."

Mary Grace and Kate left Barry in the car, Kate following behind her mother as fast as her crutches would allow. Mary Grace introduced herself to the attendant. "My son Ryan was evacuated to this town. We want to know where he lives and if he's in school here."

The attendant picked up a clip board. "What did you say his name is, again?" she asked.

"Ryan Murphy. Probably in third form."

The woman perused the list. "No one by that name here," she said.

"Oh dear. How about two others from Surrey, Tom and Francis Harris. Twins."

"Yes, I know them. They're in Mr. Johnson's class. They'll be coming out soon."

"Thank you. You wouldn't happen to have information about the placement of other children in the town, would you?"

The woman shook her head. "Sorry. They all arrived together on the train. I understand every boy found a home, though."

Kate's spirits sank. Her intuition had been right. *Something's wrong.*

At that moment, hordes of boys streamed past them out of the building. "Tommy Harris!" Mary Grace shouted. The boy stopped, Francis on his heels.

"'ello, Mrs. Murphy," Tom said, with a look of surprise. "What are you doing 'ere?"

"So glad to see you boys," she said. "We're here to look for Ryan. Do you know where he is?"

"No," Tom said. "We 'aven't seen 'im—'e got picked up like the rest of us at the train station. I saw a big man take him away. Rough sort. Looked like a farmer."

"A farmer? And Ryan has never been to school?"

"No. You know, Francis and me don't stay at the same place. Francis likes 'is family. They give 'im lots of ice cream, and they have 'orses. I don't like mine so much. What's the news from 'ome? 'ow's Mum? Any bombs yet?"

"No bombs, and your parents are fine, Tommy." Turning to Kate with a pained expression she said, "Seems no one knows where Ryan is."

"We'll find him," Kate said brightly. "He's not at school, but he wanted to leave anyway. Let's go back to the pub, have a drink, and decide what to do next."

"If you'll excuse us, we 'ave to get back," Tom said. "I get in trouble if I'm late. Nice to see you, and I'm sorry about Ryan. We miss 'im, too. Is Mum coming to visit us soon? I wish she would."

"I'll tell her you asked," Mary Grace said.

The boys tipped their caps and ran off. Kate thought Francis looked healthy and well-dressed, while Tom appeared thinner and wore ill-fitting clothes.

Back at The Kings Arms, Kate ordered drinks, cider for herself and her mother, and a pint for Barry. The pub soon filled with locals, mostly men, but the chatter and laughter of the throng around them made Kate uneasy. They were there on a mission, not to have fun. Mary Grace clenched her hands around her glass.

"We've got one clue," Kate said. "Tom told us he saw a big man take Ryan, someone who might be a farmer."

"I've just remembered," Mary Grace said. "Tomorrow's Saturday. Farmers used to come here to sell their goods on Saturdays. Maybe Ryan will come to the market. If not, perhaps the bartender or the innkeeper knows who the local farmers are."

They ordered fish and chips for supper. After the meal, Mary Grace, saying she felt exhausted and wanted the next day to come soon, went up to bed.

"I'll be up directly," Kate called after her.

"Would you like another glass of cider?" Barry asked.

"Yes, I would," Kate replied.

As she watched him push his way through the crowd, Kate thought how generous and steady he was. He had no reason for taking the long trip other than to help them. He had driven carefully, kept them safe, and allayed her mother's fears. *A good man.*

He handed her the cider and sat down beside her. "To finding Ryan."

"In good health," she added.

They smiled at each other and clinked glasses.

"It's really kind of you to help us," said Kate.

"I'm glad to, and besides, it's great for the car to have a long run." He hesitated. "It's an opportunity to spend time with you."

She blushed. "Uh . . . yes," she said, downing several sips of her drink.

The fire glowed in the corner, and Barry moved closer. "You've been so patient waiting for that foot to heal. I thought you might like a chance to get out a bit."

"I wish I had a happier reason for getting out. I hope it's not a fool's errand."

He put his hand on her shoulder. "It won't be."

She stood up. "Good night, and thank you, again."

He stood in turn, pulling her towards him, and gave her a brief kiss on the forehead. "Allow me to escort you to your room."

He held her arm, assisting her as she bumped up the stairs. "Sweet dreams," he whispered, handing her the crutches as she opened the door. Her mother was already asleep. Tiptoeing through the room, she got ready for bed. She lay awake for a while thinking about him. Did he consider her a girlfriend? The possibility vaguely appealed, but brought back vivid memories of Tony and the anguish he'd caused her. She wasn't good at relationships. But she shouldn't worry. Barry was different—more of a family friend than a heart throb—and she wasn't falling in love. *So he can't hurt me.*

CHAPTER 16
November 1939

At six o'clock, eager to start the day and find Ryan, Kate dressed quickly, then left her sleeping mother and crept downstairs. No one was in the breakfast room, and it was still dark outside. A low fire burned in the grate. Kate hopped to an armchair beside it, sat down, and picked up a newspaper. Pictures of British Expeditionary Force soldiers in Belgium and an article about the British battleship HMS *Royal Oak,* torpedoed by a German U-boat in October, filled the front page. She read it with horror. The ship had sunk in Scapa Flow in Scotland, the main British naval base, and so difficult to navigate and well-protected that it was thought impenetrable by enemy vessels. But somehow a German submarine had entered the harbour and destroyed one of the prize British battleships. So far, the Royal Navy had sunk only a few U-boats. It did not appear Britain was winning the war. *Why is the news always so late? It's not new, at all. A misnomer.* She heaved a sigh of irritation, threw the paper down, and waited impatiently for Mary Grace and Barry to join her.

They appeared an hour later and ate a hurried breakfast. Through the window, Kate could see vendors setting up tents and tables in the square outside. Daylight arrived, damp and chilly, and the travellers bundled up in hats, coats, and scarves before venturing outside.

"We'll leave you here while we search the aisles," Mary Grace told Kate. She took a seat on a bench, and laid her crutches beside her. From there, she could see vegetable stands, fish laid out in rows, and three red chickens in a cage. In the early morning only a few customers shopped, mostly women, with baskets over their arms. After fifteen minutes, Mary Grace and Barry returned.

"Perhaps this is hopeless, like looking for sunshine in the rain," Mary Grace said, slumping onto the bench beside Kate.

A van drove up and a large man and a boy started unloading containers of milk onto an empty table.

Kate's chest tightened. She grabbed Barry's arm, stood up, and pointed. "That's Ryan!" she said breathlessly.

"Wait here, Kate," he said. "We should check the surroundings before we approach him. We don't want to raise the alarm."

Barry steered Mary Grace behind the parked van. Kate could hardly restrain herself from calling out to her brother. She moved closer.

"All right, try to get his attention, but be careful," Barry said quietly to Mary Grace, who nodded and crept forward. "Psst . . . Ryan!" she called softly, peeping round the vehicle. He didn't hear her and bent to lift another urn.

"Hey, *Ryan*," Barry called.

Ryan raised his head, turned round, and caught sight of his mother. His face broke into a wide smile.

"Mum! What are you doing here?" he said, straightening.

"We've come to take you home."

"You found me! How on earth . . . but that's splendid, and I'm *so* glad!"

He rushed to Mary Grace and gave her an enormous hug. Tears rolled down his cheeks as he embraced her. Then his face lit up as he saw Kate.

The large man strode towards them. "What's this all about then? No huggin' the customers," he roared. He was unshaven, with wild hair and eyes.

Ryan released Mary Grace and stood beside her, his arm around her shoulder.

"This is my mother. Mum, this is Mr. Turner, my host."

"How do you do?" Mary Grace said.

"What's yer mum doin' 'ere?" he growled. "She let you go. You're an evacuee. You're mine now."

"Thank you very much for keeping him, but he's coming home now," Mary Grace said.

Mr. Turner's face reddened, and a leering smile lit his face.

"Oh no, 'e ain't. 'E's my billet. S'posed to stay fer at least six months, maybe till the end o' the war."

"But I'd like to go home now, Mr. Turner. You can't stop me," Ryan said.

"Can't I, now? I 'ave me rights. I'll report you to the police. It's kidnappin.'"

Barry stepped forward. "Excuse me, Mr. Turner. The boy has told you what he wants to do. It's not kidnapping if he goes home with his own mother—"

"You keep out o' this!" he bellowed. "'Tis my affair." He lunged at Barry, hitting him squarely in the eye and knocking him backwards. Kate screamed. Ryan grabbed the man by both arms.

"Stop this!" he yelled. In the struggle, they crashed into the table, knocking urns off the table, and hit the ground, wrestling. The milk gurgled onto the cobblestones.

A crowd gathered around the stall, talking and pointing. Whistles sounded, and three policemen arrived.

"What's all this about?" one of them asked sternly. "Oh, it's you, Dick Turner. What are you fighting about this time?"

Ryan sat back on his haunches and Turner pulled himself up. "They're takin' away me billet. They've no right doin' that."

"Who's taking your billet away? This young fella, you mean?" he asked, pointing at Ryan.

"I took 'im on, just doin' me duty to save the kiddies, and now 'is mother wants 'im back."

The policeman cast his eyes around. "You his mother?" he asked. "Do you have proof?"

"Yes," Mary Grace said. From her handbag she produced Ryan's birth certificate.

Kate marvelled at her mother's forethought. *Thank goodness for that.*

"Ryan wants to come home," Mary Grace continued. "There's nothing wrong with that, is there, officer?"

"Not that I know of. Do you want to go home then, sonny?"

"Yes, please. *Rather.*"

"All right. It makes sense. I've heard of others leaving. There're no bombs at home, so no need to evacuate, they say."

"Thank you, officer," Mary Grace said.

Facing Turner, the police officer said, "Are you going to behave yourself, or are we going to have to take you down to the station again?"

"I'll be'ave. Need to get my milk cans sorted now."

Kate watched the man scowl and spit on the ground after the policeman left.

"Bloody coppers," he mumbled as he stamped away to pick up the overturned urns.

Barry sat up, holding a hand to his eye.

"Are you hurt?" Mary Grace asked. She pulled his hand away gently. His eye was swelling and a trickle of blood ran down his cheek. "Looks like he gave you a black eye. What a brute. We'll get some ice."

Kate turned to look more closely at Barry. He looked shaken, but managed a thin smile.

"I'm all right," he said, standing up.

She felt a momentary twinge of guilt that Barry had been hurt helping her brother when she had given him such little encouragement for a closer relationship. But her excitement at finding Ryan soon overtook any feelings of self-reproach, and she beamed as Ryan came over to her.

"So good to see you here, but what's this with the crutches?" he said. "Playing wounded soldier, are you?"

He wrapped his arms around her.

"Fell out of a tree. Tell you about it later," she said. "So glad we found you."

They proceeded to the pub, Ryan linking arms with Mary Grace. "Too bad about the lost milk," he said, "though it serves the blighter right. What's the saying? Don't cry over spilt milk? Anyway, he's got plenty more where that comes from. Good milk, too. Jersey cows."

Back at the pub, everyone took seats at a table. Mary Grace asked for ice for Barry. Kate looked Ryan over. He wore dirty trousers and a frayed blue pullover under a shabby overcoat, but his weather-beaten face had a healthy glow.

"What were you doing, selling milk? Have you become a farmer?" Kate asked.

"Not exactly. Quite a long story," Ryan said.

"Well, tell us everything. Would you like something to drink or eat?" Mary Grace asked.

"A cup of tea would be nice. Your friend here was a big help," he said, looking at Barry. "Sorry you took a punch. The bloke's a monster. Who are you, by the way?"

"Excuse me. I should have introduced my friend. This is Barry," Kate said.

Barry extended his hand. "Pleased to meet you, Ryan."

"Go on. Tell us your story, son." Mary Grace said.

The tea arrived and Ryan began. "As you know, we arrived here by train. Host families were waiting at the station to choose the boys they wanted. They lined us up like cattle and chose the younger boys and girls first."

"*A crime*. Not what they promised us," Mary Grace interrupted.

"No," Ryan said. "Mr. Turner picked me. He owns a farm outside the town, and several acres of land for cows, pigs, and a few crops like cabbages. He told me he needed help, and I looked strong and healthy. It was too far for me to get to school from the farm, and I told him I didn't care if I didn't go."

He scowled. "But he worked me hard. Farming's tough, I've learned. I don't mind if I never muck out another pig sty. Those animals stink! I probably do, too. Didn't have many baths. His wife never talked much, just cooked meals and did all the washing."

"Was he good to you?" Mary Grace asked.

"Not really. Sort of a bully. He told me he'd report me if I tried to run away. I had no access to a telephone or way of contacting anyone. This is the first time I've been away from the farm since I got there. He needed my help at the market today."

"Don't they have any other children to help out, or farm workers?" Mary Grace asked.

"No children, but there's a man who helps milk the cows. He usually comes to market with Mr. Turner, but he didn't feel well today, so I came instead. Lucky I did."

"I'll say," Kate said. "Sounds like forced labor, for God's sake. Horrible. Did he pay you?"

"Course not. He gave me room and board, didn't he? And did his part for England, saving a child." Ryan grimaced. "Anyway, you've all rescued me," he said, the corners of his mouth curving to a grin.

"It's wonderful!" Mary Grace smiled, refilling his teacup.

Ryan gulped the steamy tea. "Thanks, I needed that. I've been up since five."

Me, too, worrying. Kate thought. *So glad things worked out.*

"Did you have breakfast this morning?" Mary Grace asked.

"Did I ever. That's one thing I can't complain about. They fed me well."

"They made you grow, anyway. You've shot up like a spring onion, and filled out. Your clothes at home won't fit you anymore."

"Least of my problems, Mum," he said, patting her hand. "It's my growth spurt. We've all got it."

"But tell me," Kate said, "if you were trapped at the farm, how did you get the postcard to us?"

"I didn't for weeks, as you know. Mr. Turner said he'd put it in the post when he went to market, but he didn't. I came across it in the waste paper bin. I asked Ted, the farm hand, to post it when he came to town. And you must have understood my secret message," he said, winking at Kate. "Thank you for that, and by the way . . ." he dug into his pocket. "Here's the moonstone. You can have it back now."

"No, you keep it. I'm glad it worked," she said, fighting the impulse to cry for joy and relief.

"We need to get on the road," Barry said.

"I agree," Mary Grace said, "but are you all right driving with that eye?"

Barry nodded. "It's fine."

"Let's get our things and pay the bill," Kate said. "Ryan, don't you have belongings you need to bring home? Things you left at the farm?"

"Nothing that matters. The only important thing is the moonstone, and we have that."

"The magical moonstone," Kate said happily. She perceived her mother's puzzled expression but offered no explanation. It was a secret she and Ryan shared.

"I'll bring the car round to the front of the building," Barry said.

While they waited, Ryan said suddenly, "Hang on a minute. I forgot something."

He vanished into the crowd in the square. The Bentley arrived and stopped by the curb. Barry jumped out and stowed the suitcases.

"Let's go," he said, opening the passenger doors for Kate and Mary Grace.

"We have to wait for Ryan. He said he'll be back in a minute," Kate said. *Where could he have gone at the last minute?*

Barry fidgeted in his seat. "Where the heck is he? We should get going."

Ten minutes passed. Kate felt her stomach tighten. *What if something goes wrong?* She avoided looking at her mother, whom she suspected shared her concern. *More worry. Nothing but worry, these days.*

A moment later, Ryan reappeared holding a cardboard box with holes in the sides. Barry got out. "Are those your clothes? Let's put them in the boot."

"Can't do that. I'll hold the box on my lap."

A loud squawk sounded from the container. Barry took a step backwards. "What have you got in there? Something alive?"

Kate and Mary Grace wound down their windows to hear. Ryan beamed.

"A chicken. We need one for eggs. She's a Sussex chicken, good for laying."

"You can't bring her in the car, Ryan. She won't make the journey home," Mary Grace said.

"Yes, she will. The farmer told me we need to be sure she has enough air and to avoid bumps. Looks like that car of yours will give us a smooth ride. I've got food and water. She'll be fine. Friendly, the farmer says. She'll be a good pet."

Ryan sat in the back seat beside his mother, holding the box. Kate couldn't help laughing, and Mary Grace edged farther away from him.

"What's her name?" Mary Grace asked.

"I'll call her Scooter."

"Never a dull minute with Ryan around," Kate chuckled. "Actually, it's a good idea to have a chicken. I heard they're going to ration eggs soon."

"That's what I was thinking," Ryan said. "By the way, quite a nice motor car you have here, Barry."

"It'll get us there, but I want to stop soon for petrol. I don't want to risk getting stuck in the moor with no fuel," Barry said. "And it's better to use the coupon somewhere where they don't know who you are."

"I wish we had time to look around the town," Mary Grace said. "It brings back so many memories."

Kate detected the wistful look on her mother's face. Someday she'd ask her more about those memories.

The chicken, after scratching and clucking for a while, settled down in the box.

Several miles down the road, Barry stopped at a village with a pump. An attendant appeared at the driver's window. Barry handed him a coupon, and the man filled the tank without a question or comment.

"I told you. They almost never ask," he said to Kate. "They're glad for the business."

Kate wound down the window and took deep breaths of the country air. Crisp sunshine touched lingering leaves of beech trees, highlighting their rich bronze and yellows against the azure sky. She smelled the aroma of wood smoke from grey smoke tendrils curling above the trees. Grassy fields across the street shone verdant from recent rains. Late harvest time, she thought. *All is well.*

Ryan climbed out of the car with the box and lifted the lid. The chicken sprang free with an ear-splitting squawk, flapped her wings, and took off running along the road.

"Hey, come back!" Ryan said, chasing after her. Kate, Mary Grace, and Barry watched, laughing. The bird eluded Ryan, twisting and turning, but eventually he caught up with her, grasped her in his arms, and held her to his chest.

"P'raps that peek was a bad idea," he said, panting.

He shoved her back in the box, pushing the top shut. After a few minutes, the chicken's shuffling ceased. "The farmer said she can go the whole way without water, but I thought I'd see how she is. She'll settle down in the dark."

"I think you've given her exactly the right name," Kate said. "Scooter. What a hoot."

They drove home without further incident. As Barry dropped the passengers off at the Holly Road house, Mary Grace said, "Come for dinner tomorrow night. It's the least we can do to thank you."

"I'd like that."

"I—we—look forward to seeing you then," Kate said.

He drove off, and Ryan carried the chicken to the back garden. Sean appeared on the front doorstep.

"Welcome home, all. How did it go? Did you find Ryan? Where is he?"

"He's putting a chicken in Hickory's old hen house. We've had a long journey," Mary Grace said cheerfully. "Let's put the kettle on and we'll tell you all about it."

Ryan's home, Kate thought. *As much as I love having him around, this means I don't need to stay. Maybe I'll join Clare in America. But not yet. After the cantata.*

CHAPTER 17
November 1939

K ate found her mother up early the next day humming tunelessly as she drank her cup of tea. Sean had already left for work. Ryan stumbled into the kitchen behind Kate, yawning. Dull, tangled hair hung around his ears. He stretched out his legs as he sat down at the table.

Mary Grace studied him with an amused expression. "You need a haircut. New clothes, too. And you could use a bath."

"I know. I'm going to enjoy a long soak. I never really got clean at the farm. They didn't have running water in the house, and the work was grimy."

"Nothing like seeing things from another perspective for making you appreciate the comforts of home," Mary Grace said.

"You're right. I had no idea. It's good to be back," he smiled.

"You stink, little brother," Kate said.

He stuck his tongue out at her. "Too tired to have a bath after supper last night. I got up at five in the morning, remember? Couldn't wait for that comfortable bed."

Mary Grace put a rack of toast on the table and Ryan took two slices.

"Would you like some porridge as well?" she asked.

"No, thanks. I need that bath." He slathered butter and marmalade on the toast and wolfed it down, drank a cup of tea, and went upstairs.

"He shouldn't be so extravagant with the butter and marmalade, but he's just home, so I'll let it go this time. I expect he'll settle down now, and stop trying to fly the coop like that chicken of his," Mary Grace said.

"We'll see. He needs to finish school."

"Perhaps he'll see the value of that now he's had a taste of the working world. Thank the Lord he's too young to be conscripted. Speaking of that, I suppose Barry will leave soon. What a nice young man. He likes you, Kate."

"Yes, he's a decent chap." Kate avoided her mother's eyes. "Have you decided the menu for dinner tonight?" she asked, eager to change the subject.

"Yes. A celebratory meal, roast beef and Yorkshire pudding with apple pie for dessert, using the last of Mickey's apples. I'll shop early. Meat's getting scarce these days."

"Do you need any help with the cooking?"

"You can peel the potatoes."

Kate sighed. That was one reason she had never been inspired to learn to cook. She had always been assigned the task of peeling potatoes, nothing more, and the dullness irked her. Besides, Mary Grace had often criticised her for not finishing the task quickly enough. She affirmed her opinion: she had no desire to learn how to cook. She took up a knife and soon filled a pan of the peeled vegetables and covered them with water, ready for her mother to boil.

Soon, freshly washed, Ryan came downstairs. His trousers rode two inches above his ankles. "I need to buy chicken feed and the coop needs repairing. Think I'll go over to Mickey's. He knows all about things like that."

Kate went to the piano. With everyone out of the house, her practicing wouldn't bother anyone. The doctor had said her cast could come off the following week, meaning the audition might soon take place. After spending a good hour going over "Sally" and "Red Sails in the Sunset," with nary a hiccup, she was ready to ask Barry to arrange another meeting with Lydia.

Barry arrived promptly at six o'clock. He wore a coat and tie for the occasion and gave chrysanthemums to Mary Grace. Kate had set the table with a white tablecloth and serviettes. She took a couple of stems from the bouquet and placed them in a vase as a centrepiece. The roast beef sat on a platter on the stove while Mary Grace stirred the gravy.

"Smells great," Barry said.

They all took their places round the table. Sean carved the meat and soon each person had a plate piled with food.

"It's such a treat to be with a family," said Barry.

"Tell us about yours. Kate says you have a brother," Mary Grace said.

"Yes. Kevin. He's a pilot with the RAF."

"Do you hear from him? Is he all right?"

"I saw him last time he came home for leave, about two months ago. The air war hasn't really started."

Mary Grace had just gathered dirty plates and put the pie on the table when the sound of sirens blasted into the house.

"God help us," Mary Grace cried, crossing herself.

"Out to the shelter, everyone," Sean said urgently. "Grab the gas masks. I'll turn off the lights and bring torches so we can find our way." They hung masks around their necks and Kate reached for her crutches.

"Let me help you," Barry said, wresting the crutches from Kate's hands. He picked her up and carried her outside, surprising her with his strength. They piled into the shelter, taking seats on the two benches on each side. Sean hung the lantern on a hook and lit it. Explosions boomed in the distance.

No one said anything. Kate's chest tightened. She cast her eyes around in the flickering light and observed the terrified eyes of her family. Her mother held her hands together, praying softly, and her father's lips were pressed into a tense thin line. Ryan's face shone full of defiance. Barry put his arm around her shoulders. A banging on the door startled her. She froze.

"What's that? Are the Germans here?" Mary Grace asked, her words full of fear.

"Who's there?" Sean shouted.

"'ello there all," a raspy voice called. "It's only me, Mickey!"

"Let him in!" Ryan said and threw open the door. Mickey's unshaven face peered down at them.

"Brought some victuals," he said. "Thought you might be needin' them, I did."

"We just might," Sean answered. "Come on in."

Mickey lumbered inside, followed by his dog. He wore his peaked cap backwards and carried two bottles. "It's me cider, just brewed. Got any glasses, 'ave you?"

"We've got some cups. They'll do," Mary Grace said, reaching for some on a shelf.

"No good, letting them Nazis frighten us 'alf to death," Mickey said. "Sit down, Pinocchio."

He poured drinks for everyone as the dog settled at his feet.

"Cosy in 'ere," he said. "Let's drink to our 'ealth. God Save the King, and us too."

They raised their cups.

"It's tasty. Not too sweet," Sean said.

"Yes. It's them apples. Exactly the right sort. Couldn't 'ave got them down without missy's 'elp this time."

Ryan caught Kate's eye and laughed.

"'Ow's the foot doing, love?" Mickey asked.

"Better. Cast comes off—" another series of explosions interrupted her.

Pinocchio barked, Mary Grace wailed, and Kate sensed a hiccup on the way. She held her breath and only a small *hic* escaped. She involuntarily grabbed Barry's arm and felt him tremble. At their feet, the dog whimpered softly. Gradually, the noise faded.

"Not close," Sean said, "and I don't hear any planes overhead."

"The war's here, finally. At least I won't miss it. Thought I would, down South," Ryan said. He took several swigs of his drink. "Could I have another one?" he asked. Mary Grace looked at him sideways, but before she could speak Sean said, "Why not? It won't do him any harm."

Ryan held out his cup.

"Another round for all," Mickey said.

"Too bad there are no windows. We can't see what's going on," Mary Grace said.

Kate laughed. "That's the whole point. Do you want an explosive blowing up in your face? Nazis peering in at you?" Mickey had been right. As she spoke, she noticed the cider had taken the edge off her fears.

Ryan stood suddenly, bumping his head on a sloping side of the shelter.

"Speaking of looking out, I need to check on Scooter," he said.

"*No.* Sit down, son," said Sean. "Like Kate said, you don't know what's out there. We're supposed to wait until they sound the all-clear. The chicken will be fine. She's inside her house roosting, isn't she?"

Ryan sat back down, rubbing his head. "Suppose you're right. Anyway, I'm not sure she'd get along with the dog."

"You bet. Pinocchio might bother 'er. No room in 'ere for fighting. But 'ow about some entertainment," Mickey said.

He produced a mouth organ from his pocket and blew. The muffled tones of the "Marseillaise" came out, the rhythm shaky. Barry and Kate broke into laughter.

"That's the French national anthem," Kate said. "What are you playing that for?"

"I like it better than 'God Save the King.' Dead dreary, that one is."

"You're right there," Sean said. "Let's have an old Irish song, or a Welsh one like 'The Ash Grove'."

"I like that one," Mickey said, and started playing. Everyone sang along, Kate's strong voice soaring over the others.

"You sing beautifully, Kate," Barry said. "We must make arrangements to see Lydia as soon as you can walk properly."

She could have kissed him.

Despite the war that raged somewhere, she felt secure in the small world of their shelter. The people she cared most about were here, all around her. Everyone's face had become flushed from sitting in the close quarters, now warm, although as she viewed them, Kate thought the cider might help boost their spirits as well.

"Haven't heard any explosions for a good fifteen minutes now," Sean said, squinting to read his watch. "I wonder where the bombing took place. Not here, anyway."

"Your cider really hits the spot," Mary Grace giggled. "Thank you for bringing it, Mickey."

He smiled his toothy smile. "You're most welcome, I'm sure."

"We were about to eat some apple pie for afters. When we get out of here you must join us."

"Much obliged," he said, tipping his cap.

Not long after they finished the cider, the all-clear sirens sounded, echoing softly at first, then more loudly. They heard shouting outside. "You can come out now! All's clear!"

"You wanted excitement, you said, Ryan? Well, you got here just in time," Kate laughed.

Sean blew out the lantern and they filed out of the shelter, Barry again bearing Kate in his arms. They gathered on the road beside the house. Kate searched the horizon for signs of fire or planes, but saw nothing in the darkness except searchlights sweeping the sky and spots of light on the ground cast by torches held by neighbours like themselves. A safety warden rode by on a bicycle.

"Go home, everyone," he said. "Danger's over."

"Hey, where was the bombing?" Sean shouted.

"Don't know yet. Listen to the news," came the reply.

"Now, how about that pie?" Mary Grace said.

Inside the house, everyone crowded into the kitchen. Mary Grace switched the lights on and cut the pie into even slices. She filled a bowl of water and placed it on the floor for the dog.

"Those apple trees of yours are worth their weight in gold, Mickey. First cider, now pie," she said, passing plates around. "We do have something to celebrate, after all. To us all, and may God keep us safe."

"Hear, hear," they chorused.

Barry turned to Mickey. "I haven't met you before. I'm Barry."

"Wondered who you was. Glad to make your acquaintance, I'm sure. Aren't you joining up, going to fight over there? Kill some Gerrys?"

"I expect I'll be called up soon."

"That's the spirit," Mickey said. "Well, I'd best be going. Thanks for the pie, Mrs. Murphy."

After he and his dog left, Kate went with the rest into the living room to listen to the news. The wireless sputtered into life.

> *This is the BBC Home Service. Air raid warnings sounded this evening because of explosions in and around central London. Police are investigating. No enemy planes have been sighted, and it appears that the Germans were not responsible for the damage. Early reports indicate that the Irish Republican Army might be involved. We will have a more information later.*

"What? The IRA? That's atrocious. My own countrymen!" Sean said.

"Does this mean we're at war with Ireland as well?" Ryan asked.

"I hope not," Sean said. "We'll know more tomorrow."

"I'll be on my way home now," Barry said. "Thank you for a most interesting evening."

"I'll see you out," Kate said.

At the front door Barry put his arms around her and bent to kiss her, a lingering kiss on the lips. She didn't resist.

"Good night. I'll be in touch soon," he said.

After shutting the door behind him, Kate stood for a few minutes leaning against it. Barry had somehow made himself part of the family. She felt a rush of warmth towards him. All in all, she appreciated having him in their lives. In her life.

CHAPTER 18

December 1939

For several days afterwards, Kate and Sean talked about the air raid warning. Kate noticed that her father's expression, usually on the verge of a smile, turned sterner, and a frown furrowed his brow.

"I still can't believe the IRA took responsibility for the explosions," he said. "I've heard that many people in Ireland are sympathetic to Hitler, more's the pity. Even though the Irish don't all like the English, fighting us now isn't the answer."

"Right. But we've learned a lesson," Kate said. "We should get more supplies for the shelter, enough to last us for a couple of days at least. Canned food, water, first-aid kits, matches, blankets. What else?"

She took up a pen.

"Don't forget torches and a lot of batteries. Those are hard to come by these days."

The war with Germany continued to be fought largely at sea. On December 13, the news came that a British naval squadron, including the cruiser HMS *Exeter*, had attacked and damaged the German pocket battleship *Admiral Graf Spee* at the Battle of the River Plate in Uruguay. This event, along with Winston Churchill's reports that the Royal Navy sank two to four U-boats each week, increased morale in the country. But no one said the war was over.

Kate's cast came off a week after the air raid incident. Relieved to be free of the encumbrance and itching skin, she needed crutches for another week for support until her foot healed completely. As she found her leg muscles returning to normal, she welcomed the regular rhythm of both feet on the pavement again. She gained a new appreciation for the freedom of walking easily and would not take her good fortune in a complete recovery for granted. *Not like some*, she pondered, as pictures of injured soldiers in the papers passed through her mind.

She returned to St. Bridget's and her classes. She received a warm welcome from her pupils, though several had been evacuated. To her relief, Hannah was still there, along with several other girls who would sing in the cantata. Teresa, one of the soloists, a tall girl with long braids and a wide smile, raised her hand.

"Miss Murphy, we missed you. Sister Mary Joseph taught us singing in your absence, but she didn't give us any songs we liked."

"That's right. No cantata, either. Our voices are rusty."

"Can we sing that American song, the one about the chariot swinging low?"

"All right, girls. Settle down. I missed you, too, but now we've got work to do if we're going to perform the Handel cantata."

Kate scheduled rehearsals after school and postponed the performance until after Christmas. She wanted a simple set and costumes; these would take extra time and work. One morning, as her mother finished the weekly washing, Kate asked for suggestions about costumes for the play.

"I'll be glad to help with those," Mary Grace said. "I can sew, but I'll need material. What style of clothes?"

"I don't know. They're all shepherdesses and hunters," Kate said.

"You'll need blouses and full skirts and, along with trousers, I imagine. I might find some things at the WVS shop. They have fabric there, too."

Kate gratefully accepted her mother's help. She asked Ryan to help build a set, perhaps with Mickey's assistance. But somehow, since her accident, her enthusiasm for the music production at school waned.

Why, she didn't know. She felt restless. It was as though after finding Ryan her own concerns seemed petty and trivial, and she was only marking time, waiting for something important to happen.

The Christmas season arrived as quietly as the first snowflakes. The shops had sparse merchandise, and no one felt like celebrating. A package with presents arrived from Clare in America: silk stockings for Mary Grace and Kate, and leather gloves for Sean and Ryan. The card accompanying the gifts showed a picture of the Statue of Liberty covered with snow. Kate set it on the living room mantlepiece. The symbolism of the statue was not lost on her.

"I suppose she's living a life of luxury," she said with a sigh. "These things are in short supply here. They don't have rationing there, I hear. Not yet, anyway."

Mary Grace sent an invitation to Barry to join the family for dinner on Christmas Day. His response, a letter delivered through the mail slot, landed face down on the doormat. Kate picked it up along with the bills and tossed them on the table. Then she saw the handwritten one addressed in a hurried scrawl to the Murphy family. She tore the envelope open.

December 20, 1939
Dear Mrs. Murphy and family,

Thank you for your kind invitation for dinner. Much as I'd love to accept, I'm afraid I must decline. My brother Kevin will be home on leave, and we'll be spending Christmas Day together. I hope you understand.

Happy Christmas! I look forward to seeing you all in the New Year.

Sincerely,
Barry

Kate plopped down, perplexed. The letter seemed overly formal. He didn't mention her. Perhaps she had misconstrued his interest, and he was just a family friend, nothing more. While she harboured some feelings of relief, she realised to her surprise that she felt disappointed as well. He had expressed interest in her. He had *kissed* her. Perhaps she didn't respond in the way he wanted. She cursed herself for her indecision and for allowing the sad business with Tony to interfere with the next possible romance in her life. Or perhaps Barry had met someone else. Her heart shrank. Feeling a sudden chill, she wrapped her arms, hugging her chest.

After a few minutes, she drifted to the window and looked at the trees, now bare. *Tony.* They had met on a school excursion to London three years ago, when she was seventeen. During the Christmas season, the teachers arranged for girls at St. Bridget's to join the boys at St. Thomas's and travel to London to see a performance of Shakespeare's *A Midsummer Night's Dream.*

They travelled by rail. As the excited youngsters piled into the carriages, Kate jockeyed for position beside a boy of about her age in a St. Thomas's School uniform. He had the bluest eyes ever, and his smile revealed deep dimples as he motioned for her to go ahead of him and board the train.

"Ladies first," he said.

Before she could thank him, he took her elbow and guided her into one of the last open seats in the carriage, then disappeared into the line of schoolgirls and boys standing in the aisle of the crowded train. She wondered who he was. After they arrived at Victoria Station, she caught a glimpse of him among the group, his head higher than the rest. To her surprise, his seat was next to hers in the theatre.

"Hello again," he said. "What luck. I'm Tony Trent."

"Kate Murphy."

They shook hands. She liked the feel of his larger grasp in hers, spreading heat through her body. When the character Bottom in the play sang, "The ousel cock, so black of hue," he whispered, "Don't you love this song?" She smiled, warming to him. He loved music, as she did. Charmed by the words, she turned to see him smiling as well. A crooked smile.

And so it began: she appreciated his assurance and his immediate understanding of her inexperience. With him she never strove to be more attractive, more worldly, or more accomplished. He simply accepted her, and in so doing, gave her confidence. Her insides fluttered whenever they touched. She loved being with him. And she was aware of envious stares from her classmates when they saw him with her. "He's handsome and charming, and you're lucky," they told her. She knew only too well. Attending a girls' school made meeting boys difficult, and she was proud to have a boyfriend.

They saw each other regularly for months, having tea at Lyons, walking in the parks, sneaking embraces out of sight from passers-by. She floated, giddy with love. Then came the day when she learned with queasy intuition that she was only one of his girlfriends, and not the first on his list. After the sickening encounter when she saw him kissing an older girl, she ran home like a wounded animal, and vowed she would never see him again.

The truth shocked her. What had she done wrong, or failed to do enough, to hold him? She decided she was not special enough, not experienced enough. He didn't love her, as she did him. To add to her humiliation, she was forced to endure the pitying glances of the other girls after she lost him.

And so she set her sights on singing. She could become accomplished at that and ease her pain. All went well until she developed the hiccups, the ongoing curse that the breakup with Tony had brought on. Or so she thought. After she left school at eighteen, Sister Mary Joseph asked if she would be willing to teach. Having no other plans, but wanting to keep music in her life, she jumped at the chance. Now she'd discovered great pleasure in sharing her love of music with her pupils and helping them appreciate the beauty and confidence it inspired in each one of them.

Then and now, the healing power of music could overcome all fear. She just needed to apply that principle to herself, she told herself, and keep going.

CHAPTER 19

January 1940

The new year brought freezing weather, biting winds, and food rationing. Kate listened as Mary Grace read the Ministry of Food's pamphlet at the breakfast table. Each person was allowed four ounces of bacon, four ounces of butter, and twelve ounces of sugar per week, and civilians were encouraged to start "Digging for Victory" gardens to grow their own vegetables. Kate sighed. *Things are going to get worse.*

"I don't need their advice on how to cook with limited ingredients," her mother complained. "I know how to make the most of the little food we have, and I already keep a vegetable garden. I can't plant yet, anyway, in the dead of winter."

"The Ministry's advice wasn't meant for people like you, Mum," Kate said.

"But I wish we had more butter," Mary Grace continued. "Margarine's a poor substitute, and baked things don't taste right with it. At least, thanks to Scooter, we've got eggs. I'll make a cheese omelette today."

"Could we eat early?" Kate asked. "Practice for the cantata starts at five, and I need to get the costumes over to the school."

"All right. I hope you reserved good seats for us tomorrow."

"I did, in the middle. That's where the acoustics are best. But Mickey wants to sit right up front, in the first row. Says he wants to see everything."

"That sounds like him. I'm sure it will be wonderful," Mary Grace said.

Mary Grace had done yeoman's work designing and making the costumes, and Ryan had built a fine set in the school gymnasium with Mickey's help.

Kate arrived at the assembly hall early. She had given the girls instructions to be at the school before five, and they were waiting for her. Tension and excitement mounted as she took her place at the piano.

"All right, everyone. We'll warm up and then go backstage so you can dress. Are any of your mothers here to help?"

Several girls raised their hands.

"Good. I'm sure we will do well. All our hard work will ensure that. Be careful to listen to one another so your voices blend. Remember, no prima donnas in the chorus. Let's start with scales."

She sounded the chords, then the first note, and the girls sang.

"Very good. Now start softly and sing louder until the end of the octave, then more softly as you descend the scale."

After they rehearsed the first pieces, Kate stepped away from the piano.

"Good. You sound heavenly. As you know, Sister Mary Joseph will play the accompaniment so I can direct you from the floor. Please go backstage now, and keep quiet once you've finished dressing. We don't want the audience to hear background noise."

The girls climbed the steps on each side of the stage, some with their mothers, and disappeared behind the curtain. Kate watched with appreciation. They *would* do well—months of preparation had paid off, and they knew their parts. Parents had risen to the occasion to help Mary Grace make costumes. Ryan and Mickey's set, a backdrop with a scene of sheep receding into the distant rolling hills, provided the country atmosphere. She was especially pleased that proceeds from ticket sales would support the war.

At seven o'clock, the curtain rose. The girls in colourful dresses had assembled in groups. Several held crooks, and two girls dressed in hunting garb carried bows. As the curtain rose, a collective gasp sounded from the audience, followed by clapping and a few cheers.

"Break a leg, my lovelies," Mickey yelled.

Sister Mary Joseph played the introduction, and Kate lifted her arm. At the downbeat, the chorus erupted into song. The opening conveyed pure joy—the explosion of summer in the idyllic country-side—and the exuberance of youth.

At the conclusion of the chorus' first song, Teresa sang an aria. She seemed nervous at first and Kate felt on tenterhooks, but to her relief the girl soon relaxed and finished her solo with confidence. The performance continued, the pace livening as the singers got caught up in the spirit of the music. Then the chorus sang "See, fair Flora hither comes," the cue for Hannah to step forward for her solo. Dressed in a lavender dirndl with a white bodice, her thick hair crowned with a wreath of flowers, she shone in the role of head shepherdess. Her silvery voice reverberated through the hall as she sang her aria, the climax of the presentation. After she finished, the audience clapped, roaring its approval, and Mickey whistled. Hannah curtsied and smiled and Kate directed the chorus to resume singing. The chorus swelled and diminished in keeping with Kate's directions from the podium on the floor. The shepherdesses circled and regrouped as they continued to sing in the imaginary pastoral setting. Moved by the girls' wholehearted efforts, Kate couldn't wait to praise them.

As the cantata ended and the singers took their final bow, the audi-ence stood and cheered. Hannah stepped forward and received spe-cial applause. At the last curtain call, the girls beckoned to Kate. She mounted the steps to the stage, then motioned to Sister Mary Joseph at the piano. Mrs. Fitzgerald appeared from the wings and presented Kate with flowers.

Kate smiled and bowed her head. She stepped up to a microphone on the side of the stage. "This production could not have taken place without all your support. Thanks to Sister Mary Joseph for supporting this production, to parents for making costumes, to the stage crew for the set—"

"Hey, that's us!" Mickey yelled. Kate paused to acknowledge him with a slight nod, then continued, "and to all the girls who worked so hard to brighten our days and offer this marvellous entertainment. Thank you for coming."

As the curtain lowered, she felt a surge of pride. She knew that music could have a transformational effect but seeing it ripple through an audience of war-weary parents, if only for a short while, made it all worthwhile. *And what about Hannah? I need to help her realise her dreams, dreams that were once mine . . . have I given them up? No! She inspires me. There's always hope.*

But there was still work to do. She ushered the girls backstage, all talking and laughing, eyes glowing with excitement. She lifted her hand to silence them.

"An excellent performance," she said. "Thanks to each one of you."

Members of the audience pushed into the space behind the stage. Parents swarmed around her, eager to congratulate her on the performance and saying how much their daughters had enjoyed being part of it all.

Sarah Bell appeared with Hannah beside her. "I have no words to thank you. This is like a dream for Hannah. *Kerzen*—candles—in the middle of winter."

Kate gave Hannah a hug. "You were wonderful!"

"But I need to talk to you as soon as possible." Sarah whispered. "It's urgent. Do you have time?"

"Not now. How about tomorrow after school?"

"Thank you. I will see you there."

Sarah wrapped an arm around Hannah's shoulders and escorted her outside.

Mickey arrived. "Girls sang like lit'l angels. A sight for sore eyes, my love." He shook Kate's hand vigorously.

Her mother and Ryan rushed to give her enthusiastic hugs.

"It was beautiful," Mary Grace said. "All those lovely girls, and the costumes."

"Well done, dearie," Sean said. "Gorgeous singing. We're so proud of you. When you're all done here, I've got a bottle of wine to celebrate."

"Wine? What extravagance." Kate said, wiping perspiration from her brow.

"Yes, but I didn't buy it. My boss gave it to me for Christmas. I've been saving it for a special occasion. This is it."

As they strolled home only one question tugged at the back of Kate's mind to mar her happiness: what did Sarah Bell want to say that was so urgent?

The following day, Kate met Sarah after school. They took seats in chairs by a window in the empty assembly hall.

"I came to ask you for a favour," Sarah said. "Time may be short for us. I will come fast to my question. Hannah admires you so much. I want to ask you if you will look out for her, if something bad happens to me and her father."

"What do you mean, something bad? Because of the war?"

"Because of the war, but more than that." She lowered her voice and looked around furtively. "I trust you to keep this to yourself. We are Jewish. They are killing Jews in Poland, and they won't stop there. Hitler and the Nazis. It is a bad business."

Sarah's shaky hands and worn small face softened Kate's heart, and she reached to touch her arm.

"I don't want Hannah to suffer," Sarah went on. "They only admitted us to Britain for a short while as temporary resident aliens. Our time is up. Your country does not want us here, and the Nazis may come for us, but Hannah must live."

"Yes, of course she must." *So must all of you,* Kate thought.

"Can you promise me you will help her?"

Kate hesitated. "This is all news to me. Are you sure?"

Sarah's face contorted. "*Jawohl.* We have friends in Germany, Jews. You heard of *Kristallnacht,* yes? We read Hitler's book *Mein Kampf.* He wants to kill us all. Hans and I, we may be deported or arrested any day."

"I *have* heard about *Kristallnacht.* Horrifying . . . I'll do my best to help," Kate said soberly.

"I believe you. One thing more. We have a relative who used to live here, my husband's sister Anna. She lives in America now. You may need this information." Sarah handed Kate a folded piece of paper, then met her eyes. "You have set my mind at rest. *Herzlichen Dank, Fräulein.*" She squeezed Kate's hand.

Goose bumps rose along Kate's arms and a cold sweat broke out along her hairline. What a story. In her heart she knew it was true. She shook her head. *What did I just promise to do? Have I taken leave of my senses?*

CHAPTER 20
March 1940

Two months later, Kate had made no progress furthering her dreams. She hated the long winter, especially this year, when moonless nights made everything darker as she bundled herself against the chilly winds and trudged home from work after late choir practice. But March arrived at last, and the spring daffodils and warmer weather raised her spirits. Things continued to worsen, however. Oranges, bananas, even paper bags, once so readily available, became hard to find, and rationing deepened.

Kate missed Sybil. She'd had almost no social life outside of school since the time she went dancing with Lydia. Though she'd written to Sybil at her parents' address asking about her, she'd received no response.

She hadn't heard anything from Barry either, and finally consigned him to the memory of a friend who was helpful at a time when her family needed him, and nothing more. Then she imagined he had been called up for service and was suffering in the trenches in Belgium. What if he'd tried to reach her, and couldn't, like Ryan? She had given Barry no talisman like a moonstone. She listened to the news on the wireless every day. With effort, she quelled her anxiety.

The war suddenly moved closer when an air raid in Scotland on March 16 caused the first British civilian casualties on land. But it still seemed very far away from Carshalton, and she hoped with all her might that it would stay that way.

Kate yearned more than ever to sing, but she resisted phoning Lydia, feeling awkward about Barry's estrangement and the lack of a personal connection with her. And she'd taken no steps to address the accursed hiccups. Lydia was out of her class, anyway. Best to let the whole thing go.

Then everything changed. On a day that promised to be no different from another, Kate took the bus to Sutton to buy meat. It had become hard to buy in their local shops, and her mother wanted to make lamb for Easter. As she stepped off the bus, she caught a glimpse of a familiar head of dark brown hair moving in her direction. Her heart flipped. *Tony!* She halted. When he approached her, his startled expression confirmed that he recognised her. He stopped an arm's length in front of her. He had the deep blue eyes she remembered, like summer sky.

"Well, hello!" he said, smiling. "What a pleasant surprise!"

She managed a dry smile. "Hello, Tony."

"How long has it been? A year? Two?"

"Three."

"For goodness sake. What are you doing? Do you have time for a cup of tea? I'd love to hear what you've been up to."

"I'm not sure . . . I'm on my way to the butcher's."

"I'll go with you, then."

She didn't tell him not to. Her breath caught in her throat, and she wondered if her face had gone white with shock. It felt white, anyway, and her knees wobbled.

"Actually, I'd rather have tea, after all," she said.

She needed to sit down, and what harm could it do, talking to him for a few minutes? *One cup of tea, then I'll get on with my shopping.*

He steered her across the street to Lyon's teahouse.

"What'll you have? My treat," he said.

They took trays and moved them along the rails past the offerings in glass cases, helped themselves to custard tarts and cups of tea, then took seats at a table in the back of the congested room.

"You look well," he said. "Are you still living at home? Married?"

"Still at home. Teaching music at St. Bridget's. How about you? Haven't you joined up?"

"Not yet. I have a deferment. I'm in medical school."

She blinked. "Really? So, you'll be a doctor. I didn't know you had any fondness for science. I remember you liked music."

"Of course, I like music. That doesn't mean I don't have other interests."

"Right. Where are you studying?"

"In Glasgow. I'm only home to see my parents."

"Very good. Medicine is a worthy profession," she said lamely.

She looked askance at him. She could imagine him as a doctor, despite her impression of him as a womaniser. He had enormous charm, but his intensity would help him focus on his work.

She cleared her throat. "I'm impressed that you've gone into the medical profession. How did you decide to go into the field?"

"I've always liked science and maths. The incentive was my younger brother's death from scarlet fever. I'd like to help people who are ill, that's all."

That's all? That's . . . so much. He was drawing her in to him again, dangerously so.

"I remember you wanted to study music. Did you?" he asked.

"No."

"Do you still sing?"

"Not anymore."

"Would you like to? I've been to many charity events where people like you provide entertainment. You're certainly attractive enough. More than attractive."

She blushed and took a sip of tea. *He's flirting with me.* She hadn't touched her custard tart.

"I don't know how to get into that business. Quite happy teaching," she said drily.

"I have friends who would love to have you at their events. They raise money to help the war effort. Why don't you come with me? I can introduce you."

She hesitated. "I'm not sure that's a good idea."

"Why ever not? Don't let an opportunity go to waste. I'm here for another week. How about Saturday? I'm invited to a cocktail party in Hampstead."

This sounded like a repeat of the earlier offer with Lydia and Barry. That had come to nothing. And, despite his appeal, she had no desire to be drawn into another relationship with him and risk another heartbreak. She shook her head. "Thank you, but I'd rather not."

His eyes, those summer-blue eyes, bore into her. "Please. You were always my favourite girlfriend. I'd love to have your company. Just for one evening."

Her resistance slipped away. "All right."

"Fine. I'll come by for you at six."

Kate sat with the small package of meat on her lap on the bus home. For the second time in as many months, she asked herself what she was doing. First, she had agreed to take responsibility for Hannah, something she didn't feel equipped to do, and now she had accepted an invitation to go out with a man she instinctively considered a bad risk. She was flirting with danger. But she did wish for a more intense life. War or no, she craved a renewed sense of living life fully instead of sitting on the sidelines. She would still like to help Hannah, besides finding an opportunity for herself to sing. Perhaps by meeting new people she could achieve at least one of her goals, even if it meant accompanying Tony to a cocktail party.

CHAPTER 21
April 1940

K ate didn't tell anyone about her arrangement to meet Tony. She wished Sybil or Clare were around to talk to. Now she anxiously awaited the day of the event, fretting about how to conduct herself. She wanted to appear sophisticated. He had already noted her more womanly appearance, and she imagined she saw a glimmer of appreciation as he appraised her. She hated that—why did men stare at a woman from head to toe without that behaviour being considered rude? But in any case, she wanted to look her best. She'd have to dress up for the cocktail party. Perusing her wardrobe, she chose a blue dress and held it up against her body. She had only worn it once before. Though not silk, it was her dressiest garment. Perhaps Mary Grace would let her borrow some pearls for the occasion.

As though reading her daughter's thoughts, Mary Grace appeared at her bedroom door.

"You need to get out more," she said, holding out a copy of the *Sunday Express*. "Lord Castlerosse says that any girl who doesn't marry in these times is just not trying."

Kate felt her face flush. "What does *he* know?" she retorted. "Some girls might not want to get married. Why marry just for the sake of it?"

"For security. Your father provides a livelihood for all of us, including you. And these days, men going off to war want a wife or sweetheart to write to."

Kate glared at her. "I have a job. I stay here because—well, because I know you want to keep the family together, not because I can't support myself. But it's time for me to leave . . ." she stopped, holding her hands to her mouth. *There. She'd said it.*

Mary Grace glared back at her. "When did I ever tell you that you had to stay? After all, I left home myself, once. Before I was your age, too."

Her mother turned to go, slamming the door as she went.

"For God's sake!" Kate said, exasperated. *She can't stop needling me. After insisting she wants to keep the family together, now she says she doesn't care if I leave. Damnation. Perhaps I'll marry Tony.*

She flopped onto the bed and threw the dress into a corner.

On the day of her appointment with Tony—she refused to call it anything else—she spent hours preparing: ironing the blue dress, putting curlers in her hair, taking a long bath, dusting herself with talcum powder, and carefully applying makeup. The dress fit and suited her. She'd manage without the pearls. She was ready early, two hours ahead of time, and sat down at the piano to while away the minutes, attempting to slow her racing pulse as she anticipated seeing him. A knock at the door interrupted her as she played the last strains of the Vera Lynn hit "Don't Fence Me In." *He's early. That's probably a good sign*, she thought.

She made for the door. On the step, smiling, his face almost hidden by an enormous arrangement of red roses, stood not Tony, but Barry.

"Oh," she gasped. "It's you."

He thrust the bouquet into her hands, then stood back.

"So good to see you," he said admiringly.

She could hardly speak for shock. "Uh, thank you very much. I thought I'd never see you again."

"I've been away. Conscripted and in training. I'm home on leave."

"I didn't know," she said. "Look, thank you so much for the flowers, but I can't talk now. I'm about to go out."

"But I've got something important to say. It'll only take a minute. May I come in?"

"Um, I suppose so, just for a minute," she said.

He followed her into the living room. She could hear her mother in the kitchen preparing supper and closed the door.

He cleared his throat. "I know this is very sudden, but I'm leaving on Tuesday, and this can't wait."

"Do sit down," she said, taking a seat on an armchair.

Ignoring her, he dropped to his knee. "You see, I love you," he blurted. "I want you to marry me."

She stood up, confused and queasy.

"This is so . . . *hic* . . . sudden . . ." *Hic, hic, hic.* "Unexpected. Please excuse me."

She dashed into the kitchen for a glass of water, dropping the roses onto the floor. Mary Grace looked away from the pan she was stirring on the stove. "Whatever's wrong?"

"Please tell Barry I can't." *Hic, hic.*

"Barry's here? What's going on?" Mary Grace asked, scurrying into the living room. "What are you doing on your knees? Are you hurt?"

Kate overheard her mother's question with despair. *How embarrassing for us all.*

"Sorry for the intrusion, Mrs. Murphy, he said. "I'd best be off. Please tell Kate I'll write to her."

Kate sat at the table, resting her forehead in her hands.

Mary Grace strode into the kitchen. "Whatever's wrong with you?" she asked, angrily picking up the flowers. "It seems you've just slighted a very nice suitor."

"Leave me alone, Mum. It's none of your business," Kate said, rising to leave.

"He told me to tell you he'll write."

"All right. Thank you."

Kate slowly mounted the stairs to her room. Barry's proposal had shocked her, and she needed time to calm her racing mind. *What a nerve he has, appearing out of the blue, with a marriage proposal, of all things.* She'd never considered him a serious prospect, especially not now. She had a date with a man who interested her in less than an hour. How could she compose herself? Perhaps she would tell him she was unwell. In her confusion, she'd messed up her hair and smeared mascara all over her face. She looked a wreck. She couldn't possibly go out now. A train sped by outside, but for once she found the familiar rattle comforting. At least the train understood her disordered life.

Half an hour later, having cleaned her smudged face and gulped down two aspirin, Kate resolved to go ahead with her plans for the evening. She expected to hear later from Barry and needed time to write a response. She would refuse him, of course. After running a comb through her hair and refreshing her makeup, she deemed herself presentable. Not quivering with excitement like before Barry's intrusion—and she did consider the marriage proposal an intrusion—but calmer. Maybe it was best this way. She did not want to allow her emotions to overwhelm her as they had the last time she'd seen Tony.

He arrived late, at half-past six. Kate grabbed her coat and called goodbye to her mother. No need to explain. Mary Grace would assume she was going dancing, and who she was with was none of her business.

Tony stood on the front step dressed in a dark coat and tie. His handsome face wore a disarming smile. The man she remembered.

"So good to see you," he said.

"And you."

"I tried to remember our last date. We went to the pictures, a Jeanette MacDonald flick, I remember. We loved the singing. I always wondered what happened to you after that. You avoided me."

"Let's not talk about it now. Where are we going, and who will be there?"

"I'll tell you on the way."

He opened the car door for her.

"Tell me more about the people I'm likely to meet."

"Actually, I won't know many. Henry Abbott, a fellow student, invited me. He has a lot of connections and thought I'd enjoy getting out and having some fun. I believe Sir Anthony Wyckham will be there. He's one of my teachers."

"Who's the host?"

"Lady Cornelia Rowbottom."

"Ah." Kate didn't keep up with the upper classes and their pursuits, but she recognised the name from the society column in *The Times*. She pondered what she would have to say to these aristocrats, but she anticipated the evening as an amusing adventure, pleased to have her good-looking and respectable former boyfriend as her escort. *Former boyfriend*, she told herself firmly.

They arrived at the wrought-iron gates enclosing Lady Cornelia's grand residence. A fitting venue for a fancy occasion, Kate was glad she had on her best dress. It would have been better if she'd worn the pearl necklace, but perhaps no one would notice her bare neck. Leaving the car parked in the circular driveway, they entered the house. The cavernous entry hall soared two stories high with marble pillars supporting the upper floors. Chandeliers glittered overhead and sconces adorned the frescoed walls. Kate speculated whether the lighted dome could be seen from the air, making it a prime target for bombs.

A silk-frocked servant took their coats and ushered them into the ballroom. A mob of perfumed guests and the roar of lively conversation surrounded them. Many of the women sported feathers in their hair, and diamond jewelry flashed from ears and throats. *I'm underdressed*, Kate growled to herself, and hoped Tony didn't care. They passed a long table laid out with platters of food and enormous vases of flowers. *Pure opulence*, she thought, *and where did they get these things?*

Tony shepherded her towards the bar on the far side of the room. "What will you have to drink?"

"How about a Singapore Sling?"

"Good choice."

He placed the order for their drinks. After handing her a crystal glass, he proposed a toast. "To my beautiful lady. Thank you for the pleasure of your company tonight."

He bowed slightly as he spoke, and she laughed at the unnecessary gallantry. "I'm a bit overwhelmed by all the grandeur," she said. "Hard to believe we're at war."

"Yes. The wealthy classes have ways of maintaining their luxurious lifestyle. I suggest you take full advantage of the offerings while you can."

A tall, mustachioed man wearing a white tie and black coat tails joined them. "Anthony, old chap. Glad you could make it," he said, shaking Tony's hand.

"Thanks for inviting me, Henry. May I introduce Miss Kate Murphy?"

"Miss Murphy, my pleasure," Henry said, eyeing her with obvious appreciation. "If you will excuse us, I need to steal Anthony to talk about some medical matters. Should only take a few minutes."

"Of course," Kate said.

The two men moved away. She scanned the room. As expected, she didn't know anyone. Her stomach growled. Something to eat would ease her discomfort. And more to drink . . . but she didn't suppose she should ask for a drink for herself. So awkward, not knowing how to behave. Kate drifted towards the food table and reached for a fig. As she did so, her finger touched a woman's plump hand aiming for the same piece of fruit.

"So sorry," the hand's owner said.

"After you," Kate replied.

"No. You're the guest." The woman lifted the platter. "I'm Cornelia. Help yourself."

"How do you do? I'm Kate. I came with Tony Trent."

"Ah yes. My grandson knows him, I believe. They're both in medical school, aren't they?"

"That's right."

"A worthy profession, and one that keeps them from fighting in this atrocious war. Doctors are in reserved occupations, I understand. No reason to go after Hitler, you know," she said.

Kate looked askance at the hostess. She had a glass of champagne in one hand and glittery eyes. Probably too much to drink. But Kate needed to make a response to the shocking disclosure.

"Uh, yes. We do need doctors," she said. "What a lovely party, Lady Cornelia."

"Isn't it? We all need cheering up, don't we? Such a nuisance, keeping everything so dark everywhere. We have to keep things going so when the Germans arrive, we can welcome them in style," she crowed.

Kate squirmed inwardly, but offered a thin smile.

"I shouldn't keep you," the lady continued. "You young people should dance and enjoy yourselves."

Swaying, she vanished into the throng. Kate surveyed the room, searching for Tony. Perhaps he would be at the bar having a drink. She wove through the bejeweled mob, avoiding eye contact. Maybe they were all Nazi sympathisers like their host. Since her conversation with Sarah, she had learned more about the Nazis' brutal treatment of Jews. Horrified, she questioned if Tony could be one of Lady Cornelia's type. All the more reason to resist him. She must find out. Discreetly.

The musicians in the corner struck up a Strauss waltz and guests scattered to allow space for dancing. As the crowd thinned, Kate spied Tony on the far side of the room and worked her way over to him.

"Ah, here you are," he said, placing an arm around her shoulders.

"Sorry for neglecting you, but I hope you're having fun. I'll try to introduce you to several people I know."

"That's all right," Kate said. "I'd really like to dance, though."

"Of course. Let's go."

Relieved, Kate allowed him to swing her around the floor. He danced well, and she relaxed into his arms. She questioned whether the music of Strauss, a native of Austria, and now an enemy nation, would be played at other English parties. Music should be universal, she thought, not blacklisted because of the nationality of the musician. Perhaps Tony had some thoughts about that. In fact, that might be a way to approach the subject of his political beliefs. Wrapped in his arms, she suddenly felt uneasy and desperately hoped he shared her views in such important ways.

And she sensed that, despite the intimacy of his touch, the magic she had always felt with him simply wasn't there. Furthermore, she recognised that she didn't really know him at all.

After dancing for a while, her disappointment growing, Kate saw no reason to linger at the party.

"If it's all right with you, I'd like to go home now. I have a beastly headache," she said.

"Sorry to hear that. Would you like an aspirin?"

"No, thank you. It's just something I need to sleep off."

"I'm sorry you're under the weather. We may be able to sneak out without offending anyone. I only came to please my colleague, and as you know, I've already seen him."

They reclaimed their coats, and with the aid of their torches, located the car. Kate experienced a surge of relief once away from the party's noise and safely ensconced in the vehicle's dark interior.

"So how did it go? Did you meet anyone interesting?" Tony asked.

"I hardly know what to say. Such an outlandish experience. Unworldly . . . I don't move in such circles," she said.

"Neither do I, but it's good to have connections in high places."

"Mmm. Useful."

Kate wanted to learn more about his connections, especially those with Nazi sympathisers, but tired out from her day's ordeals, she chose not to pursue the matter then. She wouldn't want to sing at an event with the people there even if asked, and possibly Tony wouldn't want to see her again, anyway. And she wasn't sure she wanted to see him, either. If he shared views with those people, she wanted none of him.

When they reached the house, he accompanied her to the door and gave her a brief hug. "Thank you for coming, and I hope you feel better soon. I'll be in touch," he said.

She fitted her key in the lock. "Thank you for the invitation."

She stepped inside without looking back.

CHAPTER 22
April 1940

The next morning, Kate lingered in bed replaying events of the previous day, questioning if everything had been a hallucination. Or a bad dream, more likely. The last thing she wanted was a marriage proposal, and Tony, the man she'd kept close to her heart for years, had turned out to be a grave disappointment.

What had happened to the fairy-tale attraction that captivated her when she first knew him? She cast her mind back to the warm July day when he took her hand as they wandered in the lavender fields south of Carshalton. She'd worn a new summer frock—white and gauzy. Sitting on a bench, they watched yellow butterflies flitting over mounds of intoxicatingly fragrant purple flowers. Her body roused when he kissed her. She'd fallen helplessly in love. But even then, the idea crossed her mind that the fluttering butterflies moved quickly from flower to flower in their endless search for nourishment. A few days later, Tony had betrayed her, sitting in the same place, kissing another girl. She'd ached with the memory ever since.

Until last night. No passionate feelings had emerged, and the promise of love in the lavender fields dwelled in her mind as a lost dream.

Her mother would want an explanation about Barry, and she needed to work out how to tell him she couldn't accept his offer. *I wanted a more active life, and now that I have one, I only want to retreat into my old familiar one.* She had obligations to her family, and to Hannah. Her mother would be at church for a while longer, so Kate had time to think. She opened the blackout curtains to discover the sun flinging rays into the awakening spring day. A walk was in order.

Sean and Ryan stood in the back garden examining the air raid shelter. She heard their laughter and didn't want to bother them. After leaving a note on the kitchen table saying she would be back soon, she stepped outside. Moving at a fast clip, she soon reached Carshalton's town centre and its two ponds, where Anne Boleyn was rumoured to have gone riding. Kate wondered if the former queen deliberated here about the wisdom of marriage four hundred years ago, just as Kate was doing now. The queen had made the wrong decision, Kate thought wryly.

Trees were leafing out, greening the branches, and framing the view of the twelfth century All Saints Church across the upper pond. An Anglican church, it was not the one where her mother worshipped. Kate had stopped going to church years ago. She meandered along the path past banks of daffodils and primroses. Songbirds, robins and blackbirds, chirped in the bushes. Could bright days like this in England be dashed by enemy planes and incendiaries falling from the sky? It seemed impossible to imagine. Perhaps, as some believed, the war would never arrive to destroy their history and quiet way of life. Momentary optimism driven by the beauty of her surroundings soothed her spirits, and as she crossed the bridge to the church, she told herself she was the mistress of her own life with the freedom to make her own choices about her future, her mother notwithstanding.

She would not marry a man she didn't love, or pursue one she didn't trust.

Her mind calmer, Kate turned her thoughts to the cocktail party. She had read in the papers about the Fifth Column, British people who supported Hitler and opposed war with Germany. Lady Cornelia implied she held those beliefs and must have presumed Kate was one of their number. Foolish on the lady's part, but she had apparently indulged in too much champagne. *But what position does Tony take about all this?* She owed it to herself to find out.

On her way home, Kate saw Mickey across the street with his dog. He waved and crossed to meet her. The dog jumped up and licked her face, tail wagging.

"Down, Pinocchio," Mickey said. The dog obeyed and sat on his haunches, staring up at his master, his head cocked. "'Ow's everything, love?" Mickey asked. Without waiting for a reply, he went on. "Saw your young man leaving the 'ouse a few minutes ago."

"My young man? You mean Barry?"

"'E's the one. Looked to be in a hurry. Drove off in that fancy car of 'is."

Oh dear. He wants an answer.

"Thanks for telling me," she said. "How are you getting on?"

"Well enough. I'll walk you 'ome." He fell into step beside her with the dog and they turned onto Holly Road. Then he said, "Those Nazis won't 'ave a chance if they cross the Channel. They don't 'ave a clue what they're up against. We're tough. They're sending up more barrage balloons to protect the cities from bomber planes."

"So I've heard."

"Good thing Ryan's back. We've got things planned to 'elp the war effort."

"Do you mind telling me what? Not more bombs, I hope."

"Nah. Best to keep some things quiet," he said, running a hand over his mouth as if to zip it shut.

Kate nodded. She'd ask Ryan later. Soon they reached number 59. She opened the gate and Mickey continued to his house. When she opened the front door, her mother's voice rang out.

"You've just missed Barry. He left you a letter," she said, handing an envelope to Kate.

She took it and headed for the stairs.

"Wait. Aren't you going to tell me what's happening?" Mary Grace called.

"Not until I've had a chance to read this."

Her mother stared after her, agitation in her eyes. *Mum will just have to wait.* She sat on her bed, tore open the envelope, and unfolded the note. The scrawled words filled two pages.

Dearest Kate,

Please forgive me for my silence these last months.

I want to let you know that my brother Kevin died shortly after Christmas. His plane crashed off the Dorset coast. As you can imagine, it was a blow. I loved and admired him, and his courage. As you know, I have no other immediate family members now. I kept the garage going until I decided to join the army. I'd rather die in a trench than drown at sea like my brother. So I've been busy training and settling things here.

I probably should apologise for my sudden reappearance in your life, but I've just learned that I will be leaving for Belgium and I didn't want to go without seeing you. I have had time to assess my feelings, and you have been on my mind night and day. I love you, and want to marry you. When, I don't know, but if you can give me an answer, it will greatly ease my mind as I join the forces abroad.

My phone number is Sutton 5761. Please telephone before Tuesday. I anxiously await your call.

Love, Barry

P.S. I have something important of interest to tell you as well.

Kate remained seated, too stunned to move. His brother was dead. Her resolve to refuse his proposal now struck her as cruel, another blow to a decent man who had only ever treated her with kindness and respect. What matter of interest did he have to tell her? She needed another walk, or perhaps a good soak would be better. After a while, her numbed senses reviving, she rose to draw the bath. She shook a bottle of lavender salts through the steam. *Why is my life so confusing these days? Old lavender memories and recent red roses don't mix well.*

An hour later, Kate dressed and ventured downstairs. A strong aroma of roast beef filled the house. She gagged, having no stomach for food.

Mary Grace opened the oven door and basted the meat with a spoon. "I've been waiting to talk to you. This is a big decision. What are you going to do?"

Kate sighed. "I will probably accept him. I wasn't going to, but I can't bear the thought of sending him off to war without hope. His brother died."

Mary Grace rubbed the back of her neck. "So he has no one. You will be a great comfort to him, Kate," she said gently. "I know he cares about you. I'm sure you're making the right decision. He's a good man."

"I know that."

"He's leaving soon, I understand."

"Yes, Mother. I'll phone today, but I'd like a cup of tea first."

She filled the kettle with water and slammed it on the stove.

"What an exciting time for you, Kate dear. Marriage—"

Kate cut her off. "Well, we can be engaged. Who knows when we will marry, with the war on."

Mary Grace threw a strained smile, but held her tongue.

Ryan breezed into the kitchen. "I'm starving. When's lunch?"

"Almost ready. You can set the table," Mary Grace said. "Wash your hands first."

Ryan turned on the tap. "I could use a cuppa," he said. "Cleaning the shelter is hard work. There are spiders in there. Lots of webs. Might be more if we don't use the place."

"Did you check for eggs today?" Mary Grace asked.

"I did. Forgot to bring them in. I'm meeting Mickey later. He might like a couple. Can we spare any?"

"Not if I'm going to make a cake, which I plan to do to celebrate Kate's good news."

Ryan stared at her. "What good news?"

"None yet," Kate said quickly.

Mary Grace opened her mouth to speak, but stopped as she saw Kate's frown.

"So what are you and Mickey up to?" Kate asked.

Ryan smiled. "Just helping the war effort."

The kettle whistled, and Kate made the tea. Mary Grace mashed the potatoes, poured gravy into a bowl, and set the roast, Yorkshire Pudding, and vegetables on the table.

"I'm not hungry," Kate said. "I'll have tea and a biscuit."

"You need to keep healthy, dear, and we're having roast beef. A nutritious meal we can't count on in the future."

"Please let me be, Mum," Kate said, taking her cup and leaving.

Kate arranged to meet Barry the following evening at the Star, the pub around the corner from Holly Road. She tripped along the street, feeling strangely reckless. *This is the boldest decision of my life.* Feeling shaky, she entered the building and saw him right away, waiting at the bar. She approached him from behind and touched his shoulder. He turned, and his eyes settled on hers, questioning.

"Yes," she said.

He blinked. "*Yes?* You will marry me?" he said, a smile radiating to his eyes.

"I will."

"Hurray!" he exclaimed, then kissed her. "You've made me the happiest man in the world!"

"You're a good man, and I'd be honored to be your wife."

The words sounded strange to her, but not unpleasant.

"Congratulations," the bartender said. "Couldn't help overhearing. How about a couple of pints on the house?"

"That's very generous. Thank you," Barry said.

"You're marrying into a fine family, my boy," the bartender continued. "Sean Murphy has been a good customer for years."

He poured two glasses of ale and passed them to Barry and Kate. "Best wishes for your happiness."

They clinked their drinks.

"I'm sorry this isn't a more romantic setting," Barry said, "and I can't give you a ring yet, but I'll make up for it, you'll see."

"It's quite all right," she said.

"I don't know when we can get married either. It depends on when I have leave. I'm going to Belgium tomorrow."

"I wish you didn't have to," Kate said.

"Don't worry. I'll be in touch when I can. There's something else I have to tell you." He paused, and Kate looked up at him in anticipation.

"Lydia gave me the name of a speech therapist who may help cure your hiccups."

"Wonderful!" she said, with an irresistible urge to hug him. She reached for his neck with both arms.

He kissed her cheek. "It's not Lionel Logue, who helped the king with his speech impediment, but a colleague, Ian Conway." He handed her a slip of paper. "I hope you look into this soon."

"I'll phone him, I promise. I can't thank you enough."

"No, I can't thank *you* enough—for agreeing to marry me. Really, Kate, you've captured my heart, and I'll go into battle stronger for that."

"I wish you all the strength in the world," she said.

They finished their drinks, and Barry took her hand as he walked her home.

"My, your hand is cold," he said.

It was true. Despite the mild April evening, her hands felt like ice. "Cold hand, warm heart," Kate said feebly.

"Come in," she said, opening the front door. "Mum will be overjoyed to hear the news."

"All right, just for a few minutes. I need to get back and finish preparations for leaving."

Mary Grace and Sean were sitting in the living room. Kate entered, Barry closely behind.

Kate cleared her throat. "We have news—" she faltered, then took a deep breath. "Barry has asked me to marry him, and I've accepted."

Mary Grace jumped up. "I knew it," she said, her eyes sparkling, and immediately rushed to give Barry a hug. Sean stood and pumped Barry's hand.

"We're so pleased to have you as a member of our family," Mary Grace said. "And we look forward to the wedding. A Catholic wedding."

Kate let the remark pass. Barry and she had not discussed the details, and he wasn't a Catholic. She'd deal with this problem later.

She watched him drive away in his car, hardly able to absorb the change that was about to take place in her life. Besides marriage, Barry had opened a door that could lead to her being able to sing again. This possibility helped mitigate any qualms she had about her impending wedding: Barry wanted the best for her. He was an extraordinary man.

CHAPTER 23
April 1940

Kate slept fitfully. She supposed that was normal for someone whose life was about to change dramatically. She respected Barry as a thoughtful, reliable man who loved her and wanted to make her happy. But a tiny voice inside told her that wasn't enough. *Cold feet before marriage are normal.* But cold hands? She wasn't so sure about that.

As she entered the kitchen, she heard her mother talking to her father.

"Do you truly think Hitler will win?"

"He'd bloody well better not," Sean replied, "but now he's invaded Norway. It's a neutral county, so why? They say he wants a foothold nearer to Scotland. Perhaps that's where he'll come first, though we've all expected London."

"Let's not talk about it. This is supposed to be a happy day."

Kate took her place at the table.

"Good morning, Kate dear," Mary Grace greeted her. "I'm going to bake a cake in honour of your engagement if I can save enough butter. We'll have some wine. It's a shame Barry won't be here to share it, but we'll celebrate the wedding soon enough, I hope."

"That's nice. Thank you," Kate said, ignoring her mother's naïve remark.

Ryan lumbered in and sat beside her. He wolfed down a couple of pieces of toast.

"No school today?" Kate asked.

"No. The teachers needed a day to discuss safety precautions. An ARP bloke is coming to explain how to keep us all safe in case of bombing. We haven't used the shelter in the school grounds yet, and it has to be outfitted with provisions. Dad and I did that yesterday for ours."

"We need more blankets," Mary Grace said. "I'll get some at the Centre. They've collected a lot of things like that, and we can't distribute them fast enough.

"Seems the Germans are getting closer," Ryan said. "I, for one, will not stand around and welcome them. Look what they're doing to our lives, cutting off our food and provisions, starving us to death. Mean bastards."

"Watch your language, young man," Mary Grace scolded.

"I've got work to do," Ryan said, rising to leave. He was through the doorway before Mary Grace could ask him what he meant. *He sounds more grown-up every day*, Kate thought.

Monday had always been washday, but since working for the Women's Voluntary Service, Mary Grace had adjusted her routine and now washed clothes on Tuesday. Kate marvelled at her mother's domestic routine. It had always been the same, year after year. Washing on Monday, ironing on Tuesday, shopping on Wednesday, baking on Thursday. Though essential, Kate considered the chores drudgery.

Mary Grace interrupted her musings. "Since you're not teaching this morning, Kate dear, how about coming with me to the Centre? I could use a hand with the blankets."

They set off together after breakfast.

"Good morning, Alison. I've got news," Mary Grace said as they entered the place. "Kate has just announced her engagement."

"That *is* good news!" Alison replied. "Congratulations. I think I saw you with your intended. A couple of nights ago. You both drove off in a car. Nice looking young man."

"That wasn't Kate and Barry," Mary Grace said. "They didn't go anywhere in a car. Not that I'm aware of, anyway. Her fiancé is a fine young man."

Kate caught her mother's puzzled expression. *She doesn't need to know about Tony.*

"Yes," Kate said quickly in a tone that precluded discussion. "And Barry has left to join the army."

At home that evening, Sean continued talking about the war.

"The British Norwegian Campaign has begun. The Navy is blocking the entrance to the port of Narvik with mines."

"Why? Norway is neutral, like America," Kate said.

"It has to do with supply lines. But things are getting more serious. They're conscripting older men starting next month. Thirty-six-year-olds."

"Thank the Lord that's not you, Sean." Mary Grace said.

"I don't know. In some ways, I wish I could join the fight. We must stop Hitler."

The front door banged, and Ryan crashed into the room, knocking a chair over.

"Where have you been, sonny?" Sean asked.

"Just out and about."

"Playing football?"

He righted the chair. "Not today. I was with Mickey."

"I see. What were you two up to?"

"Helping out. We took down road signs. Lots of them. Especially ones pointing to Sutton and Carshalton. We don't want the Nazis marching through here, do we?"

Kate and Sean laughed.

"Not sure that's your responsibility, but it's the right idea," Sean said.

Mary Grace gulped. "Ryan! What if someone caught you? What if that's a crime, stealing signs?"

Sean gave Ryan the thumbs up sign behind Mary Grace's back.

"We didn't steal them. Just left them by the roadside," he grinned. "No one saw us."

"Heaven help us," Mary Grace said. "All we need is for you to go to jail."

"Don't worry, Mum. I missed tea time. Is there anything left to eat?"

"I think Mickey is a bad influence on you," she said, pursing her lips as she opened the pantry door.

Kate considered the conversation. So many secrets, things she didn't understand. About the war. About her own life. And, as her mother said, she was supposed to be happy. She wasn't sure she understood that, either. But she would get married, a bold move that promised a future for her, and make a small contribution to the war. Barry would now leave with a sweetheart to come home to.

CHAPTER 24
April 1940

K ate watched as her mother made a list of ingredients for the cake to celebrate the engagement.

"What sort of cake?" Kate asked.

"A Victoria sponge. You like it, and it's special. I've got enough butter. I'm inviting the neighbours. Is there anyone else you'd like to ask?"

"Not really. Sybil, but I don't know how to reach her."

"Let's go out to tea tomorrow," Mary Grace said. "You'll be leaving home before long, and this will be a chance to have a chat. Just the two of us."

"All right, thank you," Kate replied. *She knows I won't be leaving for months, so why?* But wanting to avoid a discussion, she simply added, "I'll come straight home from school."

The next day, she and Mary Grace strolled along Holly Road, stopping at a tea shop on High Street. They took seats at a table near a bow window. Mary Grace ordered a pot of tea, sandwiches, and biscuits.

"You know your father and I are happy about your engagement," Mary Grace said, "and all we want is your happiness."

Kate took a sip of tea and set the cup on the saucer. *What is she getting at?*

"I understand that," she said.

Mary Grace clasped her hands on the table. "All the same—and I don't mean to intrude—I can't help questioning if marriage is what you really want."

"What do you mean?"

"Well, marriage to this man."

Kate looked away. "I've made my decision, Mum. It'll be all right."

"There are other men, and you're young."

"*Of course* there are others. I can't break his heart."

Ah, so that's what this is about. She's concerned about a rival for my affection. Kate supposed she could thank Alison for this conversation.

Mary Grace unclasped her hands and leaned forward, looking Kate squarely in the eye, "You don't have to marry someone just because he asks."

Kate swallowed. How unlike her mother, suggesting that she not marry. "It's all right, Mum. Don't worry. I could do a lot worse. You know that."

"Yes. I like Barry. He has a generous soul. Not all men do."

"You're right, Mum."

Kate had no desire to discuss the matter any further and thought it surprising that her mother would broach such a personal matter with her. Kate owed her a smidgeon of appreciation, however. She was showing concern and unusual sensitivity.

They drained the teapot, and Kate nibbled at a sandwich.

"You need to eat, keep up your strength. You're getting too thin," Mary Grace said.

"All right, Mother. Enough. I'm not a child anymore. Let's celebrate my engagement tomorrow and hope for the best." *That's all anyone can do these days.*

When Kate and Mary Grace arrived home, they found Sean and Ryan listening to the news on the wireless. "I don't know what to believe," Sean said. "Half the time the news sounds like propaganda. Chamberlain gave a speech today, said that Hitler has 'missed the bus,' to defeat us while we are unprepared. Meanwhile, it seems Germany has invaded Denmark and Norway, and Quisling, the former Norwegian Minister of War, has formed a Nazi party in his own country. Doesn't make sense."

He switched the wireless off.

"All very confusing," Kate said, "but now we can't call it the Bore War any more. The Germans are aggressive. I've heard they want *Lebensraum*—room to grow."

"Yes. Plundering monsters," Ryan said. Kate stared at his brown-stained face, trousers, and boots.

"Go and wash," Mary Grace said. "How was football?"

"Muddy." Ryan grinned.

What has he been up to? Taking down more signs? Kate wondered.

The next morning, she arose to the aroma of sweet butter emanating from the kitchen. The cake. Her mother had invited neighbours to the party: the Harrises, Mickey, and Pamela and Bill Warren. Everyone arrived at three. No one except Mickey had met Barry, and the guests wanted to know more about him. "Where is he from? What does he do? Is he handsome? When's the wedding?"

Kate answered perfunctorily, without elaborating. She felt out of sorts, her eyes blurry. People helped themselves to sandwiches and sausage rolls, and Sean poured the wine. Several made toasts, wishing the couple happiness. She acknowledged their good wishes, then sat in a corner of the room wondering why she was so unlike others. She wanted more out of life than marriage, and being in the spotlight for engagement toasts was a far cry from singing on stage. But she reminded herself that Barry had given her the ticket to success, and she owed him for that, at least.

Mary Grace handed out slices of cake, plates, and forks. Everyone stopped talking while they dug in.

"Yum. It's so light and spongy," Pamela said.

Mickey winked at her. "That's 'ow it's s'posed to be, love. *Sponge* cake, you know?"

Kate watched her mother's glowing face, knowing she enjoyed enhancing her reputation as a baker.

Conversation among the women soon turned to the evacuees. The Harris twins were still in Devon, and their mother wanted them home. "What's the point of them being there? We thought the war would be 'ere by now. I'm talking to the authorities. After all, Ryan's back, none the worse for wear."

"And I'm so glad," Mary Grace said.

"I hope Tommy and Francis do come home 'cause I've missed my mates," Ryan added.

"I'm grateful I didn't send Rachel," Pamela said. "No good splitting families, I say."

"We don't know what level of schooling our boys are getting in that place. They don't tell us much in their letters. What do you know about the schools there, Ryan?" Mr. Harris asked.

"Don't know. I didn't go. Worked on a farm."

"Right. This evacuation scheme might not have worked for everyone," Mr. Harris said.

"The government thinks they know what's best for us, but I don't see any real leadership there," Pamela said. "Chamberlain talks nonsense. Says we're winning, but where's the evidence?"

"Wait a minute, everyone. This is Kate's party. Let's make another toast," Mary Grace exclaimed. "To Kate and Barry!"

Kate stood up, forcing a smile while the guests lifted their drinks.

After everyone left, Kate collected the glasses and plates and stacked them by the sink. "Thank you for the party, Mum. You go and put your feet up. I'll clear up. The cake was delicious."

"Don't mention it. I wish we could do more to send you off, dear. These are such trying times."

Kate yawned and plunged her hands into the soapy dishwater. What was it the Germans said about women's lives? *Kinder, Küche, Kirche,*—children, cooking, church.

Not for me. But that's my secret.

CHAPTER 25
April 1940

A fter she finished cleaning up, Kate escaped to her room and took out a journal. She supposed it wasn't really appropriate for a Mass Observation submission and she wasn't accustomed to writing, but doing so might help sort out her feelings—or possibly, she thought with dismay, to find out if she had any. Since accepting Barry's proposal, she felt oddly removed from life, as though she were floating high, like a barrage balloon. She had no strong emotions, just a flat, dead feeling. She wished she might talk to Sybil or Clare, people who understood her. How had Clare behaved before her marriage? Kate could conjure up only one image: her sister like the Cheshire Cat, with a smile that remained even after she left the room. As she'd already thought, in all likelihood Clare had talked about marriage with their mother, but while her sister would have welcomed a cosy chat, Kate could only resent it.

Instead of spilling her thoughts into a journal, she wrote a letter.

Dear Clare,

I have news. I'm engaged. His name is Barry Collins. He's a decent chap and everyone approves, especially Mum. I wish I could talk to you about marriage. I have so many questions, and don't know what to expect. Are you happier now than when you were single? Do you have any advice? I miss you so much, and now it

looks as though I won't come to America anytime soon. Barry is a
local boy. He's joined the army and is on his way to Belgium. We'll
marry when he comes home on leave.

   Looking forward to your reply. Much love,
   Kate (Caterpillar)

She sealed and addressed the letter and fell into a deep, exhausted sleep.

Next morning, she tore the letter up. What would be the purpose of sending it? She needed an in-person conversation with her sister. Or anyone she could trust.

Kate announced her engagement to the staff at school. Sister Mary Joseph asked if she would continue teaching after her marriage, and Kate told her she expected so. Mrs. Fitzgerald organised a party, and Kate accepted gifts of tea towels and embroidered pillowslips from the staff. It all seemed strange and unreal. Would she really set up a household?

She received a letter from Barry, sent before he crossed the Channel with his regiment. He thanked her for accepting him and vowed his eternal love. At the end he wrote, "P.S. Don't forget to make an appointment to see Mr. Conway. No hiccupping allowed at our marriage ceremony!"

What a kind man. He looks out for me, even from afar, when he has difficulties of his own. I've done him a disservice, worrying about marriage, depriving myself of happiness, she scolded herself.

Kate pocketed the letter and slipped out of the house. Within minutes, she reached the nearest telephone box and called the number for the speech therapist's practice.

"I'm Kathleen Murphy. A friend referred me to Mr. Conway because I have a speech problem. I'd like to make an appointment to see him."

"Certainly," a woman answered. "How about two o'clock on Thursday? We're at 249 Harley Street in London."

"I'll be there."

Kate hung up the receiver. At last!

On Thursday she took the fifty-minute train ride to Victoria station. A bus carried her to Harley Street, a fashionable area with stately five-story townhouses and polished brass plates listing the doctors' surgeries inside. She mounted the steps at number 249. There was no doorbell. She rode the lift to Mr. Conway's consulting rooms on the third floor. The sign on the door read IAN CONWAY, SPEECH THERAPY.

A tall woman with a slight limp answered her knock. "Kathleen Murphy? Mr. Conway is expecting you," she said.

Kate entered, holding her hands to her sides to keep them from trembling. A grey-haired man with finely chiseled features and light grey eyes stepped towards her and offered his hand. She raised her left hand to grasp it, then quickly replaced it with her right. She saw his eyes flick from side to side, as though he had detected the exchange.

"Pleased to meet you, Miss Murphy," he said. "Please take a seat."

She eased herself into a chair while he sat behind a desk. She glanced around, noticing the wood paneling and small windows in the room. Even in the daylight, it appeared dark. A lamp on the desk provided a warm glow. He took up a pen and met her gaze. A handsome man with a caring face, she thought.

"Please tell me about yourself, and the reason for your visit," he said.

"I have dreadful episodes of the hiccups. I sing, and I would like to perform, but when I start the hiccups erupt. I realise it's only an inconvenience for most people, but for me, it's a disability. It's lasted for years now, and I thought I would grow out of it, but I'm twenty, and it's not going away."

"I can see that would be a problem. How often are these episodes?"

"Not very often. Mostly when I'm nervous."

He cupped his chin in one hand and regarded her. "It's not the usual symptom my clients present me with, but some of my methods may work. It all depends on your willingness to go along with my treatment programme. Understand that my methods are my own, and I prefer that you not talk about them."

"I'm very motivated, and I can keep confidentiality, but I'd need to know how long, and . . . uh, there's the matter of the cost."

"Don't worry about that for now. May I ask your occupation? Do you work?"

"I'm a part-time music teacher at a girls' school."

"Hmm. I take it the pay isn't high."

She shook her head.

"And you're not married?"

"No. Engaged, but not married yet. My fiancé is in the armed forces."

"All right." He narrowed his eyes. "Are you willing to come and see me every week for a month?"

"Certainly."

"Good. This will be a short meeting for me to assess your condition. My assistant Mrs. Wood will set up future appointments."

"So you will see me?" Kate asked, not sure she believed what she was hearing.

"I will. I'd like to help."

"Thank you," she said, rising to leave. "I'm most grateful."

After arranging her first appointment for the following month, Kate almost skipped down the street. She liked this man with his kind eyes, and she determined to follow his instructions and defeat her longstanding affliction. Perhaps she would finally achieve a singing career. And tell Barry: no hiccupping at the wedding.

CHAPTER 26
May 1940

With Barry in service, Kate followed the news more closely. Her family, anxious and subdued, gathered around the wireless most evenings for the nine o'clock BBC Home Service broadcast news. On May 7, Parliament held a debate about the possibility of invasion and shortly afterwards passed a vote of no confidence in Chamberlain, who had advised peaceful negotiation. On May 10, Germany invaded Holland and Belgium. Within days, Chamberlain resigned, and Winston Churchill replaced him as Prime Minister. Holland surrendered. On May 13, Churchill gave an inspiring speech, saying Britain would win, but warning citizens to expect "blood, toil, tears and sweat."

Kate understood that her own concerns paled compared to the worsening situation in Europe and Britain, and she questioned if she could justify making efforts to cure her hiccups. But life went on until it didn't, wasn't that so? She worried about Barry. How was he faring in Belgium? They had no information about the troops abroad. She could do nothing more than carry on.

And so she travelled to London for her appointment with Mr. Conway.

When she arrived, he greeted her, as before, with a firm handshake. She offered her left hand this time.

"You need to be comfortable," he said, smiling. "Comfort is important, and we will work on how to stay comfortable, even when certain situations cause *dis-ease*. To begin, I must ask you a few questions about your condition, your hiccups. When did they first occur?"

Kate gripped the sides of the armchair and said nothing.

"All right. I understand this is difficult," he said. "Let's talk about times when you've had recent episodes."

Kate blushed. She'd rather not tell him about the time Barry proposed marriage. That was her private business. "Uh, we had an air raid warning and had to go into our shelter."

"That makes sense. Everyone is jittery these days." He gazed at her with soft eyes, his head tilted.

Then she told him the truth. "The first—and worst time—was when I auditioned at the Royal Academy of Music. Three years ago. I wasn't able to continue, and I lost the opportunity for a scholarship."

"How disappointing. I love music, too, and I know a bit about singing and breathing. It all has to do with the diaphragm, you know. I can teach you how to relax."

"That's exactly what I need to re-learn. I didn't feel nervous as a child."

"That's good. It means we have fewer years of a problem to correct."

"True. I hadn't considered that—actually, I think the spasms only began after I broke up with my first boyfriend. I suddenly became insecure. I was seventeen."

"Ah." Conway nodded. "You will overcome it, but you need confidence and motivation to continue the treatment. Let me explain the nature of your condition. Hiccups are caused by an involuntary contraction of the diaphragm. Each contraction is followed by a closure of the vocal chords which produce the 'hic' sound. The spasm is like an electric pulse, and we have to find a way to interrupt that."

"I understand. What do I need to do?"

"First, stand up and take a deep breath. You can feel your diaphragm underneath your ribs. Now exhale slowly."

Kate followed his breathing instructions, breathing in and out, and noticing the calming effect. After the first session, Kate caught herself grinning on the way home. It was a long way to London, but who else could treat her? No one she knew had disabling hiccups, and Mr. Conway had said he could help her.

One Saturday evening, a waxing moon arose, infusing leaves with an olive glow. Kate sat with her mother in the back garden sipping gin and tonics. The wind sighed in the trees. The soft moonlit air caressed her hair as strains of Debussy's beautiful *Claire de Lune* ran through her head. *I'll play it one day*, she thought. Mary Grace extolled the progress of her garlic, whose young shoots had already pushed through the soil on top of the air raid shelter. Ryan's chicken clucked and scratched in the coop.

Mary Grace put down her drink. "If worries about the war didn't consume our minds, I'd say this is a perfect spring evening," she said.

"I agree," Kate said. "We don't often have warm nights like this."

She almost added, *I don't often have moments like this with you either, Mum, when we're in perfect harmony with each other.* Perhaps things would change after she married.

"Too bad Clare's not here to enjoy this. I can't imagine life in New York could be any fun. Besides, she's a gardener like me, and she writes that there are no gardens surrounding the high-rise buildings in the city. She must miss England in May."

Kate pictured Clare and Mary Grace working together, weeding and planting, laughing as they knelt in the soft brown soil and clutching it in handfuls to inhale the earthy scent. While not something that had given Kate pleasure, she recognised the value of the work. Her own work, too.

"Imagine if, instead of the railway, we had a view of water," Mary Grace went on. "How much better our lives would be. The sound of the sea, the tides that wash away the rubble . . . but the ocean is treacherous, too."

She caught her mother's thoughtful expression, now grown sober. Her pale eyes appeared watery in the moonlight. Kate sensed a gentle tug in her heart. She considered talking about visits to Mr. Conway, the man who was making things better for her, but as she started to speak, the train to Victoria whistled, then roared by. *Clickety clack, clickety clack*, the wheels rattled, halting her words.

Sean called from the kitchen door. "Kate, someone's here to see you."

What bad timing, Kate moaned inwardly. She wanted to continue this special conversation, but rose from her garden chair and went inside.

Tony stood in the front hallway, twirling his hat in his hands.

"Sorry not to be in touch sooner," he said. "It's hard to reach you since you're not on the phone."

"I know. Let's go for a walk."

"What a lovely evening. Romantic," he said.

That smile. His tall, straight figure. She needed to keep a cool head and not waiver.

"Just taking a stroll," she said to her father. "Back soon."

"Aren't you going to introduce your visitor?" he asked.

"Sorry. Dad, this is Tony Trent, an old friend."

Tony stepped forward and offered his hand. "Nice to meet you, sir."

"As I said, we won't be long," Kate said, pulling Tony's sleeve as she made for the door.

The linden trees bordering Holly Road shimmered in the breeze, the sweet fragrance of their lemon-coloured flowers wafting in the air. They reminded Kate of earlier times, of lavender fields, and long rambles with him through ancient beech woods.

He reached for her hand. She pulled it back.

"Tony, there's something I have to tell you. I'm engaged."

He halted. "What a surprise—uh, congratulations, I suppose."

"Thank you."

She took a breath, congratulating herself for not weakening and falling under his spell while trying to ignore the conflicting feelings whirling in her head. Now might not be the best time to ask many questions. She concentrated on one.

Turning to face him, she said, "I have to know. Who were all those people at the party? Are they good friends of yours?"

"Not really. I don't share their beliefs about the war, about many things."

"So you don't have sympathy for Hitler?"

"Absolutely not. As I told you, I went to that event because my colleague from school asked me to. Those people frighten the life out of me."

"I'm glad you think so. Anyway, thank you for introducing me to a different way of life."

"I'm sorry I can't show you more of that good life. With better people. I expect to enjoy it myself, someday."

"Well, there's more to life than luxury."

"True. Look, I'd best be getting back. I wanted to see you, but . . . I've got work to do."

They turned round and ambled back to the house. He started to say something else, but stopped, and she didn't encourage him to go on. They reached her house.

"I'm glad you've discovered a profession that suits you, Tony. Best of luck," she said, as she opened the front door.

"To you, too."

He grasped her hand, seeming reluctant to let it go, then with an undecipherable expression, dropped it, spun around, and left.

I'm glad that's over, she said to herself. Why had he come to see her? Did he want to resume their relationship? Perhaps he wasn't a scoundrel after all, but the way she reacted around him scared her. He was an enigma. Or perhaps no more than an adolescent crush. Anyway, she had made her decision and would honour her commitment.

And somehow now, the enchantment of a rare evening sitting with her mother chatting about things that mattered had given her a new sense of hope for her uncertain life ahead.

As the month of May progressed, people waited, glued to the wireless, eager for news about the war. In the staff room at St. Bridget's, she listened with growing concern to the daily exchange of information among the teachers.

"Queen Wilhelmina has fled the Netherlands. Our royal family say they won't leave, though."

"The Nazis have taken over Belgium and are marching towards the coast."

"I heard our troops are trapped at Dunkirk."

Each day without fail, Kate practiced the exercises Mr. Conway had taught her using them as warm-ups before singing. They steadied her as the days went by with no word from Barry. She waited impatiently for the post and wrote to him every day, but with no address to send letters to, they lay in a growing stack on her dresser. She told him how much she admired him and that she looked forward to their life together. Writing it would make it true, she thought. *Perhaps he's at Dunkirk. Yes, that's where he must be.* Nerves strained to breaking, she postponed her appointment with Mr. Conway. She questioned if there would ever be a wedding. She heard rumours about something called Operation Dynamo. Anyone owning a vessel could join the campaign to rescue the soldiers at Dunkirk. All would cross the Channel together in a civilian convoy. It seemed like an extraordinary plan, but better than allowing the ruthless slaughter of the brave men on the beach. *Maybe Barry is safe and will return home.*

She couldn't bear thoughts of any alternative.

CHAPTER 27
June 1940

K ate overheard her father's raised voice one morning.
"I'm going, and that's all there is to it."

"Oh Sean, not you. It's not safe. *You can't go.*"

"I can, and I will."

The door slammed.

In the kitchen, Kate found her mother slumped at the table, her face etched with worry.

"He wants to go to Dunkirk."

Kate nodded. She wasn't surprised. "But where will he find a boat?" she asked.

"Mickey has a friend who's got one. He keeps it in Dover. They're driving down together, the three of them, to find it."

"Well, I understand it's risky, but if Dad could man a lifeboat to rescue ships in storms, he can sail across the channel to rescue stranded soldiers in France. I'm proud of him for wanting to go." *And a little envious.*

"But it's not safe," Mary Grace wailed. She sat, twisting her wedding ring around her finger.

Kate wanted to remind her that nothing about the war was safe, not even right here in their own home. Long ago, Sean had given up his seafaring career because Mary Grace had asked him. It was too much to expect him to cater to his wife's wishes now, when he might to save a life, perhaps even Barry's. Kate left her mother to her distress.

* *

Kate supposed she would feel enthusiasm for her wedding as she became used to the idea of marriage. But she remained sullen, ate almost nothing, and rarely sang or played the piano. She wandered around the house and stared at the walls. Once so quick to shut the blackout curtains each evening, she forgot them, and their ARP warden scolded the family for leaving a light on in an upstairs bedroom. She wished she could accompany her father to Dunkirk and make a contribution. But when she approached Sean with the proposal, he shook his head.

While Kate floundered, her mother seemed to gain strength. The work at the WVS had given Mary Grace a new purpose in life. While Kate had never confided in her mother, she had sometimes talked to her father. But she didn't feel inclined to talk about her impending marriage, and shunned any overtures he made to bring up the subject.

In the middle of June, she received a letter. After reading it with growing alarm, she flew into the kitchen.

"I've heard from Barry," she cried. "Rescued from Dunkirk, but wounded, and now at Queen Mary's Hospital for Children. I must visit."

"Of course you must," Mary Grace said. "Does it say anything about the nature of his injuries?"

"Nothing. The note came from someone else writing on his behalf. I'll go as soon as I can and learn more."

"Queen Mary's Hospital for Children, you say? He's not a child."

"No, but that's where he is. At least it's in Carshalton."

Ryan lumbered into the room. "Has something happened? You look ill."

"Barry's been wounded."

"No! How?"

"I don't know."

"Those damned Jerrys. Can I have something to eat? I'm famished."

"Have a piece of bread and margarine. There's no marmalade."

"*No marmalade? This bloody war.*"

The next day Kate dressed carefully in her best summer frock. It wasn't new, but Mary Grace had come across it at the WVS shop and it fit perfectly. She tied her long curly hair back with a ribbon and dabbed some rouge on her pale cheeks.

"The dress suits you, Kate dear," Grace said. "I take it you're going to visit Barry. Take some slices of gingerbread with you."

"I wish I had more to give him, but I don't know what he needs," Kate said.

"I'm sure your presence will be more than enough. Good luck."

Kate took the bus to Queen Mary's Hospital for Children with trepidation. At the entrance she produced her letter, and the guard gave her directions to a wing that had been converted to space for wounded soldiers as an Emergency Military Hospital.

"Do not talk to people about this place," the guard warned. "It's not widely known, and it's important to keep secret."

Kate remembered the Official Secrets Act—the one Sybil had signed. Perhaps she would have to sign. Her feelings of dread increased. She peered through a glass door leading to a room filled with men in metal beds, most lying still under blankets. Through another door marked POW, she saw more patients.

A nurse moved towards her. "May I help you? Who are you here to see?"

"My fiancé, Barry Collins."

"He's here. Prepare yourself. He has a bandage over his eyes and a severe wound in his chest. He can hear, though. Is he expecting you?"

"No. The letter only arrived yesterday."

"I'll bring you to him, then. I'm Jane Fletcher. He's one of my patients. A nice boy."

The smell of antiseptics hung heavy in the ward and Kate wanted to hold her ears to block the sounds of men crying out in pain. Some lay with vacant stares; others slept. All had bandages on limbs, heads, or torsos. Kate's knees wobbled as she searched for the bed with Barry's name.

Nurse Fletcher stopped at the foot of a bed indistinguishable from the others. "Here," she said, and stepped back. Kate gasped.

Barry lay still, eyes obscured by a white bandage. His right arm lay lifelessly at his side. His thin body appeared thinner. Kate's spirits sank as she watched his chest slowly rise and fall. *He's alive, but just barely.*

The nurse bent to him. "Private Collins, you have a visitor," she said.

He moved as if to sit up. His lips curved into a slight smile. "Kate?"

Kate knelt beside him and touched his face. "Yes, it's me. I came as soon as I heard. I'm so sorry. How are you feeling?"

"Happy now you're here. Just wish I could see you," he rasped. "Come around to the other side so I can hold your hand."

The hand that grasped hers was ice cold. She barely recognised the long, sensitive fingers. Violinist's hands. A wave of sorrow washed over her.

"Tell me all about yourself," he said, with effort. "I don't want to talk about me. What have you been doing? Have you started singing yet?"

She tried to sound cheerful. "Not singing yet, though I have seen Mr. Conway. He says he can help me. Thank you for the referral. I like the man, and plan to see him again soon."

"Best news I've heard in years," Barry said, his smile broadening. He coughed before continuing, "How's everyone else in your family?"

"All fine. Mum's doing better. She volunteers with the Women's Voluntary Service and that's doing her some good. She's found a new purpose in life. It helps that so far, no bombs have fallen, and she's less fearful now."

"Glad to hear that. Are you still teaching?"

"Yes. Nothing has changed since you left, actually. The war so far has been fought at sea and in Europe."

"Yes. Dunkirk wasn't a pleasant experience," he drawled, drawing down the corners of his mouth. "The rescue was extraordinary, though. All those small boats blazing across the channel. Have you heard about it?"

"Not much. We suspect the government doesn't want us to know much to keep up our morale. It's easy to believe the Germans will win this war."

"They'd better not," Barry said, grimacing and clearing his throat. "Despicable bastards. Hitler—what a brute." He made a fist with his good left hand.

"I'm so glad you escaped. You must get well soon."

"Doing my best. It helps to have you here," he said, squeezing her arm.

"Mum sent you some gingerbread."

"Good of her. Food here isn't the best, but beats what we had in the trenches. Just glad to be alive."

"I'm glad you are, too."

Nurse Fletcher arrived at the bedside.

"I hate to break things up, but this is enough for today. Private Collins has to gain back his strength."

"All right. I'll come again as soon as I can," Kate said, standing to leave.

"Please do. It's like a tonic, that musical voice of yours."

She smiled briefly at the compliment, then broke into guilty tears as the nurse escorted her out.

"Will he ever be able to see again?" Kate asked shakily.

"Too early to tell. The doctors are more concerned about the wound in his chest."

"But when will we find out?"

"Sorry, but I don't know. We'll give him the best care we can."

Kate wiped her eyes. "I'm sure you will."

Kate slipped out of the room, trying to ignore the cries and moans. She had never witnessed such suffering in her life, and didn't know what to make of Barry's condition. How long would he remain in that state? His life in limbo—hard to understand in one so young. Her sorrow weighed upon her like a soldier's pack as she passed through the gate.

"How is he?" Mary Grace asked.

"It's serious, and they didn't say when he'll recover." *Or if he'd ever recover.* It was sad beyond measure, and Kate didn't want to say the words aloud. "His eyes are bandaged, and he may lose his sight. I know you're eager for a wedding, but there's no point in making plans anytime soon." Her voice faltered, and she let the tears flow. Her mother said nothing, but folded Kate in an embrace.

That evening, Churchill delivered a speech to the House of Commons, saying, "we shall never surrender."

I won't give up on Barry either, Kate vowed.

Later that week, Sean announced he wouldn't be going to Dunkirk after all. He had seen Mickey's friend's boat and deemed it unseaworthy. He wasn't foolhardy, he said.

Kate kept her appointment with Mr. Conway. She wanted to report to Barry that she'd followed his recommendation to overcome her affliction. It seemed a feeble gesture, given the serious nature of Barry's troubles, but it was the best action she could take to improve his spirits.

She travelled to Harley Street. As before, Mr. Conway shook Kate's hand. "Would you like a cup of tea? Or whiskey, perhaps?'

"No thank you," Kate said. She had not expected to be offered refreshments, certainly not whiskey.

"Make yourself comfortable," he said.

That's what he advised last time. *Does he just offer tea and comfort? If so, I won't learn a thing,* Kate thought, as she took a seat in the plush leather chair.

"I sense resistance," he said. "It's important for us to understand what we're aiming for here. May I ask what's important to you now, at this time in your life?"

Kate coughed. *How can he read my mind?* "I have to admit things are different now," she said. "My fiancé was rescued at Dunkirk. He's in hospital, seriously wounded."

"Ah. So you have other matters to preoccupy you just now. It might be better if we wait a while before we begin our sessions. They require your full attention, and, as I mentioned before, the belief that you can succeed."

"I understand," she said. "But part of my fiancé's recovery may depend upon his knowing that I can overcome this problem. He supports my longtime goal of a singing career, and . . ." despite herself, she couldn't help smiling. "The last thing he wants is those ridiculous hiccups when we say our marriage vows."

Mr. Conway returned her smile. "Fair enough. But you know it's essential that you want this outcome as well. Do we agree?"

She nodded.

"All right then. To begin with, don't take yourself too seriously. Don't try too hard. Consider what makes you comfortable, whether that's clothes, the food you eat, the music you listen to, the people you're with. That's my lesson for today. Come back and see me when you've thought about those things. Take notes."

"That's all you want me to do?"

"That's all, along with the breathing exercises we discussed last time. Come and see me when you're ready."

She left, puzzled. *What a strange man.* Still, he made few demands of her, and she supposed she could focus her mind on comfort and make a few notes. It was true: she hadn't given such matters much consideration in recent months, and she had never before deemed her hiccups the least bit amusing. Maybe it was time to open her mind to new ways of doing things.

CHAPTER 28

June 1940

K ate opened the back door to insistent knocking. "I've got a job," Mickey said proudly as she let him in.

Ryan held his hand against his mouth to contain his laughter. "Now that's news. What are you doing? Stealing signs for pay now? Supplying the troops with cider?"

"Enough of that," Mary Grace said. "Mickey deserves some respect. Have a seat and tell us more."

"I'm a Local Defence Volunteer, better known as the 'ome Guard."

"Sounds impressive," Ryan said. "How do I sign up?"

"They want older blokes like me," Mickey said. "I've got to be trained first. Told them I didn't need training to remove road signs."

"I should say not," Ryan said, laughing. Even Mary Grace stifled a smile.

"Good for you. You're going to the aid of our country," Sean said grandly. "Churchill says the government ought to explain more about the war to us all. Will that be coming from you?"

"That's it. We're going to pass out leaflets soon. I think they're called, 'If the Germans Invade Great Britain.'"

"We certainly could use more information about that, God help us," Mary Grace said.

"Who will look after Pinocchio if you're out working?" Ryan asked.

"I'll take 'im with me. 'E's a fine watchdog."

"That reminds me of something I heard at work today," Sean said grimly. "The Nazi party wants the Jews to 'die like dogs.'"

Kate stared at him in horror. *Not Hannah and her parents.*

"Cor blimey. It's easy to 'ate them Nazis with their ugly swastika flags," Mickey snarled. "My dog won't let anyone 'ere die like a dog. And Pinocchio won't die like a dog, anyway. 'E'll 'ave a proper funeral when 'is time comes."

Yes, Kate thought, thinking of Barry. *It's very easy to hate them Nazis.* And, given the promise she had given Sarah, whatever fate the Bells suffered would affect her, too.

Kate's singing class dwindled. More girls had withdrawn from the school, either headed for evacuation overseas, or had simply stopped coming. No one kept track of attendance anymore. Listening to the girls' sweet voices raised in song always gave Kate's morale a boost. While lost in the music's beauty, she forgot about her troubles and responsibilities at home. She encouraged the girls to breathe deeply and sing freely. The girls rewarded her with whoops of cheerful laughter as they filed out of the hall. No one hearing them would have guessed war was close at hand.

Hannah stopped private lessons after the concert, but her voice and confidence continued to strengthen, and Kate had to remind her more than once that when singing with a choir, she should blend with the others and not ring out like a soloist. While Kate understood Hannah's impatience to sing solo again, she would have to wait until the next performance. *If we're still here, and if I'm still teaching.*

Her third session with Mr. Conway continued in the same format as the others. He greeted her politely, ensured her comfort, offered tea or whiskey, which she refused, and asked about Barry.

"He knows I'm seeing you, and he's pleased. But Barry may be blind, and his chest wound doesn't seem to be improving."

Her eyes stung, and she fumbled in her handbag.

He handed her a handkerchief. "I'm sorry to hear this. You need to keep your spirits up. You teach singing, you say. Does that help?"

"More than anything," she sniffed. "That's what gives me comfort."

"Good. Are you singing at all, yourself?"

"Not really. As you know, I can't commit to any public performances until I overcome my problem."

"I recognise that you question what I'm all about," he said. "I've done a fair amount of work with patients with conditions similar to yours, and it's essential to understand the underlying causes."

She stiffened. He'd read her mind again.

"It may help if I explain some things about singing. There are enormous benefits, some of which you already understand. What you may not know is that the act of singing releases dopamine, which allows other hormones to escape, like oxytocin. These reduce tension. Singing helps people cope with grief. It can also overcome speech impediments because many find it easier to sing words or phrases than say them. So it goes without saying that part of your treatment will include singing. *You* singing, not the choir."

"I didn't know about all these benefits, and lately I haven't been singing much at all. But I understand I should start. That won't be difficult once I set my mind to it."

"Good. Before our next visit, I'd like you to sing. Anywhere—in your garden, in the bathtub, on your way to work. Keep a record of what and when."

Kate left the consulting room strangely elated. Mr. Conway's unconventional methods made sense. She hummed softly in the bus on her way home, then when she alighted at the stop at the top of Holly Road, she raised her voice and sang: "Morning has broken, like the first morning. Blackbird has spoken, like the first bird . . ."

* *

But the news offered nothing to sing about. On June 22, France surrendered to Germany. By the end of the month, Germany had bombed and invaded the Channel Islands. *The Times* reported that all the Dominions—Canada, South Africa, New Zealand, and Australia—were encouraging evacuees to leave Britain and flee to safety in their countries. The Government established the Children's Overseas Reception Board to assist in these evacuations. Within two weeks, over 200,000 parents applied to send their children to safety overseas.

Kate sat down at her piano, not caring whether her mother or anyone else was within earshot. She played the introduction to "Goodnight Children Everywhere." Mr. Conway had told her she must sing. And sing she did.

CHAPTER 29
June 1940

The front door banged shut as Kate was practicing the piano one afternoon. Mary Grace stormed in.

"Kate, it's outrageous," she fumed. "I never knew children could live with such awful health conditions. Lice, scabies, impetigo, all infections that keep them away from home and school."

"Where are those children and how did they become infected?"

"Most are returning home from their billets. We've set up a sick bay to care for them until they're no longer contagious. They're bored, sitting in bed all day."

"My goodness," Kate said. "Good for you, Mum, for dealing with this."

"I could use some help. I was wondering if you'd entertain them."

"You mean play with them?"

"No, sing with them. They range in age from five to eleven."

"Yes, I think I can do that. How about tomorrow? I'm down to only two classes at school, both in the morning."

"That would be so helpful, dear. Around two, then?"

This is a welcome distraction, Kate thought. *Sick children usually get well.* She rummaged through her collection of music scores and wrote down the names of all the children's nursery rhymes she could remember. She doubted the eleven-year-olds would sing along with the younger ones. If not, she should be prepared to separate them into age groups.

Mary Grace accompanied her to the sick bay. Kate surveyed the room. Some children lay in bed, while others played on the floor. Older ones appeared bored, staring at the walls, though a few sat at tables reading books. Several had shaved heads, and she saw from their shining faces that they had recently been scrubbed.

She clapped her hands to get their attention. "Hello, I'm Kate. We're going to sing together. Let's see if we can make enough noise to scare the unicorn from the roof."

A few of the younger children giggled. "There's no unicorn there."

"Pshaw. There's no such thing as a unicorn," an older boy said.

"You'd be surprised." Kate said. "He might fly right past the window."

"I want to see one. I've got a picture of one in my book. He has a long horn."

"All right. We'll sing to the unicorn. That means you have to sing with your whole self, not just part of it. We'll start by singing something everyone knows. Join in as soon as you want."

"Old Macdonald had a farm," she began.

"Ee i ee i o," two girls sang along,

"And on that farm he had a cow,"

"Ee yi ee yi o," more joined in. Then others chorused, "With a *moo moo* here, and a *moo moo* there, here a *moo,* there a *moo,* everywhere a *moo moo . . .*"

And so the youngest ones sang the song, all the verses. They clapped their hands, but the older boys didn't join in. They looked at one another with disgust.

"That sounded good," Kate said, ignoring them. "Do you think the unicorn heard us?"

"Of course he did!" a small boy shouted.

Kate left with the echoes of the children's voices in her head. She would enjoy this volunteer experience and the small children's high spirits impressed her. She'd come up with songs for the older boys. War songs like "Tipperary." Visiting these young casualties of the war had been a comforting experience, something worth mentioning to Mr. Conway.

Kate visited Barry as often as her schedule allowed. She became accustomed to the stretchers carried with white sheets drawn over them and closed her ears against the groans. Barry always brightened when she arrived, but she sensed he suffered great pain. His eyes remained bandaged.

"I wish I could see you," he said, one day. "You're so beautiful. Come close so I can feel your face."

She perched on the bed, and he reached for her with his good arm. He fingered her nose, lips, and eyes.

"What's this, tears?" he asked.

She kissed his hand briefly before moving hers to wipe her cheeks.

"I'm so awfully sad for you," she murmured.

"Don't be. I'm alive," he said. "Not like some of my friends in Belgium."

He told her about his experience in the trenches, about the driving rain, the mud, sparse meals, and the futility of it all. She asked him about the rescue.

"I waited on the beach for days, like everyone else, hoping. We didn't know when or if we would get home. Finally, the boats came and we all ran into the sea to meet them. I wasn't wounded until right before I got on a fishing boat with two strong men aboard. The German planes bombarded us, and the fishermen pulled me in. I was lucky I didn't drown. Heavy seas made the voyage back dangerous, but I fell in and out of consciousness and don't remember much of it. There were three of us, all privates. They took us to St. Thomas' Hospital in London. The queen visited us."

"Did she? So how did you end up here, in Carshalton?"

"I asked if they could transfer me to a place nearer home. I wanted it to be easier for you to visit me."

"Good thinking," she said, "but you know I'd have come to London, too."

"I'm not sure when they will let me out of here, but let's plan our wedding soon," he said. "What's the weather like? We can get married outside."

"It's June, summer, and the roses are out."

"Roses. I brought you some. Twice. Flowers of love, despite their thorns."

Her throat caught. "Yes."

Kate did not wish to discourage him, but she could not see much improvement in Barry's condition. Would he ever be able to see again, and repair engines? Play the violin? It was heartbreaking.

To her tender surprise, she had come to love him. Her acceptance of this truth was so new, so extraordinary, that she didn't know how to tell him yet. She sat at his bedside, her heart bursting, warm tears flowing down her cheeks. She took his hand in hers and kissed it.

He fell into slumber, a faint smile on his lips.

"Do you have any singing engagements yet?" he asked during Kate's next visit.

"No, but I'm making progress with Mr. Conway. He's strange, but I like him."

"That's good news. You know, we heard Vera Lynn at the base during training. She gave us all such a gift with her lovely voice. Sang 'We'll Meet Again.' It gave me hope. You should contact Lydia again. She still organises charity events, and you'd be an asset at one of those."

"I'm not ready, but I'll keep it in mind. Meanwhile, I'm volunteering with the Women's Voluntary Service, leading singing sessions with returning evacuee children."

"Evacuees are returning?" he asked. "Do they think the war's over?"

"Not at all, but parents are anxious to have their children back, especially as they've been gone for months now, and no war here. Some children weren't treated well at their billets. Remember Ryan?"

"Of course I do. Is he all right? Still in school?"

"Yes. Thank you again for driving him home. We're all grateful. Mum would like to visit you soon."

"I'd like that. And Kate, my love," he said as she kissed him good-bye, "don't give up on singing. You might need to sing for both of us."

She made no reply, but an ominous chill enveloped her.

The next day, she found Barry slumped against the pillows, a grey pallor to his cheeks. He coughed, a deep, rasping cough. He placed a frail arm on his chest. Kate watched helplessly, full of anguish as he took each labored breath.

"Does the doctor know about your cough?" she asked when his spasms subsided.

"Said it might be pneumonia. My lungs are infected."

"I'd better let you rest," she said. "But I'll be back tomorrow."

He smiled weakly. "I'll look forward to it, my love."

Kate feared this rapid deterioration and she wanted a medical opinion. She scoured the room. Nurse Fletcher stood at the far end perusing a patient's chart. Kate strode over to her.

"Excuse me, may I have a word?"

The nurse replaced the chart at the end of the bed. "Yes. Kate, isn't it?"

"I'm worried about Barry."

The nurse led Kate to the corridor.

"He has developed a nasty cough and says he might have pneumonia," Kate said.

"We know. We're treating it as best we can, but the prognosis isn't good. His chest wound isn't healing properly. I'm so sorry."

Kate's heart sank. "Let me give you a phone number. Please call if things change for the worse."

She scribbled the number of the school on a scrap of paper. "It's where I work. We're not on the phone at home."

The nurse nodded.

* *

The call came the next day while Kate taught her class. Mrs. Fitzgerald came into the assembly hall and tapped her on the shoulder. Singing stopped abruptly.

"Phone call for you," the older woman said.

Icy dread seized Kate's heart.

She tore to the office and picked up the receiver. She listened to the voice on the line, then let the phone drop to the floor.

Barry was dead.

CHAPTER 30
June 1940

K ate genuinely grieved for Barry. She had grown to love him, but realised it too late, and never told him. *How could I have let him die without telling him?* she chastised herself. She wouldn't forgive herself for not saying the important words, but with all her being, she hoped he knew. Even though she doubted all along he would survive, she came around to the idea that if he did, she would happily marry him. His lack of self-pity, concern for her, and courage endeared him to her. She felt profoundly sad about his shortened life and hoped he had not lost his life in vain. He had loved her, and she was glad for that. For both of them.

She cast around in her muddled mind for explanations. Her early affection for Barry was more like her love for Ryan, brotherly love based on protective feelings. And she'd felt a sense of duty towards this man who had shown such generosity, not only to her, but to her family. But with time it became something deeper. She understood she would have a true companion if she married him. But why did it take her so long to accept her feelings? Perhaps she was still a caterpillar after all, encased in a cocoon, unable to release herself and fly. And her conscience reminded her that, so far, she had contributed little to the war.

The school allowed her to take time away from teaching. After the shock wore off a few days after Barry's death, she drifted, distracted and despairing. The man she had promised her future to now had no future to offer her. She sat in her room with a book on her lap without reading it. She stared out the window, watching songbirds and mar-velling at their energetic search for food. Why did they sing? For pure joy? Her mother carefully avoided upsetting her, and encouraged her to practice the piano, but Kate continued to languish. She remem-bered her earlier belief that Barry would never be the cause of hurt feelings. How wrong she had been about that.

After three weeks of watching her do nothing more than go through the motions of life, Mary Grace convinced Kate to resume work with the children in the sick bay.

"Get dressed, Kate. You're coming to the clinic with me today."

"No thanks, Mum. I'm tired."

"Kate, the children need you. You can't honor Barry's memory by sitting at home."

Her mother's unusually harsh tone startled her into rising from her chair.

"We're all hurting, Kate. It doesn't bring him back. So do some-thing useful."

Mary Grace was right. Bringing smiles to the small ones' faces cheered her, and the childish voices that made the music sweet and pure comforted her. In her sorry state, she had completely forgotten Mr. Conway's instructions, until one day they came back to her in a flash: she needed to sing, herself, and commit to his process for recovery.

She began bit by bit. Each day she spent time in the dining room, singing every song she knew. She warbled up and down the scales, hearing the tone strengthen along with her spirits. On some days, Mary Grace set a glass of water by the piano and stopped to listen. Soon Kate deemed herself ready for another meeting with the thera-pist and told her mother how much he had helped her.

At her fourth meeting with Mr. Conway, she accepted his offer of a cup of tea.

"Without milk," he said. "Milk has a thick consistency that will affect your throat and compromise your singing."

She sipped the tea, enjoying the taste even without the milk.

"I see you like tea," he said.

She set the cup on the desk. *What is he getting at this time?* "Yes. Doesn't everyone?"

"No. What does tea represent to you?"

Kate shrugged. *What does tea have to do with singing?* But she understood he must have a reason to ask. She allowed herself to delve, and found the answer.

"My mother. She drinks tea all day long. Rationing has been hard on her. Tea is probably her main source of comfort, especially these days."

There it was again: the concept of comfort. "Actually, I wish I shared her love of simple things like good food. It has always been a source of contention between us."

"Aha. Does she like music?"

"Not really. That's another source of contention."

"Have you ever talked to her about music? Why you love it?"

"No," she snapped. Then softened her voice. "She has no interest."

"What are you practicing these days?"

"A Chopin Prelude, Number 15." In her lap, her right hand gently mimed the first notes.

"'The Raindrop Prelude,'" he said. "A lovely piece. There's much to learn from it."

She gazed at him in surprise. *He knows a lot about music.* "I haven't mastered the measures with strong chords yet," she said. "The ones that sound like thunder."

"But you will, with practice. How about the melody, played with single notes?"

"That's easier, mostly."

"Easier in some ways, yes. But what's all-important is the rhythm, the repeated A flat that represents the raindrops. All the chords follow the gentle pulse—monotonous, but persistent. Like a heartbeat."

She sat still, breathless. "Yes. Like daily life," she whispered. *And I've belittled its importance for so long.*

Mr. Conway took a long look at her.

Suddenly all the anger, frustration, pity, concern, and love she had felt for her mother crowded into her mind. She slumped in the chair, her mind in turmoil. A waterfall of emotions washed over her, almost drowning her with its force. Then she understood. *I've been at war with myself all these years.* She closed her eyes to allow the revelation to sink in. When she remembered where she was, she opened them. Mr. Conway hadn't moved. His kind expression hadn't changed. Words failed her; she basked in the wonder of it all. It was like the blackbird's song welcoming the dawn.

"Well, then. Time to progress to the exercises that will cure you," he said.

CHAPTER 31
June 1940

Hannah arrived on the Murphy's doorstep late one evening, wearing only pyjamas.

"Whatever's happened?" Kate asked at once. "Come in."

Hannah was sobbing. Kate immediately folded the girl in her arms.

"They took *Mutti* and Papa away," she stammered. "Put them in a van. *Mutti* told me to hide, so the men didn't see me. She told me to come to you after they were gone."

"You poor dear," Kate said, suddenly jolting into action, her muscles tense. "Let's go into the kitchen so you can tell me more." The moment Sarah feared had come, and Hannah was now her responsibility.

Mary Grace joined them. "Whatever's the matter?" she asked.

Hannah sat at the table, her head in her hands, crying so hard that her teardrops made small pools on the wooden surface. Kate mopped them up with a dishcloth, gave Hannah a handkercheif, and stroked the top of her head.

"Hannah's parents have been deported, I believe," Kate said to her mother, then whispered, "Sarah told me this might happen. She asked me to promise to care for Hannah months ago."

"Dear Lord. Why? This evil war, there's no telling what will happen. She can stay with us for a few days. We can make up a bed for her in the attic."

"Yes, that's best." *A few days? Longer, but that conversation can wait.*

Mary Grace left to ascend the stairs and Kate sat with Hannah until her sobs subsided. "You know we'll take care of you. I promised your mother," she said. "Meanwhile, we can try to discover where they took your parents."

"Thank you," Hannah said, wiping her eyes.

"We'll have to get you some clothes. Do you think we can go back to your house to collect them?"

"*No. Mutti* said I shouldn't return. They might take me away, too."

"All right. Let's see what we can do about clothes. I have some savings, and my mother can probably find some at the WVS Centre."

"If it's all right, I'd prefer to stay here with you for a while before going back to school."

"Fine. Would you like something to eat? How about some warm milk?"

"Maybe some milk."

Kate put a pan on the stove. After Hannah drank it, Kate led her to the attic, pausing to point out her own bedroom on the way in case Hannah needed her in the night. Mary Grace had already made up the bed in the attic and taped paper over the dormer's tiny window so the light from a small lamp on a trunk beside the bed didn't beam through.

"Good night, dear," Kate said, as she tucked the girl into bed. "You're safe here. Try to sleep."

When she peered into the room half an hour later, she found Hannah fast asleep. While glad that Hannah could rest, Kate expected she herself would have another sleepless night. The terrifying intrusion into the Bells' family home at night disturbed her deeply. Who knew such awful things happened in her own country? There was nothing she could imagine doing now except offering as much comfort as possible to the grieving and frightened girl.

Sean arrived home from work later than usual that evening. Kate waited up for him to tell him about Hannah's arrival.

He took off his wet coat and draped it on the stairwell banister.

"We don't have room for another person. Where did she come from? Why is she here?"

"Mum made up a bed for her in the attic. It's a long story. Perhaps Mum can tell you more in the morning. I hope you will agree that it will be all right for Hannah to stay with us for a while."

Sean looked puzzled, and his tired eyes had told her that a full discussion would best wait until later.

Both parents had already left for work when Kate arose the next morning. She busied herself in the kitchen assembling bread and eggs, thinking Hannah would need to keep as well-nourished as possible. Following her mother's example, she would provide Hannah a substantial breakfast to fortify her for the day. Surprised by a new maternal instinct, she took a deep breath. *Hannah is my responsibility*, she told herself again, *and I won't let her down*. She remembered that Sarah had a relative, her husband's sister Anna in America, who would welcome Hannah. She'd look for the contact information.

At eight o'clock, Hannah appeared sleepily in the kitchen doorway.

"Good morning," Kate said. "Did you sleep well?"

"Yes, thank you. I couldn't remember where I was when I woke up, but then I did . . . my parents are gone, Miss Murphy." Her eyes filled.

"We need to get some food into you. How about eggs and toast?"

"That sounds lovely," Hannah said.

"Sit down. I'll have breakfast ready in two shakes of a lamb's tail."

"Two shakes of a lamb's tail? I never heard that expression."

"Old country saying. Perhaps there's an equivalent in German."

Hannah drew her brows together. "Maybe, but I'm starting to forget my German. *Mutti* wants me to speak perfect English so no one will suspect my origins."

"Very wise. She wants the best, to ensure a good life for you."

"I know. I wonder if I will ever see her again . . ." her eyes filled once more.

We're going to wonder about many things in the weeks ahead. "We have to believe you will, Hannah." Kate scooped scrambled eggs onto a plate and set it down in front of the girl. "Dig in," she said. "Toast's on the way."

Ryan stumbled into the kitchen, hair tousled. He stopped as he saw that his usual chair was occupied. "Hey, who's this?"

"This is Hannah. She's staying with us for a while. Her parents had to leave," Kate said.

His stepped back to look at her. "Blimey, don't I know you? You're the girl who sang a solo at the school performance."

Hannah wiped her eyes, put her fork down, and stared at him. "Yes."

"I'm Ryan. Kate's brother. Jolly pleased to meet you again."

Kate noticed the questions in his face, but shook her head. He sat down beside Hannah.

"What a change to have such pleasant company for breakfast," he said, smiling wickedly. "Not used to it. Kate's so sad these days. We could all use some cheering up."

"That's enough, Ryan," Kate said, frowning. "Would you like me to make you some eggs, or do you want to make them for yourself?"

"Well, if you're offering, I'll take them."

Ryan bolted down his breakfast. "I'll feed Scooter, then I'll be on my way. See you later, I hope," he said to Hannah.

Hannah stood up. She had hardly touched her food. "He's nice," she said. "Let me help with the dishes."

"Thank you," Kate said. "Perhaps you'd like to have a bath, then we can go over to my mum's place of work and find you some clothes. I'll lend you some of mine in the meantime. They won't fit, but at least they're not pyjamas."

"You are all so kind to me, Miss Murphy. *Mutti* said you are a good woman. '*Eine gute Frau,*' she said."

"Please call me Kate. You're part of the family now."

Kate and Hannah arrived at the WVS Centre in the late morning. Mary Grace came over to them, introduced Hannah to her co-workers, and held up a pile of clothes.

"I've chosen these for you. Decide if you like them and see if they fit. If not, I can look for more."

Hannah picked up each item of clothing, examined it briefly, and set it down.

"Everything's nice," she said. "May I change into some of these new things now?"

Mary Grace showed her into a dressing room. Five minutes later, Hannah emerged wearing a dark blue dress. The style suited her, and heads turned as she crossed the floor.

"She's a pretty girl," Mary Grace said.

Kate glanced at Hannah with approval, and beckoned to her mother. They moved to a corner of the room.

"Did you talk to Dad about our keeping Hannah?" Kate whispered.

"I did. He worries about our finances and the extra expense, but for now he's accepted the idea of her staying. He remembers her from the play."

"Thank you for talking to him, Mum, and for Hannah's clothes. I'll take her for a walk. There's time before lunch and it's a fine day. We can visit the ducks in the pond."

"I'd like that," Hannah said, when Kate told her.

Mary Grace had folded the clothes and stowed them in a suitcase. "I'll bring them home for you. Go on and enjoy your walk. It'll do you both good."

They walked for a while in silence. When they left the shops on High Street and reached the river Hannah said, "You left school for a while. May I ask why? Were you ill?"

"No. My fiancé died."

"So sorry. Now we both have sadness. Is that what your brother was talking about at breakfast?"

Kate nodded. "I'm going back to school this week, though. Perhaps you would like to come to my singing class. School will be out for the summer soon, but I'll keep directing the choir. The nuns want the girls to sing at church. I can talk to Sister Mary Joseph about it, if you like."

"Yes, please." Hannah grasped Kate's arm. "But whatever you say, don't mention that my family are Jews. We mustn't mention that to anyone, not even your family. It could be dangerous for them."

"I understand. My lips are sealed."

Oh dear, I hope my promise to care for Hannah won't put the family at risk, Kate thought, lowering her head and avoiding Hannah's eyes.

They reached the upper pond and watched the mallards as they quacked and dipped their heads in the water. A few tufted ducks dived and then surfaced, crests raised like unruly hairstyles.

"I can't swim," Hannah said.

"Can't you? Then I'll have to teach you. It's fun."

"I've always been afraid of drowning."

"There are swimming baths nearby. We can go there, if you'd like. You can learn to overcome your fear. Then someday you will go to the seaside and swim in the sea. It's lovely in summer. We used to go every year when I was younger. We made sand castles."

"Castles out of sand. That sounds like a dream to me. I remember the dark castles, terrible places, full of giants and dragons, in Germany. I used to have nightmares about them."

"Sand castles can't do anyone harm, and anyway, they wash away with the tide."

"I'd like to build one. I'd like to have happy dreams again."

"You will."

But will she? Kate thought. Nightmares seemed more likely.

Hannah tossed a stone into the water causing a ring of ripples that rocked the ducks as they swam.

"We have to be like ducks," Kate said. "See how they float, bobbing up and down, getting on with their lives and letting water run off their backs? I admire them."

"I like them, too, but I'd rather be a songbird. Now I'm hungry. Can we go home and have lunch?"

She sounds childish just now, Kate thought. *She's usually so precocious—though at twelve, she's barely more than a child.* An orphan, missing her parents. But singing. They shared that goal, the one her grandmother Ellen had urged for Kate. Having responsibility for Hannah added new purpose to Kate's life. She had spent the last several months worrying about Barry, and almost made herself sick in the process. She allowed school to become a dull routine, even letting the pleasure she felt at hearing music fade. Now Hannah needed attention. Helping her might be the tonic they both needed. The girl was good company, and she wanted lunch.

When they arrived home, they encountered Mary Grace in the kitchen. She had piled tea-making ingredients on the table. She reached into the pantry shelves, muttering to herself.

"What on earth's the matter, Mum?" Kate asked. "I thought you were working at the Centre all day?"

"I came home early. I'm weighing tea. What rubbish. This stupid war. Do you know what they've done now? *They've rationed tea.* Two ounces a week. *Only two!* We usually go through half a pound. How are we going to manage without tea?"

"Oh dear. Most upsetting, I agree. But why are you putting tea on the table?"

"I want to see how much we have. We must economise. We've got enough for two days."

"It's all right, I don't need tea, Mrs. Murphy," Hannah said. "We drank coffee at home." Her tears smarted, and she made for the attic.

Kate met her mother's eyes. "Best leave her alone. She doesn't want to be a burden."

"I must admit, it won't be easy, having another mouth to feed," Mary Grace said.

Kate said nothing. Her mother spoke the truth, and Ryan, a

growing boy, was eating more than his share of rations these days. But what choice did they have? She'd eat less herself, if necessary.

"It's lunch time. Can I help?" she said finally.

"Let's get these things off the table. I made vegetable soup yesterday, and there's some left over. At least they're not rationing bread yet."

Kate climbed the stairs to tell Hannah lunch awaited her. The girl lay on her back on the bed, one arm covering her eyes.

"I'm not very hungry, thank you."

"Please. You said you were, and it's important to stay healthy."

"Maybe later."

Hannah removed her arm from her eyes. Kate noted the tear-streaked face and went back downstairs. *It takes time to stop grieving, and this is only her first day,* Kate thought sadly. She had lost a fiancé, but not her parents, and she was twenty, not twelve. She would do all she could to ease the girl's pain.

CHAPTER 32
July 1940

R yan arrived home for supper in football boots and a sweaty shirt. "Starving," he said, taking a seat next to Kate at the kitchen table.

Mary Grace glanced at him from the sink. "I'll have Welsh rarebit ready in a little while. Take those filthy shoes off. Have you been playing with the twins?"

"Only Tommy. His head lice have cleared up now. Had a terrible time with his billet. Told me he slept in the kitchen. They didn't have a bathroom, only an outhouse, and he only had a bath every few weeks. Dirt poor, the family was. Surprised they took him in, but they made him work for it."

"I treated him at the clinic," Mary Grace said. "Felt bad for him. What about Francis? Why didn't he play with you?"

"Francis lost interest in football. Seems he stayed with rich people and learned to ride. Thinks he's too good for us," Ryan said. "All he talks about is horses. He wants to work with them and says he's going to Epsom to see the race horses soon. He almost didn't come home, his life in Devon was so much fun. The twins turn fourteen next month, so they can leave school and home as well."

"Their mother won't like that. What's Tommy planning to do?"

"He doesn't know. Might work on the railway like his dad."

"I don't know what to think these days," Mary Grace moaned. "You and your friends left as boys and came back young men. You'll be fourteen yourself, soon."

He grinned. "Well, I'm not leaving school. Not yet, anyway. Do I get a cake? With candles?"

"A small one. Too expensive otherwise."

"Hey, no fair."

"Why don't you make yourself useful and go upstairs to tell Hannah supper's almost ready? And wash your hands."

He left the room, taking the stairs two at a time.

"I'm glad he's decided to stay in school. I wonder what he'll do when he grows up," Mary Grace said.

"He said something about being a vet," Kate replied. "Ryan learned a lot at that farm. He doesn't want to be a farmer, but he likes animals."

"Hmm. He does take good care of that chicken, I must say."

Later, at supper, Ryan said, "I see Hannah's sleeping in the attic. She might be more comfortable in my bedroom. I don't mind swapping rooms. I've always liked the attic. Used to play up there with my trains."

"That's nice of you, but I don't want to disrupt the household," Hannah said quickly, putting down her fork.

"Really, it's no trouble. I had worse accommodations at my billet."

"The government's Pied Piper scheme wasn't such a good idea after all," Mary Grace said angrily. "Child abuse, I call it."

"I understand there's a new government programme to send children to safety overseas," Kate said. "The papers this morning had an announcement. They need volunteers to interview parents who want their children to go. They're also looking for escorts to accompany them."

"Why on earth?" Mary Grace exclaimed. "Whose parents would send them so far away? It was bad enough packing them off to the country. And there hasn't even been any bombing."

"But there will be."

Mary Grace crossed herself. "You've finished your meal, Hannah dear. Good for you."

"Mum, they want me back at school tomorrow," Kate said. "Can Hannah stay here with you while I'm gone?"

"Yes, that's fine. I'm not expected at the WVS clinic until later this week."

"Fine. Now I'll go and change the bedsheets."

"I'll help," Hannah said.

As they left, Kate overheard Mary Grace say softly to Ryan, "That was a kind gesture. Thank you," and Ryan's whispered reply, "I like her."

"So kind of Ryan to give me his room," Hannah said to Kate and Mary Grace at breakfast the next day. "I slept better last night than for as long as I can remember."

"The trains didn't bother you, I hope," Kate said.

"I heard them, but I went back to sleep after they passed."

"You'll get used to them. What would you like to do today while I'm at school?"

"How about if I help your mum cook? I love cooking and want to learn more about English recipes. I'd like to learn about gardening, too."

Mary Grace stared at Hannah, a new appreciation in her eyes. "A girl after my own heart," she said. "Now, if you really mean it, how about peeling apples for an apple crumble? We can make it for pudding tonight."

"Happy to do that. Perhaps I could make *rugelach* for you sometime."

"I've never heard of that. What's in it?" Kate asked.

"It's a kind of pastry. Let me think a sec. Flour, butter, cream cheese, jam or cinnamon to make it sweet. And sugar and walnuts." Hannah smiled with obvious pride.

"Sounds delicious," Mary Grace said. "We'll make it for a special occasion, then. Here are the apples. You need to wash them, then peel, core, and chop them into slices."

"Just thinking. Perhaps I won't go to school today after all," Kate said. "I might learn more about cooking, along with Hannah. I'll run along and tell them. They can get by without me, and school's almost out for the summer, anyway."

"Good," her mother said. "We'll wait for you."

Kate didn't want to say anything in front of Hannah, but since Hannah was her responsibility, Kate wanted to be there. She spoke briefly to Sister Mary Joseph, who understood. When she returned home, Hannah and Mary Grace were sitting at the kitchen table drinking tea.

"All right. Let's get started," Mary Grace said, putting her teacup in the sink.

Kate noted how deftly Hannah prepared the fruit. Mary Grace made the topping by rubbing margarine into the flour to the consistency of breadcrumbs. Then she added sugar.

"When you've finished chopping, we'll spread the crumble on top. It will cook quickly, and then I'll go shopping for fish for supper. We'll have to queue up, I expect. You can come with me, if you'd like."

Hannah nodded.

"We'll both come," Kate said.

The house smelled of apples as they left. Mary Grace carried a shopping bag, and they strolled along Holly Road to the shops on High Street. A line of women waited outside the fishmonger's.

Mrs. Harris, standing at the end, greeted them. "And who's this?" she asked, glancing at the girl.

"Hannah, a family friend, staying with us for a while," Mary Grace said.

"Nice for you to have another girl at 'ome, I'm sure. My boys only just got back, and now they want to leave again."

"At least they came back from their billets."

"Right. Changed. Not sure for the better. Tommy told me you 'elped 'im with 'is lice."

"Yes. Nasty."

Another woman joined the queue leading a large Alsatian dog.

"Wait a minute! You can't stand 'ere with that animal," Mrs. Harris shouted. "That's a *German* dog."

"Yeah. It ought to be shot," another woman exclaimed.

Kate winced. *Foolish women*, she thought. She watched Hannah's face turn white, then grasped her arm and led her away. "Let's forget the fish, Mum," she said. "We can have bangers and mash instead."

Hannah trembled. "People hate us, Kate."

"Not you. The Nazis."

But there was little comfort she could offer. As the war progressed and news of the Germans' success and fear of invasion increased, people's rage mounted. Kate wanted to understand more about Hannah's family's past in Germany, but this wasn't the time to ask.

CHAPTER 33
July 1940

Since Hannah and Mary Grace seemed to get along, Kate returned to school the following day. To her relief, Sean had expressed no thoughts that the girl should leave. He had asked about her best subjects in school and smiled his ready smile when she told him, "Music, with my favourite teacher Miss Murphy."

Perhaps it was time to find out if her sessions with Mr. Conway and the exercises she had practiced would allow her to perform without the dreaded hiccups. Barry had urged her to keep singing and to contact Lydia about opportunities. She rummaged around looking for Lydia's phone number in her pigeon hole at school, cursing herself for her disorderly ways—ones her mother rightly abhorred—before finally unearthing the piece of paper. She'd call soon.

Back home at the end of the day, she discovered her mother measuring scoops of tea.

"That's two teaspoons," she said. "I'm keeping these for testing. Pamela Warren told me you can make twenty cups of tea from two ounces by re-using the leaves. Maybe I can squeeze more if I use less. As you know, when I'm home, I drink tea all day long. Keeps me going. My one luxury. This rationing is a real hardship for tea drinkers, you know."

"It is. Where's Hannah? How did it go today?"

"She's upstairs. We had a lovely day. She's good company. But she worries about staying here. She persists in thinking everyone hates her, especially after that incident yesterday with the dog."

"Well, no wonder she was upset. She believes she's not welcome in this country and has proof of that, too, with her parents being taken away."

"How much do we know about that?" Mary Grace asked.

"Not much. When Hannah's stronger, I'll ask her more. I told her I'd make enquiries about their whereabouts."

"I feel sorry for her. We must help her."

"Thank you, Mum. She won't stay forever. Her mother told me she should go to live with her Aunt Anna in America."

That night on her way to bed, Kate stopped by Hannah's bedroom door and heard muffled sobs. *Better not to disturb.*

The following day, Kate again left Hannah with Mary Grace. Pleased that things continued to go well, Kate turned her thoughts to singing. Surprised, she realised that the music she heard as she traipsed to the phone box to call Lydia was herself humming. *Maybe I'm happier these days.* She had been following Ian Conway's exercise routine, and his words echoed in her head each time she practiced: "Pause. Concentrate on breathing. Make your mind blank. Relax all parts of your body." *Remember to be comfortable, and don't try too hard*, she told herself.

She dialed Lydia's number, deposited the coins, and waited. Lydia's voice came on the line.

"Lydia, Kate Murphy here. Do you remember me? Barry's friend."

"Kate? Yes. You and he were engaged, I heard. Tragedy, his dying."

"I know. He asked me to contact you about something."

"Anything for Barry. What?"

"A singing engagement. He said you might want someone to perform at a charity event."

"Forgive me. I had forgotten. We do have something coming up, a benefit to raise funds for Spitfires. This Saturday. Are you interested?"

"Yes, but I understood you would want to try me out first."

"Actually no. There's no time. What would you sing?"

"Anything popular."

"Excellent. Seven o'clock at the Casterbridge Hotel."

"I know the one. I'll be there. Thank you."

She hung up the receiver. *What have I done?* She asked herself. *I must be crazy. What if I fail? What if I hiccup?* Then she told herself firmly: *I just need to follow Mr. Conway's instructions.*

At tea time, Mary Grace reported she had enjoyed another day with Hannah. They'd worked in the garden weeding and gathering beans, lettuce, and radishes.

"She loves all the fresh vegetables," Mary Grace said. "Her family didn't grow any. Didn't have a garden, she said. We're fortunate that way, and this year the yield is better than ever."

"Probably on account of all your hard work, Mum," Kate said.

Her mother beamed. "I suppose so, but the chicken manure from Ryan's bird helped, too."

The front door banged, and Sean strode in. "So much to do at work these days," he grumbled. "With four of the younger staff off to war, the load on the rest of us has doubled."

"At least you still have a job, and you're over the age limit for conscription," Mary Grace said. "Let me fetch you a pint."

"I won't say no," Sean said, sitting down and yawning. He took up the mug of brown ale and drank a few mouthfuls. "The lads asked me to join them at the Sun, but I told them I had to be getting home. It costs too much to drink there—and we have another mouth to feed."

Kate heard her father's veiled complaint and started coughing. Telling herself to remain calm, she paused, took a deep breath, and managed to contain the hiccup that fought its way into her throat. She sighed with relief. Perhaps she would succeed at her singing engagement.

"I'm not teaching tomorrow," she said to Mary Grace. "I'll take Hannah off your hands, if you like."

"No need for that. I like her company."

"We can share her, then. The weather is so warm, I'd like to take her to the baths. She told me she wants to learn how to swim."

"I could teach her," Mary Grace said, "although I'd prefer to bake with her tomorrow. She has a special pastry she wants to make for us. This will work out well. I'll go shopping for the ingredients tomorrow while you're at the baths."

Kate could hardly believe she was competing with her mother for Hannah's companionship, but that was a good thing. She broached the subject of swimming later that evening.

Hannah clasped her hands. "You know I'm terrified of water. I got seasick on the voyage from Germany from the fierce waves rocking the boat."

"The water in the pool will be calm, and you can overcome your fear," Kate said. "You'll see . . . I would never put you at risk."

The next morning, they set out for the public baths. It was a fine summer day, not something to count on in England even in July, and the women milling around wore summer clothes—cotton dresses, hats, and sunglasses. Gardens of roses, phlox, and Canterbury bells brightened their way. In the women's changing rooms, Kate handed Hannah one of her old swimsuits and a towel.

At the pool, the potent smell of chlorine wafted towards them. Hannah stood at the side and stared into the aqua-coloured water. She dipped a toe. "Not cold."

"I'll get in first, then help you. This is the shallow end. You'll be able to stand," Kate said. She sat on the edge of the pool, then slipped in and swam to the other side, turned, and came back. She swam almost without splashing, her arms arcing gracefully as she glided through the water. "It's lovely," she breathed. "Now let yourself down the ladder. I'll be right here beside you."

"I'm really afraid. I'd rather watch you swim. You make it look so easy."

"It *is* easy, once you know how."

Just like baking, once you know how. But you have to be interested, or it's difficult for anyone to help you, Kate thought. *How could I have resisted for so long?*

Despite her jitters, Hannah gripped the rail and stepped backwards onto the first rung of the ladder. When she reached the bottom, she looked around for Kate.

"I'm here." Kate wrapped her arms round Hannah's slim body and gently pried her from the rail. "See, you can stand. Now, put your face in the water. Like you would in the bathtub."

Hannah obeyed. Her dark hair splayed down her back in thick strands. There were few other swimmers in the pool and the water stayed calm.

"Now hold my hands and let your legs float up behind you."

"I'm not sure I can do that."

"You can. I'll hold you. You won't sink."

Hannah steeled herself and grasped Kate's hands strongly, pulling her closer.

"It won't work that way," Kate said. "First give yourself a second to pause, take a breath, put your face in the water, and stretch your arms out. Then let your legs float to the surface."

Hannah tried again. This time, it worked. "*Heavens,*" she shrieked. "I'm a fish!"

Kate laughed. "Good progress. Let's repeat this."

After a while, Hannah began to shiver, and they climbed out of the pool.

"I enjoyed that," the girl said. "Let's come again."

"We will. You'll be swimming in no time, you'll see."

That afternoon, Hannah measured the ingredients for *rugelach*. Kate and Mary Grace watched.

"It's an easy recipe," Hannah said, "but *Mutti* told me you have to be careful not to mix the dough too much or the pastry gets tough."

Mary Grace nodded sagely and turned on the oven.

Hannah weighed the flour, butter, cream cheese, and salt and made a soft dough. Then she divided the mound into three parts, flattening each one into a circle. While letting the dough rest in the pantry, the coolest part of the house, she chopped walnuts and combined them in a bowl with sugar, raisins, and cinnamon. Finally, she rolled the dough into twelve-inch circles, then spread the walnut filling on top, pressing it in with her fingers. She cut the rounds into sixteen wedges and rolled each one into a crescent shape.

"These look delicious," Mary Grace said. "How long should we bake them?"

"Until they get brown."

While Hannah arranged the pieces on a baking sheet and placed them in the oven, a knock sent Mary Grace scurrying to the door to answer.

"You're good at baking, Hannah," Kate said, then noticed the girl's moist eyes. "What's wrong?"

"It's just—making these things brings back memories," she sniffed. "We used to sing while we worked."

"All right. Let's sing now."

"Not now. It'll only make me sadder. You won't know the songs, anyway."

Kate handed her a handkerchief. *Oh dear. Perhaps letting her bake and triggering old memories is a mistake. I should know. Better to let some things go.* She cast a worried glance at the girl.

Mary Grace blustered into the kitchen, their neighbour Pamela Warren following close behind.

"Pamela brought us some tea," Mary Grace said, placing a package on the table.

Pamela scraped back a chair as she took a seat. "We don't drink it as much as you, and I know you can use it."

"How thoughtful of you," Mary Grace said. "Hannah, our young friend here, is baking. Perhaps you'd like to try one of these special pastries. They'll be ready in a few minutes."

"They smell wonderful," Pamela said.

"Would you like something to drink?"

"Not tea," Pamela said. "A glass of water would be fine, thank you. You know, I've been busy, working on my M.O. submissions. It's amazing how many things you notice when you have to write them down."

Kate studied Mrs. Warren's expression. *Perhaps she's a good observer. Too good.* She'd heard about neighbours passing information about suspected spies to the government. She felt a slight uneasiness as they waited for the pastry.

Soon it turned brown and the buttery filling sizzled, spilling on the baking sheet. Hannah took a mitt and reached into the oven. "Done," she declared. "Shall I put the kettle on?"

"Please do, dear. She's such a help to me," Mary Grace said, catching Pamela's eye.

Hannah brought plates, cups, and milk, transferred the sticky pastries to a platter, and set everything on the table.

Pamela delicately picked up a pastry. "What do you call these?"

"*Rugelach.*"

Kate and Mary Grace declared the sweets delectable, but Pamela made no comment.

"Thank you so much for sharing these," she said. "I must be on my way."

"I'll see you out," Mary Grace said. Kate followed, and they passed into the hallway. Then Pamela reached and shut the kitchen door firmly behind her.

Lowering her voice to a whisper, she said, "I've had these confections before, in Germany. They're delicacies that Jews make. Is Hannah a Jew?"

Kate looked sharply at Pamela but held her tongue.

Mary Grace scratched her head. "No, I don't think so. Her parents are German—but the truth is, I have no idea."

"Hmm. I'd be careful if I were you. Many people dislike Jews in this country. You've heard about what Hitler is doing over there in Germany."

"Yes. Killing them. Anyway, thank you for coming, and for the tea."

Kate kept silent, but looked anxiously at her mother. *Should I tell her?*

After supper, Mary Grace invited Kate upstairs to her parents' bedroom. "I have to know. Is Hannah Jewish?"

Kate plunked down on the bed. "Yes. Hannah told me not to tell anyone. She knows the danger to us all and to herself. Now that you know, we will have to be careful not to let word get around. Best if you and I keep this to ourselves. Can you trust Mrs. Warren to be discreet? We don't want her reporting that a Jewish girl is in hiding here."

Mary Grace frowned. "I'll talk to her."

"Listen, I think the best plan would be for Hannah to join her aunt in America. We must work out a way to get her there. I'll make some inquiries. Maybe she can go as part of the new CORB Programme."

"I hate to see her go. I'm becoming attached to the girl—but I suppose that's right."

Kate didn't sleep well that night. Things had become complicated, and now more frightening. The thought crossed her mind that it would be difficult, and perhaps impossible, to keep her promise to Sarah Bell and keep Hannah safe, let alone follow her own dreams at the same time.

CHAPTER 34
July 1940

Later that week, Mrs. Fitzgerald talked to Kate in the staff room between classes.

"Have you read about CORB, the Children's Overseas Reception Board?" she asked, holding a newspaper.

"Yes, a little. That's the programme for sending children overseas. It costs money, doesn't it?"

"Only if children attend private or parochial schools like ours. It's a clever idea. Until now the only children who've gone abroad have been from well-to-do families. The government recognises that's unfair, and children of all classes, including those at state-supported schools, should have an opportunity to go, free. They're recruiting escorts, too. I'd volunteer, but I'm too old."

"What do you mean, too old? What are the requirements?"

Mrs. Fitzgerald opened the paper. "Under fifty-five, experience with children, good sailors, available at a moment's notice."

Kate sat up, alert. She fit the qualifications exactly. "What requirements for the children?"

"Between five and sixteen, fit and suitable, with excellent references from teachers."

"What does suitable mean?"

Mrs. Fitzgerald ran her eyes down the column. "Well-behaved, presentable as ambassadors for Britain."

Kate guffawed. "Ambassadors? At five years old?"

"The paper says seven thousand parents a day apply for their children. Need both parents' consent, no war orphans or children of German refugees, or Jews."

Kate's mind whirled. No children of German refugees. Or Jews. So Hannah couldn't go. *Or could she? No one at school would guess. Her English is perfect.* And perhaps she, Kate, would go as an escort. But how might they raise funds for Hannah's passage?

On Saturday morning, Kate warmed up to prepare for her singing engagement that evening. She drank several glasses of water to lubricate her throat, then practiced the exercises Mr. Conway had taught her, remembering to pause first.

Hannah's face peered round the door of the piano room. "It's nice to hear you singing again. You're practicing. Are you performing somewhere?"

"Hush. Don't tell anyone. I'm singing at a charity event tonight."

"Wonderful! Are you nervous?"

"Trying not to be. I have to admit I suffer from stage fright."

"No good, being frightened. You must take the plunge, as I did at the pool this week. I was scared of the water, but once I got in, it was fine with you there to help. Will anyone go with you to the concert?"

"No, but that's all right. If no one knows me, I won't be embarrassed if something goes wrong."

"Nothing will go wrong. Good luck."

We're both taking risks these days, confronting our fears, Kate thought. At least, thanks to Mr. Conway's tutoring, she felt prepared for this experience. She dressed for the event in a nice blouse and skirt, letting her hair fall in soft curls around the shoulders. She slipped into low-heeled pumps, and hoped her appearance was suitable for the occasion.

The sliver of a new moon rose over the rooftops. After telling her mother she was going out, she caught the bus, which took her straight to the Casterbridge Hotel. An enormous banner displayed at the entrance read SPITFIRE FIGHTER FUND. Several expensive cars parked outside. Another gathering of posh people, she supposed. Straightening her shoulders, she strode in.

The large hall held an assembly of well-dressed guests. Most held drinks, and cigarette smoke clouded the room. Kate located Lydia among her friends looking impossibly chic in a sparkly dress and a bright barrette in her hair. *That's probably the sort of outfit I should wear*, Kate thought, then caught herself. *It doesn't matter. My voice is the star, not my clothes.* She approached Lydia, forcing a smile.

"Kate, so glad you could make it. Let me get you a drink."

"Just water, please."

She examined the room. A microphone stood on a podium at one end. With a twinge, she thought how much easier things would be if Barry were at her side accompanying her as she sang. *Sing for both of us.* Lydia handed her a glass.

"I'll introduce you and encourage people to be generous with their donations, then you can start."

Kate stepped to the podium, her stomach fluttering. Lydia tapped the microphone, then spoke in a clear voice. "Welcome, everyone, and thank you for coming." Feeling light-headed, Kate hardly heeded the host's words until she heard her own name followed by applause. She grasped the microphone, paused, listened for the first note in her head, took a deep breath, and then began to sing: "We'll meet again, don't know where, don't know when . . . "

An audible sigh came from the audience as they recognised the popular tune. As she sang the last words and the sounds died away, the audience applauded. She bowed slightly in acknowledgement. *That went well*, she thought with relief. *I only need to keep it up.* She conjured a mental image of Mr. Conway. *Pause. Breathe. Sing as if my life depended on it.* She sang again. Louder applause. Her confidence grew with the next song, and even more with the third. As she sang, her anxiety receded and she felt the thrill of her voice rising, taking the audience with her.

Finally, she lowered the microphone and took a deep bow.

"Encore!" someone shouted.

"Yes! Encore!"

What should I sing for my last song? She hadn't prepared, but then she knew. Breaking from Vera Lynn's repertoire, she began.

"Morning has broken, like the first morning. Blackbird has spoken, like the first bird . . ."

That brought people to their feet. She had done it—all without a single hiccup.

Lydia stopped her as she stepped down from the podium and gave her a hug. "You're every bit as good as Barry said," she gushed. "You truly uplifted our spirits tonight. I can't thank you enough. Please do come again."

Kate could hardly utter her thanks as emotions flooded through her veins. It was almost as though Barry were there, urging her on. As she floated into the starry night, she couldn't contain her happiness. She had spread pleasure to others and experienced in herself the richness that only music could provide when she gave it her best. Barry had thrown her a lifeline and she had caught it. She felt intensely and gratefully alive.

The Casterbridge Hotel wasn't in the best neighbourhood. Litter and sandbags lined the streets beside dark buildings that loomed overhead. Kate hurried to the bus stop, glancing at her watch. Ten o'clock. She wondered how late the buses ran in that area and scolded herself for having failed to check. She rummaged in her handbag for money, not sure if she had enough for a taxi. She didn't. She shifted from one foot to the other, her impatience growing, while sensing something threatening in the almost moonless night. She'd read stories about single women facing attacks in some parts of London. She scanned her surroundings. In the dim starlight she saw a man in a derby hat drawing near. He appeared respectable, and she considered asking him to wait with her at the bus stop, but he seemed in a hurry and sped past before she had a chance to halt him. Few cars passed, their headlights dimmed.

How she wished she had asked her father to accompany her. Or Ryan. Now her desire to keep her life private might jeopardise her safety. Her earlier buoyant mood evaporated. She sat down on the curb. Perhaps no one would bother her if she resembled a dark mound on the ground. She sat for a long time, hugging her knees. It was past eleven, and no bus. The charity event at the hotel had ended by now, the wealthy attendees whisked away in their limousines. Kate pulled herself up. She would walk.

She set off down the street. Best to keep to the main roads and avoid side streets and alleys. Her pumps tapped her rhythmic stride: *tap, tap, tap.* Unexpectedly comforting, the sound of her footsteps— like music, she thought. Then she discerned louder treads behind, drawing closer. *Don't look back. Pause. Take a breath*, she told herself.

"Hello, young lady. Want some company?" a coarse voice boomed.

She jumped and ran, her hair flying in the wind, as fast as her feet could take her. Ahead, she spied blue lights. *Thank God! A police station!*

She almost fell up the steps leading to the door and pushed it. Thankfully, it gave in to the pressure. She collapsed at the entrance.

An hour and two cups of strong tea later, she arrived home. The police gave her a lift after admonishing her about the danger of walking alone at night in London in the blackout. Her family and Hannah listened soberly to her shaky account of the experience.

Almost completely lost in the telling was her wonderful success in singing at the charity event.

CHAPTER 35
July 1940

The news in early July did nothing to raise anyone's hopes for Britain's victory over Germany. On July 10, the Battle of Britain began in the air. The Luftwaffe bombed the Channel Islands, Wales, Scotland, and Ireland. Hitler announced plans to invade Britain under the code name Operation Sea Lion. Suddenly, the war seemed closer.

A parcel arrived addressed to Kate. It contained the few possessions left by Barry in the hospital. Inside she found photographs, one of his Bentley, and another of his parents and brother Kevin, all marked on the back, taken on a sunny day in the country. Kevin resembled Barry, with the same dark hair and thin frame. Their smiles touched her. Good people. Something rattled at the bottom of the box. A key. Puzzled, she took it out and examined it. Then she saw an envelope. She tore it open.

Dear Miss Murphy,

Barry asked me to give you this key to his car. He said he has nothing else to give you and wants you to have it. His address is 33 Surrey Road, Sutton.

My condolences on your loss.

Sincerely yours,

Jane Fletcher, RN

Kate stared at the box and its contents, fingering the small key lying cold in her hand. She regretted again her failure to tell him she loved him. That would surely have eased his last days. She hoped again that he knew, perhaps even before she did.

But what would she do with the car? No one in the family had learned to drive, and they couldn't afford lessons, even if they wanted them. The car might come in useful, though, and she was grateful.

Following her frightening late-night street experience, Kate felt more sympathy for Hannah's troubles. Having lived a sheltered life, she had little understanding of the difficulties Hannah and her family must have faced during their escape from Germany, and she was eager to learn more. She wanted to discover the Bells' whereabouts and longed to ease the girl's pain. But where to begin?

"Hannah, you're aware we're all concerned about your safety," Kate said after school one day. "I understand it may be difficult, but it would help if you told me more about your life in Germany before you came here."

Hannah's narrow shoulders stiffened. "What do you want to know? My mother said I should keep it to myself, and she didn't tell me much. I was a child."

"Listen, what happened to your parents here is horrible. We want to discover where they live now. What could have prompted an arrest in the middle of the night?"

Hannah lowered her gaze. "Nothing my parents did, I'm sure of that." She paused, squeezed her eyes then opened them, meeting Kate's urgent stare. "All right. You're my friend. If you promise not to talk to anyone about this, I'll tell you what I know."

Kate moved closer to her on the couch in the living room, leaning her head towards her to assure her they were co-conspirators. Hannah fiddled with the sleeve of her cardigan.

"We had a nice life in Berlin. My father had a job and my mother had lots of friends and parties. She collected paintings, lovely ones, and we had them on our walls. Papa loved music. He played the piano and went to the opera."

"So that's where you inherited your talent," Kate said.

"I suppose so. Then one day, we learned he couldn't work anymore. We couldn't pay our bills. Other men, friends of Papa's, lost their jobs, too. We saw smashed windows in shops all around us. Nasty words appeared on walls with stars of David. I stopped going to school after my school friends made fun of me. They called me *Schweinhund*. Pig dog."

Kate sat speechless. Her mind swept back to the time in her childhood when she had been bullied. Her unruly red hair and freckles made her a target, and older girls called her carrot top, forcing her to block her ears and run away as fast as her small legs would carry her. They had teased her about her left handedness as well. Her teachers considered it an abnormality that she needed to correct. Mary Grace held it against her, saying people would call her southpaw. The nuns at school snatched pencils from her left hand. Kate was forced to adapt to the right-handed world and learn to write as everyone else did. She endured this humiliation in private, not daring to tell her mother, who worried to death about everything. But as she remembered her own painful experience, Kate knew that the persecution of Jews in Germany had gone far beyond the level of name-calling and harassment of people who were different. Kate's troubles were not life threatening, but perhaps Hannah's were. Her anger flared anew at the shame and injustice imposed on innocent victims.

"People can be cruel, even school children," Kate said, her eyes burning. "They often learn from adults, who should know better. How old were you?"

"Seven. Papa said we had to leave. He spent hours waiting to see a man called Herr Foley who he said could get us visas to go to England. They cost us everything we had. Papa sold the paintings, the big piano, his music scores, most of *Mutti's* jewelry. Finally, we got our visas, and came here on a train and then a boat. We changed our name from Belowitz to Bell. My parents said we were the lucky ones. Terrible things are happening now to the Jews in Germany."

"Where did you live when you arrived here?" Kate asked.

"At my *Tante* Anna's house. Then she went to America. She wanted us to follow her, but we didn't have enough money. *Mutti* said if anything happened, I should go."

"Hmm. Let's think about that. But where's the house, the one you've left?"

"23 Hornet Avenue. You must promise not to tell anyone."

"My family will want to know your story, but I suppose it's best that we not say anything."

Hannah screwed up her face. "I've said too much already."

"I may need their help, if I'm to discover where those men took your parents, and I'd have to tell them your old address, at least."

Hannah gave Kate a savage stare. "*You mustn't go there.* People might be watching. I couldn't bear it if something happened to you."

"All right. I won't go. But perhaps someone else can, someone we trust. Leave it to me."

"I don't know . . . those people are mean. When they took *Mutti* and Papa, some people were shouting awful things, like 'good riddance, dirty Jews,'"

Here in England? Kate thought, horrorstruck. "So, is it possible your neighbours betrayed you and notified the authorities?"

Hannah hung her head. "Maybe. *Mutti* said it's hard to know who to trust."

Kate had heard more than enough. Her own neighbour had guessed Hannah's Jewish heritage. And she hadn't seemed sympathetic.

It was time to do something. Fast.

Clearly, Hannah had to leave. If she needed permission, possibly Mary Grace and Sean could sign as guardians, and Kate could accompany the girl as a CORB escort. Kate wasted no time locating the instructions in the newspaper about applying. Escort duties included travelling with up to fifteen child evacuees and ensuring they followed the rules for safety and good hygiene. Applicants would be interviewed and selection would be rigorous. Passports were not required.

She would have to talk to her parents and Ryan about her plan. Having gained Hannah's permission to tell the family more about the plight of Jews, Kate sat down with them over dinner. Hannah preferred not to join them for the discussion. When Kate had told them all she knew, they sat silently for a few minutes.

"An awful situation. I had no clue . . . " Mary Grace said. "The poor family. Hannah."

"I've heard rumours, but they're hard to believe," Sean said. "Now we know. All the more reason to keep fighting. But our own countrymen treating innocent people so badly . . . that's unforgiveable."

Ryan jumped up. "I'll go and investigate what happened to the Bells," he said, his eyes blazing. "I'm not afraid. My time in Kingsbridge taught me a thing or two about bullies. I can stand up to them, anytime. Tell me where they lived, and I'll go."

"No. It's too dangerous. Hannah warned me," Kate said.

Ryan stormed out of the room, slamming the door.

Kate braced herself and faced her parents. "Hannah wants to go to America. If you would be willing to sign for her as guardians, we can try to have her accepted into the CORB Programme. And I plan to accompany her as an escort."

Mary Grace's face fell. "Oh Kate. It's not safe. U-boats sink our vessels every day, and not only naval ones."

"I know. But nothing's safe anymore. If Hannah stays here, they may send her away somewhere worse. She's willing to take the risk, and so am I."

"Do you mean you want to leave for good?" Mary Grace asked, her voice rising.

"I'd like to stay with Clare. She invited me. There's no war in America, not yet anyway, and I may have an opportunity to sing there."

"*What?* Clare never told me. How could she ask you to leave us?"

Sean put a protective arm around Mary Grace's shoulders. "Let Kate go, Mary Grace," he said gently. "She's almost an adult and has a right to her own life. None of us know about our future here, but it doesn't look hopeful."

"Thank you, Dad," Kate said, sighing with gratitude. "Mum, I have to go. Something bigger than this family is calling me."

She had told her mother at last.

But Sean faced Kate with a stern expression. "You're asking us to sign for Hannah as her guardians? I don't think that's legal. We might pay a penalty for that. Not sure I want to go along with your plan. Remember, I work for the government, and I have to follow the rules. I can't afford to lose my job over this."

"I understand," Kate said. "But look at it this way. It's best for all of us if Hannah leaves. Do you think they check the signatures carefully?"

"I don't know," Sean said, frowning. "Let me think more about this."

Ryan fulfilled his promise of tracing the arrest of the Bells. Mickey went along with him, saying he could fight to the death if people got nasty. The family's neighbours were happy to provide information. Plain-clothed employees of Scotland Yard had come for them, hustling them into a police van and driving away. Mrs. Bell's screams had alerted neighbours, who came outside to watch. Some cheered. The house had been looted, emptied of the few valuable possessions that remained. No one knew where the couple had been taken, but rumours of the Isle of Man abounded.

Kate understood her scheme might fail. Hannah was German and Jewish, and wouldn't be eligible to emigrate with the CORB Programme. Sean and Mary Grace weren't legal guardians, either. But with luck, and if they signed, no one would know. She completed the applications—hers as an escort and Hannah's as an evacuee.

One night soon afterwards, she overheard her parents arguing in their bedroom. They rarely disagreed, and the sound caught Kate's attention as she held her ear to the door, scarcely daring to breathe.

"It's most irregular," her father said. "I work with forms and bureaucracy all day, and we keep to the rules."

"But where else would Hannah go? Do you want to send her away, to hosts like Ryan's, or worse? We're better than that. If she doesn't leave, she can stay on here. I like her."

Kate listened closer. *Good for you, Mum.*

"No. That's not the solution," her father said.

"So where else would she go?" Mary Grace asked again.

Kate exhaled and couldn't make out his reply. But when the forms arrived, he signed along with Mary Grace, saying to Kate that they were already acting as guardians, anyway. And, he told her, as an Irishman living in England, he'd been the object of discrimination himself and had more than a little sympathy for Hannah's plight.

"Thank you, Father," Kate said, giving him a hug. *He always comes around in the end.*

The government representatives interviewed Kate and Hannah at the end of July. Kate's teaching experience gave her an advantage, and Hannah's poise, enthusiasm, and strong endorsements from her teachers impressed the interviewers.

"When will we hear from the government?" Hannah asked.

"In a few weeks. But if they approve, we will leave quickly."

Mary Grace fretted around the house, arranging and rearranging the cushions on the couch and stuffed chairs. Kate knew she was trying to be brave and appreciated her quiet acceptance of the planned departures. Kate took frequent walks and played the piano.

"I think it was wicked of Clare not to tell me of her plans," Mary Grace said one day. "It was shocking enough that she kept her decision to give up nursing and move to America with Stan a secret, but to take you away from us as well, Kate . . . it's unforgiveable."

Kate swallowed hard. She had never witnessed her mother speak so critically of Clare. Despite all the times she had resented Mary Grace's singing Clare's praises, Kate found herself wanting to soften the blow and spare her mother's feelings. After all, soon both her daughters would live three thousand miles away. "It's all right, Mum," she said. "She only wants to keep me out of harm's way. What's wrong with that?"

Hannah approached Kate as she was starting out for her walk the next day. "I can help with the expense of my passage."

"That's nice, but how?"

"I have *Mutti's* diamond ring. We can sell it."

"No, Hannah, but thank you for offering." Kate smoothed the girl's hair. "I have another solution. I plan to sell Barry's car. That will pay for everything. You may need money later, and I'd hate for you to give away a precious reminder of your mother."

Hannah stared vacantly at the ceiling. "You're right. The only thing I have of hers. Not even a photograph."

Kate told Mrs. Fitzgerald about her impending departure. She hugged Kate and complimented her bravery. School ended for the year, and the summer holidays began. Hannah lived each day in a state of agitation.

"I wish *Mutti* and Papa could go with us, Kate," she said softly, then added, "If we go."

The wait for news seemed as long as childhood.

CHAPTER 36
August 1940

The telegrams arrived in the middle of August. Kate tore them open and read them, her eyes shining. "They've accepted us! We have to be ready to go in two weeks!"

Hannah said excitedly, "I can't wait to see *Tante* Anna again."

"They don't say exactly where we're going, somewhere in Canada, and we'll have to travel to New York from there."

The usual slow pace of the household turned into frantic activity: clothes needed to be chosen and washed, toiletries gathered, and shoes polished. All their belongings had to fit into two small suitcases. Kate posted the photo of the Bentley at the WVS Centre, and it sold almost immediately. Once again, Barry had come to her rescue. Rich people like Lady Cornelia Rowbottom's friends might have bought the car and unknowingly made a contribution to Hannah's freedom, Kate thought. She smiled as she conjured up the image of Lady Cornelia and her Fifth Column Jew-hating friends.

Kate sent a telegram to her sister about her proposed arrival: *Coming to New York. Arrival uncertain. Probably within month. Please confirm. Kate.*

The reply arrived two days later: *Thrilled. Phone upon arrival. Clare.*

Kate sent a similar telegram to Hannah's aunt Anna Belowitz in New York City. To Hannah's delight, a response welcoming her came almost immediately.

Mary Grace assisted them with stoic smiles. She said she hated to see them go, that she thought of Hannah these past few weeks as a third daughter. Hannah darted around, telling Kate the excitement about going to America distracted her from sad memories of her parents. She did not want to suffer as they did, she said, and perhaps in America they would treat people like her better. But Kate saw beneath the veneer of Hannah's demeanour. *She doesn't dare dwell on her parents and their fate.* Kate waited for the day of departure with more than a little trepidation.

A few days before they left, Mary Grace knocked on Kate's bedroom door. Her mother rarely went into the room to talk, and Kate opened the door with surprise.

Mary Grace sat on the edge of the bed. "I owe you an apology, Kate. I've been unfair to you, wanting you to stay, and belittling your desire for a singing career. You've had a hard time of it lately, and you're doing a brave thing, taking Hannah to safety. I know I have to let you go, with grace."

Kate blinked back tears at the words she'd never expected to hear from her mother.

"Thank you, Mum," she said, her voice breaking. "We've had our differences but we're family, and I understand the importance of that. It's one of the reasons I want to help Hannah reunite with her relatives."

"Good luck, dear. I'll miss both of you," Mary Grace said soberly. "And your birthday, a special one, your twenty-first. Let's celebrate before you leave."

"No, Mum. Thank you, but it's all right. There are more important things to do."

"But we should do something. How about a cake, at least?"

"All right." She could allow her mother that. It was a special birthday: the age of majority. The official end of childhood.

Kate arranged to visit Mr. Conway before she left. She made the trip to his office one bright morning.

"Come in, come in," he welcomed her. "Lovely morning. Tea or whiskey?"

"Too early for whiskey. How about tea. With milk, since I'm not singing."

He poured two cups from the teapot on his desk and added milk.

"Not singing, you say? Forever, or just for today?"

"Just for today." Kate smiled. "I couldn't let all your work go to waste."

"Not only my work. Yours, too. Tell me, how are things going?"

"Fine. I sang at a charity event with not even one hiccup. Your programme works! I came to thank you."

"My pleasure." He poured himself a small glass of whiskey. "Cheers! What's next?"

"I don't know really. My fiancé died, and I'm leaving for America soon to join my sister in New York. I hope to have opportunities for singing there."

"I see. My condolences. A great loss. And your mother? How is she?"

"She's not happy to lose another daughter, but it's all right. We've reached the beginning of an understanding."

He nodded. "That takes time. Most of my clients have history to overcome."

"And," she paused. "I owe you for something else you taught me: to stop trying too hard."

"Ah, yes." He contemplated the ceiling, then faced her with his kind eyes. "That can get in your way, too."

"And then there's the matter of your fee—"

"Don't worry about it. I have wealthy clients who pay more than they should. Best of luck to you."

"I can't thank you enough," she said, as they shook hands.

What could she ever say that would be enough? He had changed her life.

* *

On August 20, the family listened to Churchill on the wireless. He commended the Royal Air Force pilots, who had fought valiantly to defend the country from the Luftwaffe attacks. "Never was so much owed by so many to so few," he said. The words moved Kate as she now had understanding of their meaning. Every man and woman's effort counted. A few days later, they heard central London had been bombed for the first time, and the RAF had bombed Berlin in retaliation. The war had come closer to home. Perhaps she and Hannah were leaving just in time, Kate thought, hardly daring to think about the risk to the family left at home.

The final long-awaited telegram arrived. Kate read the instructions: *Take 07:00 train from Carshalton to Victoria on 28 August. CORB officials will meet you.*

That's tomorrow! It's really happening, Kate thought. *But they still haven't told us where we're going.* She went to inform the family, waving the telegram as they waited for the nine o'clock news. Mary Grace abruptly left the room, Sean shook his newspaper, and Hannah glowed.

"Flying the coop at last," Ryan said.

Kate suspected that no one slept well that night. In the pale dawn, the household awakened and gathered downstairs. Mary Grace made tea and cooked breakfast. Kate couldn't help comparing the morning to the one not long ago when they said goodbye to Ryan. The stakes were so much higher now but, true to her name, her mother seemed to be managing the departure with grace. She watched as Hannah gulped down only a few bites of eggs.

"You must eat," Mary Grace said. "You don't know when your next meal will come, and you have a long journey ahead. I'll pack you sandwiches and potato crisps to take along. I made a fruit cake, too. Pamela Warren gave me the raisins. It'll keep. Save it until you need it."

Mickey knocked at the kitchen door and looked in. "Today's the big day. Brought a spot of cider to keep your spirits up. You might need it later."

He handed Kate two green bottles. "Who's going to see you off?"

"Not me," Mary Grace said quickly. "I hate goodbyes."

"I'll go," Ryan offered. "You stay here, Mum and Dad."

"I'll come as well, then," Mickey added. "Ryan and me'll be proper gentlemen and carry your suitcases."

"Very gallant," Kate said. "Time to go."

Her mother gave her a tight hug, squeezing her eyes shut. "Take care of yourselves, give Clare my love, and let us know when you're safely there. I'm proud of you, daughter."

Kate smiled at the words she'd always wanted to hear from her mother. "Thank you."

Sean folded Kate in his arms. "I'll miss you and your green eyes. Keep singing, Katie."

Mary Grace pinned a white label with Hannah's name and CORB number on the girl's coat and gave her a hug.

"Thank you for letting me stay with you, Mr. and Mrs. Murphy," Hannah said.

"Good luck to you, lass," Sean said.

Kate slipped the cord of her gas mask over her neck and watched Hannah do the same. Less than a year ago, Kate had given up her dream of leaving home and never could have imagined then going under such circumstances. She grasped Hannah's hand. They were in this together now. Neither looked back as they crossed the street towards the railway station.

"You can sing 'Tipperary' and keep everyone's spirits up, love," Mickey said as they reached the platform. "That or 'Pack Up Your Troubles in Your Old Kit Bag.' I like that one."

The train pulled into the station as they arrived. Brakes squealed and carriage doors banged. A few passengers disembarked.

"So, this is it," Ryan said. He gave Kate a hug. "Take this," he said, tucking a small object into her hand. "It kept me safe, and it'll keep you safe, too. I'll see you again, I know."

She opened her hand. The moonstone shone in her palm. She wiped the tears that sprang to her eyes as she fingered the precious object.

"Thank you, dear Ry."

"Better 'urry up or you'll miss your boat," Mickey said.

"Goodbye, Hannah, and the best of British luck to you," Ryan said.

"Bye, Ryan. I wish I had a brother like you," Hannah replied. He grinned and blew her a kiss.

Kate and Hannah climbed into the carriage, and Mickey and Ryan handed them their suitcases. Kate found seats for them and, after waving goodbye, closed the window. To her surprise, no other children or teachers from St. Bridget's had shown up. Whistles blew, doors slammed, and the train puffed slowly away.

Kate sat forward to view the school and her old home as they passed. Her mother stood in the back garden beside her rose bushes, head tilted upwards as she watched the train go by. She lifted her hand in farewell. Kate imagined the tears on her mother's face as she grieved for her emptying nest. Kate eyes filled again, and her stomach clenched. She was leaving her old life behind at last, and she hoped she wasn't making a big mistake.

The train took them to London's busy Victoria Station, where a group of evacuees waited. The children, aged five to fifteen, wore coats with white labels pinned on and carried gas masks and luggage. Some of the younger ones held teddy bears or dolls, and a couple held all their possessions in paper bags. The older children stood together, wide-eyed with curiosity. Few parents were present. Kate knew they had been advised not to see their children off to avoid emotional goodbyes.

A large woman in a nurse's uniform approached. "Are you Kate

Murphy?" she asked. "We've been expecting you. I'm Gladys Hill, and I'm coordinating the evacuation. Let's get started, shall we? You can help me check the names on this list."

"This is Hannah," Kate said, looking for the name and checking it on the list. Hannah clung tightly to her suitcase. Kate bent to whisper, "Don't worry. I have some responsibilities to attend to now. Stay near me."

Hannah nodded.

Kate called out the names, and soon all twenty children were accounted for. She and Gladys helped them into the buses that would take them to nearby Euston Station. Most of the evacuees chatted noisily, excited by the new adventure, but Hannah sat next to Kate in silence. Sensing the girl's anxiety, Kate told her again not to worry, knowing she was saying it as much for herself as for Hannah. At Euston, they headed for the platform where another train would take them on the next stage of their journey. There were signs to indicate the direction the trains were taking, but no place names. Theirs was heading due west. Kate couldn't suppress a smile as she remembered Ryan and Mickey taking down road signs. *We didn't steal them. Just left them by the roadside.* They had made a contribution. Now she was making hers.

After organising the children in their seats on the train and telling them not to wander in the aisles, Gladys took a place next to Kate and Hannah.

"Let's talk a bit about what's happening next, Kate. You will be responsible for fifteen girls, whom you will meet later today. We will all stay tonight in accommodations that have been arranged for us and the children will have a medical examination, probably tomorrow, before being allowed on the ship."

"Will Hannah be one of my girls?"

"I believe so. You were her teacher at school, weren't you?"

"That's right."

Kate discerned an expression of relief on Hannah's face and squeezed her arm.

A tall woman entered their carriage ushering a girl of about five years old clutching a doll. Her white name tag read LUCY LANE.

"Good afternoon, Jean," Gladys said to the woman. "Why don't you sit here? I'll move farther back, where I can oversee the other children. This is Kate, another of our escorts."

"Pleased to meet you," Jean said, lifting the small girl onto a seat opposite Kate and Hannah. "We're in expert hands with Gladys," she said. "We went to nursing school together. They try to recruit as many professionals as possible to travel with the children, you know—nurses, doctors, teachers. I understand the selection process is rigorous—only a few are chosen out of the thousands who apply. You must have some special skill to offer."

"I teach music."

"Splendid! We'll have singing, then. That will help morale, I'm sure."

Lucy stood on her seat and leaned out of the window. "Why is Mummy standing outside? Come in, Mummy. I've saved a seat for you," she said. The train began moving. "Stop!" she shrieked. "My mummy's not on the train, and we're leaving her behind!"

Jean stood up, reached for the girl, and shut the window. "Sweetheart, she's not coming with us. You'll see her later." Then, turning to Kate, she whispered, "That's why they advise parents not to come to railway stations to say goodbye."

The child crumpled into the seat, tears streaming from her eyes and dropping her head, holding her doll closer. "She's not coming, Annabelle," she whimpered softly.

Kate watched in dismay. Maybe this entire scheme was a mistake. She glanced at Hannah, whose face had lost color.

"Here," Kate said, offering a gum drop to Lucy. "Would you like a sweet?"

Lucy shook her head sorrowfully, and Kate and Hannah exchanged glances. "This child is too young to leave her mother," Hannah said. "She can sit on my lap."

She reached for Lucy, who didn't protest, and sat quietly with Hannah cuddling her doll. Kate, impressed by Hannah's kindness, offered her a sweet as well.

They ate the food that Mary Grace had given them, and several hours later the train arrived at Liverpool. One of the older boys recognised the city and shouted the name excitedly as they passed the buildings on the outskirts. *So that's where we're embarking on the ship*, Kate thought. She had never been to Liverpool, but knew it had a sizeable port.

Gladys stood up. "Hush," she said. "No more yelling." To Kate she hissed, "We're not supposed to talk about where we're going. Remember, careless talk costs lives."

The train screeched to a standstill at the terminal. Kate and the other escorts ushered their group onto the platform. Taxis waited to take the evacuees in a caravan to their next destination. After driving through the city, they passed through tall wrought-iron gates with a sign CAVENDISH SCHOOL surrounding an imposing Georgian building and extensive grounds.

Stepping from their taxi, Hannah nudged Kate. "Reminds me of St. Bridget's," she said.

"I suppose they've evacuated the pupils," Kate said. "This is a posh private school. The parents could probably afford to send their children away."

"I can tell some of our group couldn't go if they weren't CORB children," Hannah whispered, casting a glance at a boy wearing shoes with holes in the toes.

The front school door opened and a tall, dark-haired man wearing glasses came out. Kate stared at him in disbelief. It was Tony.

CHAPTER 37
August 1940

"Tony! What are you doing here?"

"Kate! Good heavens, I might ask the same of you."

"I'm an escort," she stammered.

"So am I. *Bon voyage* to us both."

He descended the steps and strode over. Her heart skipped a beat. *He still has a hold on my emotions*, she thought with a flash of annoyance.

"Let's talk later, over supper. I have to meet my boys now. Grand to see you here. This will be an adventure in more ways than one."

Kate sat down on the steps to regain her composure. She had never expected this. Her feelings vacillated from excitement to anxiety and she wondered for the second time that day if this journey would prove to be a huge mistake. But it wasn't all about her, she reminded herself. It was mostly about Hannah.

"Are you ill, Miss Murphy?" Kate glanced up. Hannah peered anxiously down at her. She had used the formal address they agreed was appropriate for the voyage.

Kate shook her head, using a hand to push herself upright. "I'm tired from the travelling, that's all. Let's collect our suitcases and find our rooms."

The school staff prepared the evening meal for the children and escorts in the large dining room. The children's eyes glowed at the sight of the spread set out on long tables: macaroni and cheese, sausage rolls, ham and egg sandwiches, potato crisps, bowls of oranges, and bananas.

"Cor blimey, we don't get stuff like this at 'ome," one boy said.

"Go ahead and tuck in," Gladys said.

No one talked, and everyone ate. Sitting with Hannah, Kate watched for Tony but didn't see him. What a coincidence, finding him here, an escort like herself. She could hardly believe it. Was he following her? She wolfed down her food and noted with satisfaction that Hannah did the same. After the main meal, cries of joy erupted as the staff placed bowls of ice cream in front of each diner.

Gladys stood to address the group. "Welcome, children. You will now meet your escort, who will be responsible for you until we arrive in Canada. Then you should all go to your sleeping quarters, brush your teeth, and change your clothes. Remember to keep your gas mask near you. Tomorrow you will visit a doctor to be sure you are well enough to undertake the voyage, and those who pass the medical exam will leave by ship on Thursday. Escorts, we will meet tomorrow after breakfast for a briefing. In case of emergency, the air raid shelters are located outside, behind the main building."

The room buzzed as the children turned to one another.

"What an adventure!"

"We're going on a big ship!"

"Quiet!" Gladys said. "I'll read out the names of the first group of boys who will travel with Mr. Trent." Tony rose while Gladys called out fifteen boys. He moved to the side of the room and beckoned to the boys to join him. Kate thought he looked distinguished.

Soon the several hundred children had been assigned to escorts. Gladys introduced Kate's cohort, girls aged five to fourteen, including Lucy.

Kate shepherded her fifteen children to the dormitory and soon helped them into bed. Tired from the day's excitement, they didn't resist. "You must all tell me your names again tomorrow," she said as she turned out the light. "Good night, sleep tight. If you need me, I'll be in the room right next door."

There would be no opportunity to talk to Tony that evening. Just as well.

The scream of air raid sirens jerked Kate awake. She sprang out of bed. Quickly assessing the situation, she grabbed her coat, gas mask, and torch, and hurried from her room to gather the children.

"Get up, everyone," she said, flicking on the lights and glancing at her watch. Two o'clock. "We must get to the shelters right away. *Now.* Put on your coat and shoes and bring your gas mask."

Lucy sat up in bed, immobile, her eyes glassy.

"Come on, Lucy. Bring Annabelle. We have to go downstairs."

Kate helped the child into her coat and shoes and held her hand as they left the room. They were the last to leave. Sirens continued to wail and the sound of planes droned overhead. The sleepy children trailed into the large shelters in the grounds. Staff passed out blankets, and everyone curled up on benches and the floor. No one panicked. Kate understood that for many, removal to a shelter was already a common experience. Kate arranged her blankets next to Hannah. Despite bursts of explosions echoing through the walls, the exhausted children slept on.

How ironic, if the bombs kill us all here, before we have a chance to get away, Kate fretted before drifting into an uneasy sleep.

Towards morning, the all-clear sounded. Kate, along with the other escorts, shook their charges awake and guided the tousled youngsters back to their beds. A few hours later, the sun shone in a perfect late summer sky, and only a few lingering wisps of smoke above the trees marred the bucolic scene around them.

They ate porridge and toast for breakfast. Kate was pleased to note that Hannah had already made friends with Sally, a girl about her own age, and they giggled together at the table. One by one, the children were called into an office for a medical examination. Most passed, but a few had elevated temperatures and were taken to a different area of the building. Some sobbed, wailing that it wasn't fair, that they wanted to go on the big ship.

While doctors conducted examinations, Gladys called the escorts together.

"First, you must know how much your service is appreciated. You're helping our country to win the war. I'll pass out lists of your duties."

Kate quickly scanned the sheet of paper. Children must brush teeth, use the washroom, wear lifejackets, attend the drills, and keep off the deck at night. Nothing that she couldn't manage to oversee, she saw with relief.

Gladys continued. "We all need to keep the children's spirits up—as you know, some are confused about where they're going, and others miss their families. We've been instructed by CORB to encourage the children to be brave. They're young ambassadors for England, after all."

A few escorts shook their heads, but said nothing.

"We will leave tomorrow on the SS *Volendam*, a luxury ocean liner with Dutch registration. She has been assigned to take our group to Halifax. For protection, a convoy will escort us on the voyage across the Atlantic. It's of utmost importance that you tell no one any details of the ship or her departure. If you leave a stamped, addressed postcard for family members, those will be sent for you after we set sail."

Kate listened with close attention. She wondered where Tony was headed. He acknowledged her as their eyes met across the room, but he made no attempt to come over and talk to her. *Just as well*, she told herself again.

All Kate's charges had been cleared for travel. On Thursday morning August 29, taxis delivered them to the Liverpool docks. Kate took

Lucy's hand as they stepped onto the wharf. Rolls Royces and Bentleys lined up on the curb, discharging well-dressed passengers. *People who can afford their own fares*, Kate thought.

The five-hundred-foot liner with two striped funnels lay at her berth in the harbour. The children gathered around Kate as they took in their first sight of the ship.

"What a monster!"

"What are those holes in the sides?"

"They're called portholes, silly."

"See all those small boats hanging from the top. What are they for?"

"Lifeboats," Kate said. *And I hope we don't need them.*

But the children had no such worries. Soon they all assembled on the wharf, skipping and jumping and dropping their suitcases.

A tall man in a three-piece suit and a white handkerchief protruding from his top pocket addressed the crowd. "I'm Uncle Geoffrey. You're here because you're special, and we want to save you. You're about to embark on a great adventure. Behave yourselves, and when things go wrong, remember you're British. Grin and bear it!"

"Who is *that*?" Kate whispered to Jean, standing next to her.

"Geoffrey Shakespeare, the Chairman of the Children's Overseas Reception Board."

"Well, I don't know. Telling children to grin and bear it seems a bit harsh."

"He's very patriotic," Jean said.

Two-by-two, the children marched towards the ship and up the gangplank. Kate and the other escorts counted their charges and followed behind. Boarding took time, but proceeded without incident. Kate stood by the railing observing the mass of humanity on the dockside below. Uniformed military men, nurses, dock workers, and passengers milled about. The air reeked of salt and tar. Seagulls wheeled overhead. Smoke from the earlier air raids hung in the sky, and damaged warehouses gaped open, exposing rubble and ruin inside. *So this is what bombs leave in their wake,* she thought sadly.

Gladys interrupted her musings. "Here's a list of the cabins where your girls will sleep. Help them get settled, then come back on deck for a lifeboat drill before we set sail."

The cabins held three beds or bunks, cupboards for clothes, and adjoining bathrooms. Kate had a room to herself. After placing the girls, she arranged her few belongings and then checked on the girls' progress. A stewardess arrived with a box of orange life jackets. She explained how to wear them and said that everyone should follow signs to the deck for the lifeboat drill. Stewards led each group to colour-coded assembly spots by the eighteen thirty-foot lifeboats, blue for Kate's group.

The Dutch crew announced the protocol. "If we abandon ship, you must immediately put on your coats and lifejackets and come to your area. *Immediately,* you understand. No dawdling. Don't bring anything else because it will be an emergency, and we can't waste time."

Kate shuddered. She glanced around at the children's faces. No sign of fear. She admired their blind faith.

The engines purred. Everyone moved to the railings to watch as the ship pulled slowly away from the dock. People on the ground waved handkerchiefs and raised their arms in farewell. Departure horns moaned.

Gladys came over to Kate and hissed urgently in her ear. "Sing! Time to sing! Please! Give these well-wishers a moment to remember. How about, 'There'll Always Be An England?'"

Kate cleared her throat and paused. Then, taking a deep breath, she belted out the words: "I give you a toast, ladies and gentlemen . . . *Join me everyone, sing your loudest!*" she implored. One by one, the children sang. Soon the entire group joined in. The onlookers on the wharf applauded. Kate caught sight of Geoffrey Shakespeare. Tears rolled down his cheeks as he held his hand to his forehead in salute. Standing in the middle of his group of boys, she glimpsed Tony, focused on her as he sang, a smile spreading across his face. Her voice, filled with happiness, sailed smoothly across the water.

The ship gradually slipped from the dock into the Mersey estuary. After a short while, the crew lowered the anchors.

"Why have we stopped?" Kate asked a sailor.

"Waiting for the convoy to arrive, miss."

"How long?"

"We'll probably leave early tomorrow morning. This is good. It'll give you a chance to get your sea legs before the swells get rough."

Kate gulped. She hoped her girls didn't get seasick. And the next day was her twenty-first birthday. No party for her, but she had much to celebrate on her way to America at last.

They had lunch and dinner while at anchor. To Kate and most of her colleagues the meals seemed sumptuous after months of rationing. Between meals, Kate sat down with each of her girls to get acquainted. There were three sisters from the Isle of Wight, an eleven-year-old from Brighton, several older girls from a grammar school in York, two twelve-year-olds from Scotland. Hannah's new friend Sally came from Croydon. Pauline, the girl from Brighton, took a liking to Lucy, saying the five-year-old reminded her of her sister the same age at home, and wanted to share her cabin. As Kate talked to them, the shining faces of the younger girls told her they were happy to go abroad, and they viewed it as the most exciting adventure of their lives.

Hannah's eyes gleamed with hope. She liked the luxurious ship. As she and Kate stood on the deck and stared at the water swirling below, she said, "I'm glad you took me to the baths. Even though I can't swim well yet, I'm not as afraid of the water now. I was seasick when we crossed the English Channel from France, and I'm not sure I would have wanted to go across the Atlantic if you hadn't helped me overcome my fear."

Kate gave her a hug. "I'm glad."

"I'm going to explore the ship with Sally now. There are so many decks!"

"All right. Be careful. Don't climb on the railings, and come back in half an hour."

After Hannah left, Kate caught sight of Tony walking towards her. "I want tell you how impressed I was by how confidently you led the singing," he said. "You're putting your talent to good use, I must say."

"Thank you."

"I'd love to talk," he said. "How about after we put the children to bed? Meet me here."

She nodded, and felt her stomach flutter.

After overseeing the girls' preparation for bed Kate tucked the smaller children into bed. She wished them all good night. Lucy reached up and hugged her neck. "You make me feel safe like my mummy," she said. Kate gave her a kiss, pleased she could provide a small measure of comfort. She forced herself to wait a restless fifteen minutes, checking her hair, her dress, her hair again. She checked the cabins to be sure everyone was asleep. She expected more of the younger ones to be frightened or crying for their mothers, but as she peered cautiously into all five cabins, she observed only the gentle rise of bedclothes and quiet breathing. She couldn't help begrudging the children's capacity for calmness and sound sleep.

Kate waited for Tony as arranged. The moon, half hidden by clouds, cast an eerie light on the deck. The ship rocked gently at anchor. Waves lapped softly against the hull, and cool breezes caressed her hair.

She heard the squeak of shoes on the deck, and there he was beside her. He touched her hair. She trembled.

"What a lovely evening," he said. "Quite romantic, but I suppose I'm talking to a married woman and shouldn't indulge in fantasies. How's married life?"

She turned to face him. "I don't know. My fiancé died from war wounds."

"Oh dear. I'm sorry."

She waved her hand in dismissal, feeling uncomfortable. But memories of Barry flooded in. That dear man, who should have been her husband. Yet even now she was aware of the powerful emotions that Tony still provoked. *Push, pull back, push, pull back.* Like the tide.

"What brings you here, on this voyage?" she asked at last.

"A sense of duty, I suppose. I took a leave from medical school. Children need to get away to safety, and I want to help. I've been leading groups of boy scouts on hikes in the highlands and want to ensure that at least some young men like them have a future."

She nodded. "Will you continue your medical studies?"

"I expect so, after we return."

His eyes settled on her face. "If I may say so, you're more beautiful now than when we first met. Enchanting."

Is he trying to flatter me, and draw me back, or is he sincere?

They stared down at the ink-black waves touched by splashes of moonlight. It was almost a full minute before he spoke again. "Are you still hoping for a singing career?"

Relieved he'd changed the subject, she said, "Perhaps, but that somehow seems less important now."

Is that true? she asked herself, surprised by her words. *He always makes me feel differently about myself, but he leads me astray as well.*

"You certainly got us all singing today."

She shrugged. "That was easy. Everyone likes to sing, with a little encouragement."

"Don't dodge my sincere compliment, please. I mean it. Are you planning to return to England after the crossing?"

"No. My sister invited me to stay with her in New York."

"Oh." His voice dropped.

He sounds disappointed.

"I do want to flee the war," she said. "Don't you?"

"Not really. Having got into this, I want to see it through. Our way of life, as imperfect as it may be, is under threat. Maybe it's a primal response, but I want to be part of the fight to protect it."

She liked his words, and let herself warm to him. But only a bit. "Admirable goals."

"I'm so glad you're here," he murmured. "I only wish we had champagne to celebrate our unlikely reunion."

"It does seem unlikely. Tell me, were you following me onto the *Volendam?*"

"What a silly notion. You and I were both chosen as escorts for good reasons."

She allowed herself a moment of pride. "True. Tell you what. Today happens to be my twenty-first birthday. I have some cider in my cabin. We could drink that."

"Cider's festive. An important birthday. Let's celebrate, then—your birthday and our reunion."

"Back in a minute."

She hurried along the deck and down the gangway, but a few feet from her cabin door, she stopped short. *Have I taken leave of my senses? I'm here to take care of young children, not to renew a romance with a man who was at best an adolescent crush. And he should know better, too.*

Kate let herself into her room, allowing the door to click behind her. She needed to shut him out of her life. Out of her heart, once and for all. She stretched out on the bed, opened a bottle of cider, and drank it, slowly savoring its rich flavor. She didn't need to share this moment with Tony. She could give herself a toast. *Twenty-one, an adult, and on my way at last.* Mickey would approve. So would Barry.

After finishing the bottle of cider, she looked in on her charges once more. Then she snuggled into bed with a dizzy, warm feeling that dispelled the coldness of the room. For the first time she felt free from the power that one man had held over her for too long. *Life is good, even in wartime.*

CHAPTER 38

August, 1940

At five o'clock on the morning of August 30, the SS *Volendam* set sail, escorted by a convoy of thirty-three ships, including a destroyer and two armoured sloops. The convoy sailed from the Mersey River north to the Irish Sea and passed east of Ireland into the Atlantic.

After breakfast, Kate helped her girls into coats and lifejackets for another lifeboat drill. The alarm sounded, and Kate's group made their way to the staging area quickly. After the drill, she organised singing sessions: nursery rhymes for the younger children, and popular songs for the older ones. They especially liked, "Run, Rabbit, Run," sung to the words "Run, Hitler, Run."

Johan, a member of the all-Dutch crew, offered to teach deck games, table tennis and shuffleboard. Kate heard Tony encouraging his boys to participate. "You can learn new skills," he said. "You never know when you may need to know how to entertain yourself in a small space."

"He's right," Johan added, laughing. "We spend weeks at sea. Sometimes there's nothing to do. We've bred true champions in these sports."

"What happens when you lose the balls overboard?" a boy asked.

"We dive in to rescue them, of course," Johan said, winking.

Tony approached her. *He wants an explanation*, she thought.

"A child needed me," she said, simply. He nodded.

The seas became rougher and turned deep green as the ship headed into the open Atlantic. During the evening meal, the wind increased and the ship heaved, causing plates to slide precariously on tables. Kate anxiously monitored her girls for signs of seasickness. Most seemed fine, but Hannah looked pale.

"Do you want to lie down for a while?" Kate asked.

"Yes, please," Hannah said. They hugged the bulkheads to keep their balance as they edged along the gangway to the cabins. Kate helped Hannah into bed. A stewardess poked her head in the door.

"Would you like a cup of tea and a biscuit?" she asked.

"No, thank you," Hannah replied. "I'm too sleepy."

"I'll check on you later," Kate said.

After the meal, Kate rounded up the girls and oversaw their preparations for the night. She helped Lucy with her toothbrush and tucked her into bed. The ship's rolling increased. She was feeling a little queasy herself as she pulled the covers over her head.

The alarm jolted her awake. She switched on the lights and glanced at the clock. Almost eleven. The ship shuddered, lights flickered, then went out. Her suitcase skidded across the sloping floor and drawers slid open, spilling their contents. She struggled to stand, grasping the bed for support. *Pause and take a breath*, she cautioned herself. *Muster the girls, remember the lifeboat drill.* She scrambled for a coat, secured her life jacket, and felt her way out of the cabin. The lights blinked on again, and she knocked loudly on the doors of her charges.

"Get up, everyone. It's an emergency. Don't waste time, and meet on the gangway."

The fifteen girls followed her instructions, hugging the sloping bulkheads. Kate counted and recounted them until they reached their assembly place on deck. It was hard going. Fumes and smoke stung her eyes, and the stench of burning metal parched her throat. The children, escorts, and crew moved efficiently. In less than four minutes, her children had gathered in their spot by the lifeboat. No one cried. No one panicked. Everyone hung onto something—the railing or one another—to keep their balance, as the ship continued to list heavily to starboard. Kate made sure each child's lifejacket was firmly buckled. Clinging to the railing, she felt anxiously in her pocket for the moonstone. She fingered it, grateful for its smooth presence, and for Ryan's words telling her it would keep her safe. She hoped its magic would keep them all safe.

The crew had already lowered several of the lifeboats to the deck, wrestling them down with difficulty in the strong wind, sea swells, and tilt of the sinking ship. Spray lashed at their faces. Kate pushed Lucy forward towards their lifeboat. "She's the smallest. Help her in first," she shouted.

Johan lifted the child, depositing her in the bow. "Here you go, sweetheart," he said. One by one, the crew assisted the girls and Kate into the lifeboat. Hannah sat in the middle, and Johan heaved himself in and sat next to Kate in the stern, taking the tiller in his hands.

"What's happened?" she shouted in his ear.

"We've been torpedoed. Those damned Jerrys at it again. They love to strike at night, the bastards. The *Valldemosa* will pick us up."

Two more sailors and an officer climbed into the lifeboat and positioned themselves beside the oars.

"All aboard. Lower away!" Johan yelled.

Kate clenched her fists. The Germans, those murderous bastards, were not going to defeat her or take the lives of her children. Her stomach queasy, she flashed on the old memory of the capsized boat in Selsey and Ryan floundering in the sea. The image had always haunted her, but now she grabbed onto it as a talisman. She had saved Ryan: they had survived and lived on. She would protect these children in her care in any way possible.

"Let's sing," she yelled. "Ten green bottles." They obeyed, their voices almost swept away by the whipping wind. Slowly, the deck crew lowered their boat to the water and released the lines. Johan grasped the tiller. Waves crashed against the lifeboat, thrusting it back against the side of the liner, but with strong strokes of their oars, two sailors guided the boat away from the sinking ship as the angry sea rose and fell in ten-foot troughs. Their rescue boat crested and fell, careening sideways, drenching them in icy spray. Several children vomited. Kate's insides churned. She desperately wanted to comfort the ones who struggled, but the violent rocking made any movement dangerous. She saw Hannah holding Sally as she heaved over the side. "Keep singing," Kate urged, and those who could, did.

She scanned the waves, trying to glimpse the liner that until now had been their ticket to safety. Orange flames erupted from ship's side, but otherwise the *Volendam* receded into the dark, starless night.

Kate lost all sense of time. All she knew was that they were at the mercy of the sea. Their lifeboat took on water, numbing their faces and feet. The waves, menacing black walls, continued to tower above them. They made sickeningly slow progress towards the *Valldemosa*, an oil tanker that waited nearby, her lights blazing. The terrifying thought that the lighted ship might be a target for torpedoes crossed her mind. A terrible but necessary risk, she saw at the same time that the ship served as a beacon for the lifeboats as they lurched their way towards her.

It might have been hours before they reached the rusty old ship. Morse code signals blinked and searchlights flashed, revealing the occasional whereabouts of other tossing lifeboats and rescue ships hovering in the distance. Kate grew colder and colder and the sick feeling in her stomach persisted. While her own spirits flagged, she couldn't allow the others to lose hope. She marvelled as she watched the shadowy figures of the sailors wrestling the oars through the waves. Such bravery and strength. *The children need to keep singing.* "Come on everyone. Sing! Ten green bottles hanging on the wall. We won't accidentally fall!" she shouted.

It was the longest night of Kate's life.

By the time the rowing crew's oars struck the *Valldemosa*'s side, Kate felt utterly exhausted. The lifeboat crashed against the side of the larger vessel, but lines thrown from above secured it. Sailors lowered a rope ladder, and the officer from the *Volendam* lashed himself to it to receive the children. Kate staggered to the lifeboat's bow to help Johan pass the children up to him. The boat bucked, and even the larger girls struggled to climb the netting, until finally only the smallest child remained in the lifeboat with Kate.

"Let's help Lucy," Kate said. "I'll go last."

Johan called for a rope and tied it around the girl's waist. She screamed. "Annabelle! My doll. I can't leave without her. She needs a rope, too."

He cast around for the doll and thrust it into Lucy's hands. "Okay, bring her in," he yelled to the crew above. At last Johan thrust Kate into the arms of the officer on the ladder, and with enormous effort she hauled herself up the rest of the way. She collapsed at the top, almost falling back into the churning sea below. Two sailors caught her and pulled her to safety.

When she regained consciousness on the ship's deck a few minutes later, she dragged herself to the railing to look down. The lifeboat was gone.

"Where's the boat? Where are the *Volendam* sailors? Are they on board with us?" she asked the nearest crew member.

"No, miss. They've gone back to save the liner."

"And I never even thanked them," Kate said remorsefully. *My girls are safe, but what about Tony. Has he survived? And how many others?* There was no way of knowing.

For the remainder of the night, the *Valldemosa*'s sailors ministered to the shivering children, serving them hot pea soup, tea, and biscuits. The tanker, equipped to accommodate twelve, was packed beyond capacity with the survivors. Kate and her girls squeezed into a crew member's cabin, sharing a handful of blankets, and falling asleep from sheer exhaustion.

Shortly after dawn, the survivors assembled on deck. The captain counted and welcomed them.

"You will all be happy to hear that on this ship sixty-two adults have been saved, along with 188 children. No one knows yet how many others have survived the *Volendam*'s sinking, but at least two other ships from the convoy stood by. We kept our lights on, and that may have helped the lifeboats find us."

Brave captain and crew, risking their lives for us, Kate thought. Though grateful, she didn't feel like rejoicing. She still needed to hear about the fate of the other passengers and children.

"What will happen now?" Hannah asked Kate.

"I'll find out. Why don't we have something to eat? I hear they're serving peaches and cream in honour of the Dutch Queen Wilhelmina's birthday."

"I don't think my tummy could stand it," Hannah said, but then she gasped. "Your birthday! Wasn't it yesterday? We forgot it."

"It's all right," Kate said. "We can sing happy birthday to Queen Wilhelmina instead. First, I'll ask where they're taking us. I can't imagine going all the way to Canada in this ship."

Kate stumbled over to an officer, holding onto bulkheads for support. The *Valldemosa* heaved in the swells more than the much larger *Volendam*.

"Excuse me, sir. Could you tell me where we're going?"

"We're taking you ashore. Bound for Scotland now," he said.

That's a relief, she thought. From what Johan had told her, torpedoing was a common occurrence. Once was enough. She shuffled around, gathering her girls and counting. Fifteen. Everyone was present.

"Let's sing happy birthday to Queen Wilhelmina," she said.

The children rallied and sang. The Dutch sailors and passengers joined in. Kate couldn't contain her amazement at the high spirits, confirming her conviction that singing empowers people of all ages, even under the worst conditions.

The seas grew calmer as the *Valldemosa* neared the coast of Scotland. Gulls circled overhead with their plaintive cries. Steeples and buildings on shore emerged into view through the mist. Kate stood at the railing with her charges with Hannah's arm around her waist. Pauline held Lucy's hand. It all felt unreal. Even though she thought she'd been aware of the danger of the undertaking, she never could have imagined this outcome. This awful, lucky outcome.

They sailed smoothly in the sheltered waters of the Firth of Clyde alongside merchant ships and naval vessels arriving at the small town of Gourock. Geoffrey Shakespeare and a small crowd of onlookers awaited them on the pier. After disembarking from the ship, the children and escorts were efficiently bundled into buses and taken to an assembly hall set up to welcome them back. Each child was given a sprig of white heather, a symbol of luck and protection from danger.

Kate swayed uncertainly as she set foot on land. Only one thought occupied her mind: to get back to Carshalton with Hannah as soon as possible. She saw that other CORB evacuees had arrived before them. Gladys, her nurse's uniform badly soiled, was already seated at one of the long tables set with food for the new arrivals.

"Gladys! Good to see you," Kate said

The nurse smiled. "What an ordeal."

"It was. Did all your girls make it?"

"Every one. Those Dutch sailors on the *Volendam* deserve medals for getting us off the ship. So brave and competent. And the *Valldemosa* crew as well. How are your girls?"

"All fine."

Gladys took a bite of a cucumber sandwich. "You should know that your escort duties are now officially over. I've talked to the CORB officials, and they agree we've all gone through enough. They've assigned new people to ensure the evacuees arrive home safely. They're providing special trains to take the English children home."

"Are you going home now, too?"

"Not me. I'm signing up again. Another liner is leaving in about two weeks' time. There are more who want to leave."

Kate gazed at her in amazement. "You're going again?"

"Certainly. Lots of people cross the ocean without any problem whatsoever."

Kate sat down, overcome with admiration. Or with disdain. She wasn't sure which.

Geoffrey Shakespeare strode over to a podium at the front of the room, now filled with children seated at tables devouring the food.

"Ladies and gentlemen, girls and boys," he began. "Welcome back. We have learned to our great pleasure that rescue efforts from the SS *Volendam* were entirely successful. Everyone was saved, including all 320 children. All without panic, I understand. You are to be commended for your bravery. You youngsters are great examples for young people to follow in Britain and across the world. There was surely a guardian angel watching over you as you kept up your spirits. Your voices swelling in song at sea at midnight have given new meaning to our lives. God bless you all."

Gladys leaned over to Kate. "You deserve credit for raising morale, leading us in singing, young lady," she said. "There are a lot of unsung heroes in this war—excuse the pun—and you're one of them."

"Thank you," she said with a brief smile.

Kate searched the room for Tony, but didn't see any sign of him or his boys. At least he was alive. Perhaps she would never see him again. She was at peace with that. He wasn't what she wanted. Their romantic meeting on the ship had given her confidence and the hope that someday, when the right person came along, she would recognise him. Tony had remained a ghostly presence in her life for too long.

Now she just wanted to go home. She looked around the room

at the children, feeling proud that she had experienced true maternal feelings for her fifteen charges. Perhaps she could now come to a better understanding with her mother. She had left almost impetuously, wanting to escape a life that she'd outgrown. Hannah had given her the excuse she needed to get away, and while she felt strongly protective of the girl and would do all she could to give her a life free from persecution, perhaps it wasn't necessary to go abroad. In any case, unlike Gladys, she thought it far too risky to undertake another voyage across the Atlantic.

Beside her, Hannah began to eat a little. *What does she think now about going to America?* Anger rose in Kate as she again contemplated the unspeakable cruelty of torpedoing a ship full of children. With new resolve, she made up her mind to stay home and fight.

She craved the satisfaction of revenge.

Kate and Hannah left Gourock the following day. They didn't talk much. The experience had deeply shaken Hannah, and she only wanted to return to Carshalton. Their train arrived at their station that evening. As they neared the familiar landmark, they saw the family on the platform: Ryan, Sean, and Mary Grace, carrying yellow flowers. Mickey stood next to them, Pinocchio at his side.

Kate flung the train door wide and hurtled down the steps. The family surged forward and enveloped her in their arms. Then Mary Grace pulled Hannah into the circle.

"Welcome back, dear," Mary Grace said. "This is your home, now."

Kate couldn't speak for happiness. *Maybe I've saved Hannah after all.*

CHAPTER 39

September 1940

Upon her return, Kate discerned that Mary Grace treated her with new respect. She no longer feared she would inherit her mother's overly anxious nature. Her experience on the *Volendam* had taught her that.

Mary Grace came to her in the dining room as she sat at the piano.

"Hannah talks glowingly of your role as escort. You gave confidence to the girls, and your singing, she says, inspired everyone."

Kate lifted her hands from the keyboard.

"I want you to know I've done you a disservice all these years," Mary Grace continued. "I'll admit I've never really understood you, but that doesn't lessen my love for you, and I'm glad you're back. One day you will leave home to start your own life, and when that happens, I'll wish you well. With all my heart."

Touched, with love spreading through her body, Kate rose and embraced her mother.

"Thank you, Mum. I'll admit I've always fretted, wanting more for myself, resenting you, and trying to escape and find freedom. But guess what? It's hard to do."

"It is. Freedom is elusive, and people sometimes make prisoners of themselves. Do yourself a favour, and don't do that, as I've done all these years."

Her mother's unexpected words of wisdom astonished Kate. She pulled her head back, saw Mary Grace's watery eyes, and gave her a kiss. There was still much for them to learn about the other, and she fervently hoped they had a full lifetime ahead to do so.

But she didn't want to stay at home any longer. Her anger at the Nazis' cruelty, fueled by the sinking of the *Volendam*, cemented her desire to stop them.

On September 7, the Blitz began. Nightly bombing started on London, and any sense of security could not last long in Carshalton. Trembling in bed, Kate heard relentless explosions in the distance and planes droning overhead. Sirens blared, but not close. Each day, the news reported heavy damage and death on the docks and in London's East End.

Later in the month Hannah returned to school, saying she wanted to sing like Kate. But Kate had told the school she would not resume teaching.

"How will I learn to sing, if you're not there?" Hannah asked.

"I suggest you apply to the Music Academy," Kate replied. "I'll support your application, and they will give you excellent instruction and train you for a singing career, if that's what you want." Hannah gave Kate a grateful smile and a hug.

Kate considered her own options. While not abandoning her desire to sing, she realised it was no longer her main preoccupation. She wanted to find employment of the kind that would have helped Barry and other victims of the war.

She visited the WVS Centre to talk to Alison. "I'd like to volunteer," she said.

"Good. We can always use more workers like your mother, who is a great help. When can you start?"

"Actually, I wasn't thinking of working here. I read in the newspaper that people are needed to drive ambulances."

"Yes. We're taking names. Can you drive?"

"No, but I'm willing to learn."

"Right. I'll pass your information on to the St. John Ambulance people. They can train you. They're desperate for drivers now, and they expect a greater need for transportation of wounded soldiers to depots and hospitals."

"That makes sense. I'll come back in a few days."

Kate returned home, glad to have taken some action, and eager to acquire a new skill. Most women didn't drive, but now she had the opportunity to learn. At the end of the week, she visited the Centre again.

"Here's the information," Alison said, handing a sheet to Kate. She read the instructions.

Women working in ambulances must be adaptable and able to undertake multiple tasks. They must be prepared for night driving. They must demonstrate competence at the wheel and may be required to perform vehicle maintenance. Training will be provided.

An application form appeared at the bottom of the page. Kate completed it and passed it to Alison.

"I'm ready to go as soon as they'll have me," she said.

St. John's Ambulance Services accepted Kate's application. She held the letter in front of her, hardly believing the words. *They must be desperate*, she chuckled, *choosing me for a job I'm not qualified for.* But desperate times call for desperate measures. She would depart in another week for training.

A few days later, she received a letter from Sybil.

> *I'll be home to visit my parents next week. Can I see you? Wednesday's best. Let's meet at seven at the Star on Carshalton Road. Love, Sybil.*

Sybil! How long had it been since they'd seen one another? It seemed like a lifetime. Only a year ago, and so much had happened in the meantime. She eagerly awaited the visit with her old friend. *What has she been doing all this time? Why so much secrecy?*

Sybil arrived at the pub on Wednesday dressed in a plain white blouse and tweed skirt. She wore her hair cut short, in a no-nonsense style. She bore no resemblance to the party girl Kate knew. But Sybil's embrace exuded the same warmth.

"It's been too long," she said, "and look at you! Not worn down by the war—you seem to be thriving. More confident, somehow."

"That's what someone else told me recently. Just glad to be alive, I suppose."

"Right. I'll get us some drinks. Gin and tonic?"

Sybil paid for the drinks at the bar and took a seat beside Kate. "Tell me everything. What have you been doing?"

Kate pursed her lips. "Where shall I begin? I've missed you and your advice, which I could have used more than once. To be brief, I got engaged to Barry. Remember him? He died of war injuries shortly after our engagement. I joined the CORB program as an escort, set sail for Canada, got torpedoed, and returned home."

Sybil gave her an incredulous look and sat back. "That's a lot to swallow. Sounds like you've been in the wars, if you'll excuse the expression," she said. "And I'm sorry about Barry. So sorry for them all. This damned war." She pulled out a cigarette and lit it. "But so far, we've survived. Cheers!"

They clinked glasses. "To Barry's memory," Kate said. She took a deep draught of her drink, then said, "I saw Tony."

Sybil blinked. "Oh my God. What happened?"

"I met him again on the CORB ship, of all places. But it's okay. I'm over him. Really."

"Glad to hear that. He almost drove you crazy. You've grown up, my friend. No longer the love-sick girl I remember."

"No," Kate said soberly. "I have the war to thank for that. Barry taught me something about true love. So what about you? Where are you staying?"

"In Buckinghamshire. But I can't talk about it. Let's just say I've been working, making my contribution. That's all."

Kate noticed a crease between Sybil's brows that she hadn't seen before.

"No relationships? No special man in your life?"

"Not now," Sybil said, "and I think things are going to get worse."

"So you're staying on to fight? Not going abroad?"

"No."

"I'm not now, either. I'm volunteering with the ambulance services here. They're teaching me to drive and repair a car."

"That's the spirit. How about singing?"

"Believe it or not, I overcame the hiccups. Thank you for giving me Lydia's name. It turned out she knew Barry, and she invited me to sing at one of her charity events. I'll sing if I have an opportunity, anytime."

Sybil raised her glass. "Congratulations! Good for you! I knew you could do it. If I learn of new charity events, I'll let you know."

"That would be terrific. Tell me, why haven't you been in touch before now? I imagined you had left for America."

"It's hard to explain. Where I work, they don't want us to talk to people outside the walls."

"Walls? Do they lock you up, or something?"

Sybil grinned. "Not exactly, though sometimes it feels that way. Please don't ask me any more questions."

"All right, but I don't want to lose touch again. Is there any way to reach you?"

"You can always phone my parents, and they can get a message to me."

"I'll do that. But when the war is over, let's get together, often. For old times' sake and for the future. Oh, and do you still hate fish?" Kate smiled.

"Not any more. Do you still hate pork?"

"Not as much." They laughed. "See, we've just proven that even longtime friends don't know everything about one another," Kate said. "Most people these days are like strangers in the fog, feeling their way to escape their fate. Or dodge U-boats."

Sybil nodded. "Which they sometimes never do."

"Well said, my friend."

As they left the pub, a lethal orange glow rose over the rooftops to the North over London. Searchlights crisscrossed the horizon, illuminating low clouds for a few seconds before angling sharply away and disappearing. A faint sound of sirens echoed, followed by muffled explosions, and pinpoints of stars blinked through the night sky. It was horrifyingly beautiful.

AFTERWORD

This is a work of historical fiction. The Murphy family and friends are fictitious, but important historical figures are mentioned in the story with some authentic quotes.

I first learned about the torpedoing of the SS *Volendam* when I read my father's unpublished memoir. He took a year off from Medical School to volunteer as an escort with the Children's Overseas Reception Board (CORB) Programme and described the torpedoing and rescue from his own experience. I only read the memoir after his death and never had a chance to discuss this significant event with him.

In my father's words: "This incident is reminiscent of the salvation of the tanker *San Demetrio* by a dedicated crew, which attracted attention in a postwar film. There is no film I know of parallel to the saving of all of our three hundred children without any casualties or panic at night from a torpedoed liner in the Atlantic . . . we could not have rescued the children one at a time from the heaving lifeboat without the strength and competence of the Dutch sailors on the *Volendam*, the officer on the ladder, the quiet bravery of the children and, let it be said, amazingly good luck for her and the two other ships of the convoy which participated in the rescue."

Although badly damaged and not fit to transport the evacuees and passengers to Canada, the *Volendam* did not sink, and the crew managed to sail her to Greenock on the River Clyde in Scotland for repair.

During investigations later, a second torpedo was discovered in the hull. It had not exploded; if it had, the ship would have sunk within minutes.

Two weeks after the torpedoing of the *Volendam*, the SS *City of Benares* left Liverpool, also as part of the CORB Programme. Four days out, she was also torpedoed. Two hundred and sixty-five people drowned, including seventy of the ninety children aboard. The tragic story of the *City of Benares* was widely reported later. However, the heroic story of the saving of the *Volendam* children has largely passed unheralded into history.

Following the sinking of the *City of Benares*, Prime Minister Winston Churchill ordered that, "the further evacuation overseas of children must cease," and so the CORB Programme ended.

The Gourock Times, reporting on September 6, 1940, after the safe return of the children from the *Volendam*, stated: "One would have thought that boys and girls, roused from their beds, rushed up on deck and passed into lifeboats, would have been afraid. What did these kids do? They sang . . . and kept on singing until they were safely aboard rescue ships."

After the declaration of war in September 1939, the government advised evacuation and actively encouraged parents to send their children away from cities to safety in rural areas. In the first few months, 3.5 million people relocated within Britain, many of whom were children. However, for various reasons, including the slow pace of the war on land, most of the child evacuees returned home by Christmas.

Depending on the source, different figures are given for the number of children who took part in the various evacuation schemes. The government's CORB Programme for sending children overseas was designed to include a cross-section of social classes. They evacuated 2,664 children over the course of three months. However, an estimated 20,000 to 30,000 privately financed children were sent overseas during the war, including the actress Elizabeth Taylor.

The CORB escorts were carefully selected. Most were doctors, nurses, or teachers. One thousand men and women were chosen from over 19,000 applicants.

Several popular singers helped raise morale during the course of the war, the most famous being Vera Lynn, the "Forces' Sweetheart." When she died in 2020 at age 103 in England, during the height of the Covid-19 pandemic, Dame Vera Lynn was given a military funeral that was widely attended.

After the Royal Air Force won the Battle of Britain in October 1940, Hitler recognised that the RAF could not be defeated and called off Operation Sea Lion. This ended his plan for invading Britain, but the war continued until 1945.

The character Sybil Thorndyke worked at Bletchley Park, the place where the Enigma code was broken, thus helping Britain to anticipate the sinking of naval vessels by the Germans. Some people working there were well-educated high-society women like Sybil. They were bound by secrecy, were required to sign the Official Secrets Act, and could be prosecuted if they talked openly about their work. The public only learned about Bletchley's important mission many years later.

Adalbert Schnee, the captain of the German U-boat that torpedoed the SS *Volendam,* received several medals for service from German authorities during the war. He sank twenty-one Allied ships. It is not known if he knew that the *Volendam* was carrying children, but he was not charged with war crimes after the war ended.

The London Blitz began as this story ends, on September 7, 1940. The bombing continued for fifty-seven days, destroying one third of London and killing more than 43,000 civilians. Relatively few bombs fell on Carshalton, located about nine miles South on the outskirts of London. However, Queen Mary's Hospital for Children, which served as an Emergency Medical Centre, and where Barry was taken in the novel, was one of the most heavily bombed medical facilities in the country.

ACKNOWLEDGMENTS

One of the most rewarding aspects of writing a book is the contact with others that inevitably results, both with those I've known, along with new people who emerge as early readers when they express interest in what I'm writing about. Like other writers, I depend upon these readers to help me ferret out holes and speed bumps that I've somehow cruised past, even after multiple drafts. Thanks to all of you: Sharron Stringer, Paige Stringer, Kathleen Kaska, John Moody, Martha Moody, Joe Kornfeld, and Mary Alden Blakeslee.

Special thanks to Celia Chandler for feedback on the musical aspects of the story and to my brother Jonathan Stewart for Brit-proofing the manuscript to rid it of Americanisms that have crept into my writing. I'd also like to acknowledge my lifelong friend Kathleen O'Callaghan Bolling for allowing me to use her family's house as a model for the Murphy family's house on fictional Holly Road. I unashamedly borrowed her first name for the protagonist in the story.

A shout-out is due to Ilene Birkwood. A seven-year-old survivor of the SS *Volendam*'s torpedoing, she later wrote a book about her experience called *The Second Torpedo*. She now lives in Washington State. Her description of the torpedoing was of invaluable help as I wrote the scene for my book.

Thanks to the team at She Writes Press for publishing *Kate's War* and for designing its beautiful cover: Brooke Warner, Lauren Wise Wait, Mimi Bark, and Julie Metz; to How It Works in Anacortes for refining the map; and to my publicist Caitlin Hamilton Summie for promoting the book.

And, of course, I couldn't have survived the difficult revision process without the unflagging encouragement of my editor Ellen Notbohm. There were many revisions, all necessary to allow the story to emerge speed bump and pothole-free.

The book is dedicated to my dear father Gordon Thallon Stewart, whose wartime experience inspired the book. He never knew that I became an author, but long before I had any idea that I would write a book, he once told me I "had a good pen." How did he know? He had a good pen, himself.

Applause to my husband Vince for his knowledge of World War II, for teaching the writing seminar where I learned to write fiction, and for his ongoing patience and support.

Finally, thanks to all the readers who buy, borrow, or pass on this book.

WORLD WAR II EVENTS
MENTIONED IN *KATE'S WAR*

1939

Sept 3, 1939 – Britain declares war on Germany. The king's speech.

Sept 3 – Sinking of SS *Athenia*. First British civilian casualties.

October – Conscription starts for 20-to 23-year-old men.

October – British Expeditionary Force moves to Belgium and France

October 14 – U-boat sinks HMS *Royal Oak* in Scapa Flow, believed to be an impregnable harbour.

November 17 – Irish Republican Army (IRA) sets off bombs in London.

December 13 – Battle of River Plate off Montevideo, Uruguay. German pocket battleship *Graf Spey* is attacked and damaged by a British naval squadron including HMS *Exeter*. Later the German captain scuttles the *Graf Spey*. Big morale builder in Britain.

1940

January 1, 1940 – Conscription starts for 24- to 27-year-old men.

January 8 – Basic food rationing starts (bacon, butter, sugar).

March – Meat rationing starts. Later jam, biscuits, cheese, eggs, and milk are rationed.

March 16 – Luftwaffe air raid on Scapa Flow in Scotland causes the first British land civilian casualties.

April 5 – Prime Minister Chamberlain announces Hitler has "missed the bus." He was widely criticized in Britain for that statement.

April – Britain starts the Norwegian campaign after PM Quisling establishes the Nazi party there.

May – Conscription in Britain extended to age 36.

May 7 – Parliament passes a vote of no-confidence in Chamberlain.

May 10 – Germany invades Belgium, France, Luxembourg and the Netherlands. Winston Churchill becomes Prime Minister after Chamberlain resigns.

May 13 – Queen Wilhelmina of the Netherlands flees to asylum in the UK. Churchill's "blood, toil, tears and sweat" speech. King George VI, the queen, and princesses Elizabeth and Margaret do not leave the county.

May 26 – Allied forces retreat to Dunkirk. Evacuation of troops begins.

June 4 – Churchill delivers "We shall never surrender" speech.

June 22 – France surrenders to Germany. The Armistice is signed on June 25.

June 28 – Germans bomb demilitarised Channel Islands and invade in the following days.

July 9 – Tea rationing begins.

July 10 – Battle of Britain begins between the Luftwaffe and Royal Air Force.

July 12 – Luftwaffe attacks Wales, Scotland and Northern Ireland.

August 1 – Hitler sets Sept 15 as date for Operation Sea Lion, his invasion of Britain. This doesn't happen, but the country is on high alert.

August 20 – Churchill's speech "Never was so much owed by so many to so few," referring to the Royal Air Force pilots who shot down many German planes during the Battle of Britain.

August 26 – London bombed for the first time by the Luftwaffe, and the RAF bombs Belin in retaliation.

August 29 – Liverpool bombed. SS *Volendam*, commandeered for the CORB program, sets sail.

August 30 – SS *Volendam* torpedoed in the Atlantic, several hundred miles off Malin Head, Northern Ireland.

September 7 – Beginning of the London Blitz. Bombing continues for 57 consecutive days and destroys or damages an estimated million buildings, causing over 43,000 civilian deaths.

Permission to publish lyrics to two popular songs was granted by Hal Leonard LLC:

There'll Always Be An England
Words and music by Ross Parker and Hughie Charles
Copyright © 1939 (Renewed) Chester Music Limited trading as Dash Music Co.
International Copyright secured   All Rights Reserved
Reprinted by Permission
Reprinted by Permission of Hal Leonard LLC

We'll Meet Again
Words and Music by Ross Parker and Hughie Charles
Copyright © 1939 (Renewed) Chester Music Limited trading as Dash Music Co.
International Copyright Secured   All Rights reserved
Reprinted by permission
Reprinted by permission of Hal Leonard LLC

ABOUT THE AUTHOR

photo credit: Mark Gardner

L inda Stewart Henley was born in Liverpool, UK, grew up in Surrey after the war, and attended school in Carshalton before moving to the United States where she completed her education. She is the author of two award-winning novels, *Estelle* and *Waterbury Winter*. She now lives in Anacortes, Washington, with her husband.